Also by Caroline Overington

Fiction
Ghost Child
I Came to Say Goodbye

Non-fiction
Only in New York
Kickback

Matilda is Missing

CAROLINE OVERINGTON

BANTAM
SYDNEY AUCKLAND TORONTO NEW YORK LONDON

This is a work of fiction. Names, characters, places and incidents are either the product of the author's imagination or are used fictitiously. Any resemblance to actual persons, living or dead, events or locales is entirely coincidental.

A Bantam book
Published by Random House Australia Pty Ltd
Level 3, 100 Pacific Highway, North Sydney NSW 2060
www.randomhouse.com.au

First published by Bantam in 2011

Addresses for companies within the Random House Group can be found at
www.randomhouse.com.au/offices

National Library of Australia
Cataloguing-in-Publication Entry

Overington, Caroline.
Matilda is missing/CarolineOverington.

ISBN 978 1 74275 038 5 (pbk.)

Custody of children – Fiction.

A823.4

Cover photograph courtesy of Getty Images
Cover design by Christabella Designs
Typeset in 12/18 pt Sabon by Midland Typesetters, Australia
Printed and bound by Griffin Press, an accredited ISO AS/NZS 14011:2004
Environmental Management System printer

10 9 8 7 6 5 4 3 2 1

The paper this book is printed on is certified against the Forest Stewardship Council® Standards. Griffin Press holds FSC chain of custody certification SGS-COC-005088. FSC promotes environmentally responsible, socially beneficial and economically viable management of the world's forests.

FSC
www.fsc.org
MIX
Paper from
responsible sources
FSC® C009448

For Mum
For teaching me to listen
and also to read

Preface

There are people who never met Frank Brooks who are pretty sure they wouldn't have liked him. Frank was a judge of the Family Court, you see, and people don't like the Family Court. They see it as a place where they have to go to get divorced and fight about their kids, or to be robbed blind by lawyers.

That said, there are plenty of people who *did* know Frank Brooks who also didn't like him. Towards the end of his career, he developed what might be called a reputation for being biased. People had started to say that he hardly ever came down on the side of mothers. He was always for the dads.

I can't pretend I've sat down and studied every one of the hundreds of custody disputes Frank had to hear, but what I can say is that I knew Frank Brooks for sixty years, and the idea that he was biased against women sounds like BS to me.

Frank and I grew up next door to each other. We lived in the Melbourne suburb of Footscray. Footscray was what people used to call 'working class', meaning people didn't lie around all day collecting the dole. They worked at factories, like Kinnear's, or else on the docks. There were five or six kids in every house; we all got dragged by our ears to the same Sunday school; we dinked each other around on the same bicycle.

Frank's mum was like an aunt to me, and Frank worshipped her. When he was old enough he married his childhood sweetheart, Betty. They had four daughters, one of whom ended up getting divorced. Given the number of women in Frank's life, I find it hard to believe that he was biased against mums.

Did he sometimes make mistakes when it came to custody hearings? I'd say he must have done, otherwise we'd all be gathered around his grave saying, 'Here lies a man who never mucked anything up.'

Did he make a mistake when he was deciding who should get custody of little Minty – Matilda – Hartshorn?

I could answer that, but in the end I think it's best that people make a judgement for themselves.

Chapter One

The last time I saw Frank Brooks was at Young and Jackson's, which is the pub on the corner of Flinders Street in Melbourne, and it was about three weeks before Frank died.

It was Frank's idea to meet. He called me after the disaster with the billboard and said, 'Why don't we have a beer, old friend?'

Now, you're probably thinking – *whoa*, what billboard? Well, for now it's best I say only that Frank called about the time my wife, Pat, did something that was pretty much out of character.

She'd arranged to have a giant billboard put on the freeway, as part of a fight she was having with our son Brian's missus. Brian is the youngest of our four boys. He's coming up for forty now, and still in the same job he had when he left school. He works on container ships, down at the docks, at Port Melbourne.

Brian was one of those boys who, instead of getting out of the house as soon as humanly possible, stayed at home with Pat and me until he was thirty.

To my mind you're a bit old to be living at home when you're thirty, but Pat was all for it.

'A young man working as hard as he does needs a hot meal on the table when he gets home,' she said.

Like Brian couldn't have cooked his own meal? He's not an invalid.

In any case, he took advantage, paying minimal rent and getting his clothes washed and dried and folded, and saving money so he could travel to Bali and over to Broome. He'd trick up old cars and put mag wheels on them. At one point we had two-and-a-half cars on the street outside, and I had to say, 'Brian, it's not fair on the neighbours.'

Just when I was thinking Brian would never move out, he met a girl, Nerida, and decided she was the love of his life.

Now, I don't want to go scratching old sores, but it's hardly a family secret that Pat struggles with Nerida, and has done from the very start. To my mind that's because Brian was Pat's baby – the youngest boy, and the only one still at home – but that's not the only thing. They clashed. Some people just do.

My Pat's not posh. Like me, she grew up in Footscray with working-class parents. As a kid, Pat's house was always as neat as a pin, and Pat's the same as her mum, polishing the glass at least once a week.

I don't know how many families there are like that any more, but Nerida's not from one of them. Nerida's mother has never been married, and when our Brian met Nerida, she and her mum were living in Housing Commission.

'Taking hand-outs,' is what Pat says about that.

Brian met Nerida at a pub in Maidstone. Pat was fine with that. Pubs are where people meet these days. But Nerida wasn't at the pub with her girlfriends, having a dance or a counter meal. Nerida was pulling the beers.

'She's a barmaid, Barry,' is what Pat said.

I remember the first time Nerida came to visit. Pat took one look at the black dyed hair and the six earrings in the top of the ear, and raised her eyebrows at me. But she's a good woman, Pat, and even when she's made up her mind about someone, she'll still be polite. She took Nerida into the kitchen, saying, 'Let's have a cup of tea.'

Nerida followed Pat into the kitchen and pulled out a pack of ciggies. Pat said, 'I'm sorry, Nerida, we don't allow smoking in the house.' So Nerida headed for the flyscreen door and lit up on the porch.

'She's standing there, half-in and half-out of the house, blowing smoke and waving a hand in front of her face,' said Pat.

'And do you know what she told me, Barry? She told me she lives in Maidstone *with a child who is four years old*. I said, "But how old are you, dear?" And she said she's twenty. Which means she had him when she was *sixteen*, Barry.'

Like an idiot, I said, 'Who's the father?'

Pat said, 'Don't you think I asked about that, Barry? Don't you worry, I asked about that. She said she has *no idea*. She said, "Whoever it is, we don't see him. It's just me and Ethan." *Whoever it is*, Barry.'

I said, 'Well, Pat. A girl can make a mistake.'

Pat said, 'Do you know where she lives, Barry? She lives with the child, and with her own mother *in Housing Commission* in Maidstone.'

I think it's fair to say that things went downhill from there.

'Have you really thought this through, Brian?' Pat would say whenever she got the chance. 'Is this a serious thing?'

Brian would say: 'Stay out of it, Mum.'

'But do you really think it's fair to the child – to Ethan – to bond with him, and then disappear from his life?' Pat would persist. 'He's had enough traumas in his life, surely? Maybe you should back off a bit.'

Brian didn't back off. Six weeks after meeting Nerida, he'd moved half his stuff over to her place in Maidstone, so he was half-living with Nerida, her mum and with Ethan.

'I really don't understand it, Barry,' Pat said. 'I mean, what goes on over there? It's a horrible place. I invite Brian home for tea and he says he's busy. Busy doing what?'

What could I tell her? Nerida was twenty years old and Brian was a healthy young man. Probably they were having the time of their life, if you see what I mean. And it didn't help that Pat made it obvious – not just to Brian, but to *everyone* – that she didn't like Nerida.

'I can't quite put my finger on it,' she'd say, 'but I don't trust that girl.'

I'd say: 'It hardly matters what *we* think, Pat. Nerida's Brian's choice.'

Six months into the relationship, Brian rang and said, 'We're coming over Sunday, Dad. Me, Nerrie, Ethan and Nerrie's mum. All of us.'

Pat said, 'What could this be about, Barry? Please don't tell me . . .' Meaning: 'Please don't tell me they're getting married.'

I remember Nerida's mum, Cheryl, coming up the path that Sunday in leopard-skin stilettos. Pat was in the front room, looking through the blinds.

'Heavens!' she said when she opened the door. 'How do you walk in those?'

Cheryl plopped herself down on a kitchen stool and twisted her foot around, saying, 'Aren't they brill? Got 'em on sale. Run down and get yourself a pair, before they're all sold out.'

How old was Ethan then? I'm thinking not yet five. Not yet in school. He had black hair, cropped short, with a rat's tail. Pat tried to engage him. 'Would you like me to cut up an apple for you, Ethan?'

Ethan said, 'I don't eat fruit.'

Pat said, 'Well, what about a drink then? Would you like some apple juice?'

Ethan said, 'Coke.'

Brian said, 'We're getting married, Mum.'

It was one of those moments like you see on the sitcoms. Pat was holding two cups and saucers, and nearly dropped them both.

I got up and pumped our Brian's hand, saying, 'Well done, son.'

Cheryl opened her arms up – there's quite a bit to see when she does that, if you get what I mean – and said, 'Well, give us a hug, Pat! We're family!' And Pat had no choice but to go into her performing hug.

Discussions turned to the wedding. With no father of the bride around, Cheryl was offering to foot the bill. But she was on some kind of disability, or workers' comp, and couldn't afford what Nerida wanted, which was 'the big white wedding'.

Pat tried to be diplomatic. 'Well,' she said. 'I suppose in a way that's fine, because, you know, with Ethan and everything . . .'

Cheryl either had no idea what Pat was talking about – Nerida couldn't have a 'big white wedding' because she was a *single mother* – or if she did, she didn't show it. Like her daughter, she was standing half-in and half-out the kitchen door, waving a cigarette with red lipstick on the butt-end, getting Ethan to fetch the lighter from where she'd put it down outside, talking about how great the wedding was going to be.

'You've raised a good boy in Brian,' Cheryl said. 'If my

Nerrie hadn't seen him first, I might even have had a go myself!'

I rushed into the conversation, saying, 'In the circumstances, we're obviously happy to help out with the costs,' and, I've got to tell you, I got in more trouble for that from Pat than I'd got for just about anything in my whole married life.

'What you should have said was, we don't *want* them to get married,' Pat said, after Cheryl had packed up her cigarettes and headed out the front door, on those spiky heels. 'What you should have said was, we think the two of them should *wait*, get to know each other a bit, before rushing headlong into something as serious as marriage.'

What could I say? There was a reason I didn't step in – it was basically none of my business! I told Pat, 'Brian's thirty years old. He's big enough and ugly enough to take care of himself. He's picked Nerida and, whatever we think, that's his choice. And he can't pick up the tab for the wedding. That's a cost you don't want to lay on a young man at the start of married life.'

Pat said, 'You can't see what's happening, can you? Our Brian's got a job. He's got his Westpac Supersaver. What's Nerida got? Nothing. So our Brian is the best thing that's ever going to happen to her, which is why she's getting her claws in.'

To Brian, she said, 'I know you think you're in love, but there are girls out there closer to your own age, girls with proper jobs, *careers*. Have you thought about how you're going to pay the mortgage? You're going to need somebody who can help with the bills.'

Brian said, 'Nerida's not on the dole, Mum. She's still got her job at the pub.'

Pat said, 'Well, that's lovely, Brian. Good for Nerida. She's got a job in a pub. But it's hardly ideal for a girl, is it, to be working behind a bar?'

Brian said, 'She likes it. Although I reckon she'll give it up when she has a couple more kids.'

Pat was startled.

'More children?' she said. 'Now, Brian, you won't want to rush into that.'

Brian said, 'Nerrie wants to have a dozen. And Cheryl's awesome with Ethan. She reckons it's the best thing having a grandkid. She can't wait to have more.'

I don't need to tell you that the wedding went ahead and it was a good one in the end. I stumped up for a spit roast and a keg, and plenty of beer was drunk, not least by me.

Ethan looked good, in a suit from the Footscray Market with sneakers and a carnation. As for Nerida – well, I thought she looked perfectly nice in her white dress.

'It's *cream*,' Pat corrected me when I mentioned it. 'Definitely cream.'

Our eldest, Scott, gave the speech, saying it was about time Brian left home, given that he'd started losing his hair. There was a cake and all the rest of it, including a bit where Nerida sat down on one of the fancy chairs, middle of the dance floor, and Brian went under her dress to get her garter off.

It was done. They were married and into a place of their own. Brian put the deposit down. He paid the mortgage. That's what a man does. Besides which, three months after the wedding, Brian announced that Nerida was five months pregnant.

Pat took it pretty well. 'It's wonderful news, Nerida,' she said. 'If you need any advice or anything, you can ask me. Don't be shy. We're family now.'

To which Nerida said, 'Well then, can you hire me a semi-trailer to haul my arse around? Doctor says I've put on thirty kilos already, and I'm barely past the halfway mark.'

Pat said, 'Well, you're eating for two.'

'More like I'm eating for five,' Nerida said. 'I'm, like, craving the weirdest shit. Hot chips and Macca's burgers and those apple turnovers, and peanut butter, and bacon. I'm sending Brian out in the middle of the night to get me ice-cream, jelly snakes, whatever's on sale at the servo, which is the only thing what's open at midnight. It's doing his head in!'

Pat said, 'Well, perhaps you should try to get some vege-tables . . . and the smoking? Are you going to give up the smoking?'

Brian interrupted. 'Don't tell me you didn't smoke, Mum, with us lot.'

'Well, it was different in the sixties, Brian,' Pat said. 'We didn't know. You can't say that now.'

Nerida said, 'First few weeks, the smell of it had me retching. Couldn't handle it. And that's not on, because I'm working in the pub and everyone is fagging. So I forced a couple down and I'm good again now.'

Six months into the pregnancy, Nerida was still smoking – and the size of a house. She'd come over for tea on Sundays, saying, 'Check out the size of me! Doc says I better stop eating or he'll have to take me down the docks to weigh me. I'm, like, alright, me hubby works there, no worries!'

The more she did that kind of thing, the more I liked Nerida, but Pat, who was standing serving, said, 'More vegetables, anyone?'

Three months on, Brian called again one night, saying Nerida and the baby were in the hospital.

'She's had him already?' asked Pat.

Brian said, 'She nearly dropped him in the dunny! Nerrie thought she needed a poo and he was half into the bowl! Half out before we even got into the car! She said, "I'd better keep my legs crossed or I'll have him on the freeway."'

Pat pushed me out of bed and ordered me to drive her across town, to the public hospital at Sunshine. We found Nerida sat up in bed, with Ethan eating potato chips, and a baby boy swaddled in a crib.

'Take a look, Pat. It's another bloody boy!' Nerida said. 'Right through the pregnancy, everyone was saying to me, "Don't worry, it's gonna be a girl. You're all out in front, and that means a girl." What am I gonna do with all the pink stuff I got given?'

I'm not sure Pat was listening. To be clear, when that little boy was born she already had five grandchildren – our eldest, Scott, had three kids, and the other boys had one apiece – but this was Brian's first and, as I've said, Brian was Pat's baby.

'What will you call him?' she said. It was like she was in a trance.

'I'm buggered if I know,' Nerida said. 'I had my girls' names all picked out. I was that sure it was a girl, I can't tell you. I was right out in front, wasn't I, Brian? And when you're right out in front, they reckon it's a girl. Shows what they know.'

'Well, what was your father's name?' said Pat, to which Nerida replied, 'No way is my kid getting named for that idiot.'

'Well then, Brian's grandfather – my father – was Herbert. Bert to his friends, of course, but Herbert is lovely, don't you think?'

I watched Nerida's face. She seemed to think Pat was joking. Then she saw that Pat *wasn't* joking, and that amused her even more.

'Bert, like *Bert and Ernie*?' she said. 'That's a top idea, Grandma Pat!'

They didn't call him Bert, obviously. He went without a name for a week and then, after they got him home and settled, Brian called to say they had called him Jett, and because he had a thick mop of dark hair, like Nerida's even before she dyed it, his middle name would be Black. So, Jett Black Harper Harrison.

I passed this on to Pat, expecting her to say, 'I do hope you're joking.' But she'd already lost her heart to that little baby.

'I really like that,' she said. 'Jett Black! It's got a nice ring to it. And with his hair, it's going to suit him well.'

The weeks after Jett was born, it was like Pat was a first-time grandma again. She took a heap of pictures of him, stopped her old friends in the street, saying, 'Would you like to see a picture of my grandson? See his dark eyes? Lashes like a foal, he's got. Long lashes, like a foal.'

Nerida didn't bother with breastfeeding Jett – 'The little bastard split my nipples,' she said – so Pat was allowed to babysit Jett from pretty early on.

'We'll get our own bottle sterilising kit, and you won't have to worry about anything,' Pat told Nerida. 'I've got a lot of experience with little boys, Brian included! So don't worry. I know what I'm doing.'

It wasn't like Nerida needed convincing. 'You want him, you have him!' she told Pat. 'You'd think I'd have remembered what it's like to have a baby around. Like, with Ethan, he can get himself up and get a bowl of Coco Pops, or whatever. Now I'm back in bottles, nappies, and the bloody crying, it never stops. Don't get me wrong, he's dead cute and all that, but Jesus, he carries on.'

'Well, I don't mind at all,' Pat said. 'It's my pleasure to help.'

By the age of two, Jett was spending as much time at our place as he was with Brian and Nerida – and to say that arrangement suited Pat is to understate it. To be honest it suited me too. Grandkids – well, it's not like having your own, is it? It's better than having your own. You don't have to worry so much. And you can give them back! And Jett was a right little character. When he started to walk, for example, Pat bought him a Superman body suit: red underpants painted on the outside, the kind of thing our Brian would never have been seen dead in. Jett put it on and, I swear, you couldn't get it off him, not even to wash it. He'd sleep in the thing. He'd walk down the supermarket with it on. Not at all embarrassed. I've got to tell you, it was hysterical.

Then, when Jett was three, and Ethan going on for eight, Nerida came around and flopped herself down in the armchair, saying, 'I can't bloody believe this. I'm up the duff again.'

'Are you sure?' said Pat, which was a fair enough question. Nerida had been saying since Jett arrived that she wasn't interested in having another baby – 'too much bloody hassle' – and she'd never lost any of the weight she'd put on with Jett, so I wouldn't have been able to tell if she was pregnant again or not.

'That's what the doctor reckons,' she said. 'One in the oven, five months cooked.'

Of course, it was another boy.

'Is that all you Harrisons have?' Nerida complained from the hospital bed. 'You've got four, Pat. Scott's got three. Now I've got another two. Don't you reckon a girl might have been nice? What the hell am I going to call him? We've got no boys' names.'

They decided, in the end, on Baxter. I don't know, but I'm told that's a name from somebody on *Neighbours*, or maybe *Home and Away*. As with Jett, Pat offered to take him a couple of nights a week, pretty much from the get-go.

'You catch up on sleep,' she said. Nerida took no convincing at all, and so, within five years of Brian meeting Nerida, and Pat deciding she didn't like her, all three of Nerida's kids – Ethan, Jett and the new baby, Baxter – were in our house three nights a week.

You reckon she didn't love it? She loved it!

Now, I'm trying to remember how old the kids were when the marriage ultimately did go south. From memory, Baxter – Bax – had started walking, so maybe he was one, or even a bit older, which means Jett would have been, what, four or five, and Ethan maybe eight or nine?

Probably it doesn't matter. The main thing is that I was home with Pat one night, feet up, watching telly, when Brian's Holden came up the road, and onto the nature strip outside the house.

'What on earth is he doing?' Pat said, looking out the blinds. 'Why doesn't he park by the kerb?'

The minute Brian got out of the car, I could see what the problem was. He couldn't *find* the kerb. Drunk as a skunk he was, so much so that he couldn't get his old house key in the lock.

'I'm gonna stay here a while,' he said when Pat opened the door.

'But what on earth has happened?' said Pat.

'Don't ask,' he said, and started down the hall, bouncing off the walls as he went.

Pat turned to me. 'Go and talk to him!' she said.

I went down the hall into Brian's old room. He was face down on the bed, with his Blundies still on.

I said, 'What's gone on, Brian?'

He muttered, but his face was in the pillow and I couldn't hear it.

'Say again?' I said.

He lifted his head and said, 'Nerrie doesn't want me any more. She's gone and done the dirty.'

'Ah, Jesus, Brian,' I said. 'That's no good at all.'

'She's a moll,' he said, and threw up on the bed.

Now, there's obviously quite a bit of pain involved when a marriage breaks up and I couldn't hang anything on Brian for getting drunk like he did that first night. It didn't actually bother me too much when he kept drinking night and day, for something like a week.

My feeling was: let him be. We'll find out soon enough what's gone on. But Pat isn't the type to let a sleeping dog lie. What exactly had happened, she wanted to know? Was this a one-off, with Nerida, or had she met somebody else? Did she want Brian to take her back? Was Brian going to do it?

'It's not your business, Mum,' Brian would slur, drunk again. But actually, it was Pat's business. She'd organised her life around caring for Nerida's boys, and suddenly they'd stopped coming.

'I don't see what your problem with Nerida has to do with me,' she'd say to Brian. 'I don't see how it means that the boys can't still come here, like they used to do.'

Brian said, 'Nerrie's got the shits with me, Mum. I said some stuff to her. Let her calm down.'

To me, Pat said, 'I can't stand this, Barry. What have I done wrong? Absolutely nothing, that's what. Why isn't she bringing the boys around to see me, at least?'

'Pat,' I said. 'This is one of those situations where we're going to have to wait and see.'

'This is your fault, Barry,' Pat said. 'I told you from the outset – this girl's no good. But you wouldn't listen. Wouldn't warn him off. Now look – first chance she gets, she's off with someone else. And who gets punished? Me.'

I said, 'There's no warning kids off their choices, Pat. You know that as well as I do. The main thing is for us to stay out of it, and see what happens.'

I might as well have been talking to a wall.

'She's going to take you for everything,' Pat told Brian, not two weeks into the separation. 'I notice she's still in the house, Brian. That house has a mortgage on it, and you're going to have to pay that mortgage, unless you want a black mark on your credit rating for the rest of your life.'

Brian said, 'Mum, I've told you. Stay out of it.'

Pat said, 'Well, you tell me, Brian. What did she put into that house? Not one cent, that's what. And she's going to walk off with it. Given what she's done, you should ask her to move out, and you stay there with the boys.'

To which Brian said, 'As if I'd do that, Mum.'

'But what's going to happen to me?' said Pat. 'I've gotten into a good routine having those boys here. They're used to me. It's not fair on them being snatched away from their own nana. And I count Ethan in that.'

'I'm planning on talking to Nerrie this weekend,' said Brian. 'Do you want me to ask her if I can take the boys – bring them here – for a couple of hours?'

'What do you mean, *ask* her?' said Pat. 'They're *your* kids! Even Ethan, he's practically your own child! You don't have to ask permission to see them!'

'Stop interfering, Mum,' Brian warned her again.

But Pat couldn't.

'What I don't understand, Brian, is why when you've done nothing wrong, you're the one being punished. Nerida's called quits on the marriage. That's fine. But why does that mean that you have to ask permission to see your own children?'

Brian said, 'I can see them when I want. It's just Nerrie doesn't want me taking them out of the house. She's mad as an axe with me. I'm in no frame of mind to see her either. I'm just letting things settle.'

Pat said, 'I can see that we've – you've – got no claim on Ethan. She holds the cards there. But Jett and Baxter – they're our flesh and blood. It doesn't seem right to me that Nerida decides when we can see them.'

Brian said, 'I'm not going to say it again, Mum. Stay out of it.'

The weekend came and went, and Brian didn't bring the kids over.

'I asked Nerrie,' he said, on the telephone, from his old house. 'She said it's best they stay here. I'm just sitting with them. Say hello on the phone. Bax, say hello. It's Nana. Say hello.'

Pat said, 'But Brian, I've cooked the chook.'

I can't tell you how that broke my heart, to hear Pat say: 'But Brian, I've cooked the chook!' Because that was always a tradition in Pat's family – to have a roast chicken on a Sunday afternoon. I remember the first ones she cooked for me, right after we got married. And she cooked chicken every Sunday after that, even when it was expensive, and even when, because of the four boys, we had to buy two.

Only when the boys moved out did Pat give the cooked chook away. Too much fuss for two people, she'd say, and you can't get a half-decent chicken in the supermarket these days. But then one afternoon, she made chicken soup for baby Baxter – this must have been before he was onto solids – from a real roast chicken.

'He ate two bowls,' Pat told Nerida. 'Good and nourish-ing.'

There had been a wishbone with the carcass. Pat wiped it down on her apron, and showed Jett how it worked. He loved it. So the next Sunday, Pat made another chicken soup and, as the boys got older and needed more than just soup, the cooked chook came back.

'What am I supposed to do with the wishbone?' Pat said, after she'd put the phone down.

'We'll put it in Tupperware,' I said. 'The boys can have a good fight over it next time they come around.'

'And when will that be?' said Pat.

A few days later, I heard her talking over the fence. 'You won't believe what happened. My daughter-in-law knows I love to see those boys on a Sunday and now she's stopped them from coming. Can you believe that? What a mean thing to do.'

I'd say a month or so went by before Brian did finally bring the kids – all three of them – over for a cooked chook on a Sunday. Pat wanted to know what had brought on the change of heart. It was only later that we found out Nerida had broken up with the bloke she'd left Brian for, and she was actually begging Brian to take her back. He told her straight: I'm sorry, Nerida, it's not going to happen.

'She's done it once,' he told me. 'A leopard doesn't change its spots.' I thought that was pretty brave of him, because whatever had happened between them, Brian still loved Nerida.

In any case, Nerida was a free agent again, and it wasn't long before she figured out that if Brian didn't want her, some other bloke probably would, and she was ready to go out partying.

'It suits her to have the boys stay here when she's not home,' said Brian. 'Which is fine by me.'

So Pat had the boys again, and she was over the moon. She'd get up early and make hot porridge, which was something they never got at home, and she let them stir Milo into milk, or else she'd sit them around her feet while she was at the sewing table, and let them play with the jar of buttons. She took them to the movies, to see *Monsters Inc.* or *Toy Story*, and let them polish the silver with a rag from the ragbag.

So, everyone was travelling along great, and to my mind everything would have stayed great, if only Pat could have stopped with running Nerida down. 'What must it be like for them, their mother out at the pub every other weekend?' she'd say to me.

I'd say, 'Shush, Pat,' because the boys were often well within earshot, and anyway, kids listen out for that kind of thing.

Pat would say, 'Oh, come on, Barry. Does she think the children don't know why they're staying with us? Because she's out all night on the booze?'

To the boys themselves she'd say, 'Where's your mummy tonight, I wonder? Not here with you!' Or else she'd tell them, 'If Mummy gets cross with you, you come and stay with Nana. Nana won't get cross with you! Nana loves you.'

Then there was the way Pat behaved with Nerida, when they were doing the handover of the boys. Pat might pack Jett's pyjamas into his backpack with a note pinned to them saying, 'I managed to wash these, Nerida, but there wasn't much I could do about the holes.'

Nerida would get on the blower and say, 'I really don't appreciate what you're incinerating, saying you had to wash the boys' clothes.'

Pat would say: 'It isn't incinerating, Nerida. It's *insinuating*. And I'm not insinuating anything. I'm merely saying that Jett came to us with his bottom hanging out of his pyjama pants, and while we're talking, Baxter didn't have a toothbrush. Are you teaching him to brush his teeth? Because it looks to me like they're turning green.'

Nerida would say, 'I tell him, Pat, and he forgets.' And Pat would say, 'Well, of course he does. He's a child. That's why you're supposed to remind him, Nerida.' And on it would go.

Now, I'm not an idiot. I get that Pat was trying to show loyalty to Brian. She couldn't believe that Nerida had gone and done the dirty. Didn't she know how lucky she was, to end up with somebody like our Brian? All of which is perfectly understandable: a mum is always going to side with her boy in a situation like that. But to my mind there's got to be a point at which you bury the hatchet, or else you'll make things even worse.

To his credit, Brian could see that. He tried to reason with his mum, saying, 'You've got to stop running Nerrie down. It's going to get to the point where it gets back to her, and then she's not going to let the kids come here.'

Pat said, 'Well, she won't be able to do *that*. I talked to

Carol down at the hairdresser's and she told me things are different these days. I mean, we may have no *legal* right to see Ethan, but you're the father of those boys, and I'm the nana, and the way the law is now, Nerida has no right keeping them away from us.'

Then came the day that Jett went home from our place to his mum and said, 'What's a gold-digger?'

'Why do you want to know?' Nerida asked.

To which Jett, poor kid, said, 'Nana says you're a gold-digger.'

Nerida was on the phone in seconds. I could hear her, shouting down the line, 'I'm a gold-digger, am I, Pat? That's what you're telling my own kids about me? Well, I've bloody well had it. You think you can poison my kids against me? You can't, because you won't be seeing them any more.'

Pat got a bit of a shock, obviously, that Jett had done exactly what I'd told her he'd do one day, but she still thought she had the upper hand.

'I think you'll find, Nerida, that you can't holus-bolus take the kids away from me. You can stop Ethan from coming, maybe, if you'd want to be that mean. But Jett and Baxter – well, I'm their nana, and grandparents these days have just as many rights as parents do.'

'You might be their nana,' Nerida said. 'But I'm their mother, and as their bloody mother I'll decide who they'll see.'

Pat tried to brush it off. 'She'll send them back,' she said. 'Mark my words, Barry, the first opportunity she gets to go down the pub, she'll be on the phone to me, saying, Pat, please can you take the boys?'

I thought, maybe yes, maybe no. Maybe Nerida would just say, Brian, you come here and mind the kids.

Maybe her own mum would say, you go out, and I'll mind the kids. Maybe she'd decide, to hell with this, I'd rather pay a babysitter.

In any case, Nerida didn't call again that weekend, meaning Sunday came and went with no cooked chook. Pat tried to get Brian to intervene, but he refused.

'I told you to lay off it, Mum, and you wouldn't give up,' he said. 'Now it's come around and bit you on the bum.'

'Well, that's fine,' said Pat, 'but Nerida's not punishing me. She's punishing those boys.'

Brian said, 'Come off it, Mum.'

Pat said, 'I just need to know that they're alright!'

Brian said, 'They're alright. Just leave things be.'

You might think Pat would have taken that advice, but no. A day or so later, Brian caught her on the telephone to Jett at Nerida's house, saying something like, 'Nana wants to see you but your mummy won't let her!'

'What the hell?' he said, taking the phone.

'Hey, son,' he said. 'Yeah, yeah, I miss you too. Yep, I'm gonna see you soon. Say hi to Bax. Say hi to Ethan. Alright. I love you. Good night.'

He put the phone down and turned to Pat. Honestly, I've never seen him that angry.

'I'm banned from having my own kids in my own

house,' he said. 'Keep this up, Mum, and she'll cut me out altogether.'

'But she can't do that, Brian!' Pat insisted. 'You ask anyone, the law's not like that any more. It's all changed! You've got rights, Brian. Fathers these days, they've got rights!'

Brian said, 'Mum, I've told you, it's not your business.'

I know there's going to be people out there saying, well, actually, Pat's got a point. Maybe Brian should have been fighting harder to see the boys. But I've got to say, I agreed with Brian. I thought he was doing the right thing letting the boys stay with Nerida, and trying to keep the peace with her, even though he felt like she'd busted up his family. And I thought Pat should stay out of it too. Don't get me wrong, I love the woman dearly, but she has a tendency to make things that much worse.

'Why don't you at least go and see a lawyer, Brian?' she said. 'My friend Carol, her boy went through the same thing. The exact same thing! His ex-wife was trying to lay down the law, push him around, take him for all he had, but he got a lawyer and they went to court, and he ended up with custody. He ended up with custody, Brian! I'm telling you, you can do the same.'

Brian wasn't much interested in getting a lawyer, or in going for custody of the boys. He'd already told me, 'No way known am I going down that path into the Family Court. I'll work out a settlement with Nerrie, the boys will stay with her and I'll see them as often as I can. That's the right thing to do.'

Pat couldn't understand that.

'If you try to do things yourself, you'll lose the lot!' she said. 'Go to court! Everybody says it's different now: you can get back everything you put into that house, and, play your cards right, you might even end up with the boys!'

Brian wouldn't have it.

'I'm perfectly happy to have the boys live with their mum,' he said. 'She's a good mum. And there's Ethan. No court's ever going to give me Ethan, so what am I going to do, take my two and leave him? I'm not going to do it. It'll make him feel second best. He'll be without his brothers. It's not right.'

Pat said, 'And what about me, Brian?'

Brian said, 'You made that bed, Mum. You lie in it. I've told you before, if you could just cut it out, things might improve.'

And could Pat cut it out? She could not. She told Brian, 'I'll take it to court myself. A grandmother has her rights!' Of course Brian wouldn't have it. 'You drag my kids through Family Court, I'm not going to forgive you.' To my mind, there was a clear message there; he was dead serious about it. I don't know if he'd heard too much from mates of his who'd walked that route – gone to court and been ruined – or whether it was that he didn't want to lose a load of money in a lawyer's picnic, or what, but he was dead set against court.

However, Pat knew where the boys lived, and she knew where they went to school, and I suppose I realised that she was seriously off her rocker about things when she started getting in the car at 7.30 am to park by the side of the road where the school lollipop lady was, to see if she might see Jett crossing the road.

'Just a glimpse of him!' she'd tell me. 'I just need to know he's alright.'

Of course, you can't go hanging around the school crossing for hours on end, not even if you're a lady of a certain age – and Pat's going to kill me for saying this – with silver hair. Before long, people got suspicious – who was Pat, and why was she sitting there for an hour every day? – and they started to gossip, and so of course Nerida got wind of it and told the school to tell Pat to back off.

'They told me I had to move!' Pat said when she came in that day. 'They came and rapped on my window like I was some kind of pervert! They said, "You can't sit here. It's like spying. It's not right." I said, "Don't tell me what's right. What's not right is my not being allowed to see my own grandchildren!"'

'Oh, Pat,' I said.

'And I didn't even see the boys!' she said. 'I didn't even *see* them, let alone say a word.'

Now, you might think that given Pat and me have been married forty-odd years, I would have been able to predict what was going to happen next, but I've got to tell you, it took me completely by surprise.

'She thinks she can lock me out of their lives,' said Pat. 'We'll see about that.'

A day or so later, I found her out on the front porch with her gardening knee pads on, bending over an old sheet from the linen press. By her side she had a can of black paint from the shed, and in her hand she had a small paint brush.

I said, 'What in heaven's name?'

'You shush, Barry,' said Pat. I looked over her shoulder. She was writing, 'JETT AND BAXTER HARRISON, WE LOVE YOU, NANA AND POP.'

I said, 'What on earth?'

Pat said, 'Don't you interfere. I'm going to wait for it to dry and then I'm going to hang it somewhere where they'll be able to see it. Maybe on that cyclone fence across from their mother's house. I'm going to make sure those boys know what's really going on.'

I said, 'Pat, this is madness.'

Pat said, 'That's right, Barry. You take her side. Everyone else is. Why not you?'

I said, 'Pat, it's not about sides. It's about what is normal behaviour. How embarrassed are the boys going to be, seeing that? And how is Ethan going to feel?'

Pat said, 'You don't think it hurts me, Barry, to have no claim over Ethan? It hurts me. Not much I can do about it, but it hurts me. But our boys – our blood and bone, Jett and Baxter – they are actually family. I've got a right to see them.'

She waited for the sheet to dry, bundled it up and drove off the next morning, planning to pin the thing with clothes pegs to the cyclone fence. Ten minutes later, the manager of the brick works, of which the cyclone fence was a part, came and told her to take it down.

'This is about my grandchildren,' Pat said.

'I don't care what it's about,' he said. 'That fence is owned by a multinational corporation. You don't have permission to stick a bed sheet on it. They've got rules about how the site has to look.'

I'd hoped that Pat would settle down after that, that she'd see what a goose she was making of herself, but that's not the way her mind was working. She was thinking, 'Okay, if I can't put a sign on the fence because it's considered vandalism, how can I put one up that's legal?' And that's when she went down to the freeway, where there was an old billboard that often had nothing on it except a sign saying 'Advertise Your Business Here!', and she got in touch with the people who owned it.

'Can you make up the billboard so it says whatever I want?' she said.

'Well, sure,' the man said, probably fooled by Pat's sweet-lady voice. 'We do that kind of thing all the time. What do you have in mind . . . is it a fete or something?'

'No, no, it's a message for my grandchildren,' said Pat. 'I want to broadcast to the world how much I love them.'

'You mean, for their birthday?'

'No, no, just for all the time!' said Pat.

'Well, that's a nice thought,' the man said. 'You send me the words you want to use, and a picture if you like. Do you have a computer? Do you know how to send a JPEG?

Provided the picture quality is up to scratch, we'll make it look great for you.'

Pat can use a computer. Who can't these days? So she emailed a photograph of Jett and Baxter to the billboard company.

'I want you to blow it up as big as you can,' she said. 'And the message on it should read: BAXTER AND JETT, NANA AND POP LOVE YOU.'

A week or so later, the bloke called back, saying, 'It looks great, and it's ready to go up whenever you are.'

Pat told him, 'Well, how about next Wednesday?' When she put the phone down, she said, 'That'll give me time to warn *A Current Affair*.'

I said, '*A Current Affair*! Are you mad, Pat? You're going to get us into trouble. It's got to be against the law to put a big picture of the kids up there for everyone to see!'

Pat said, 'If there's a law against a grandmother telling her grandkids how much she loves them, I'd like to see that law.'

I was that tempted to tell Brian what his mum was planning. Maybe the only reason I didn't was because it was a struggle getting my head around the idea that she'd actually do it. But do it, she did. Up the billboard went, and everyone in Melbourne saw it, not just because it was on a busy freeway but because pictures of it were broadcast all over the TV.

Pat had made good on her threat to call *A Current Affair*. I'd hoped that they might say: 'Oh, thanks, love, but that's not really our thing.' A granny fighting over her grandkids – it's got to be the most common story in the world when you're dealing with divorce. But how naive am I? What they actually said was, 'What a brilliant idea! And can we offer to pay half the cost in exchange for an exclusive interview?'

'Would you really?' said Pat. 'That's incredibly generous.'

'Not at all!' they said. 'What you're doing is very brave! And, if you think about it, you're not just speaking up for yourself. You're speaking up for grandparents all over Australia who find themselves missing out on their time with the grandkids when their own kids get divorced. What you're doing, it's granny power!'

'*A Current Affair*'s right behind me!' Pat said when she put down the phone. 'Unlike you, Barry, they get exactly what I'm trying to do.'

I told Pat, 'They're not behind you, or right behind anyone! It's the story they're after. They don't care for the rights and wrongs of it. I'm telling you now, this is going to make things that much worse.'

'They're coming to get me,' Pat said. 'They're sending a car!' And so they did, and they did an interview with Pat on site – we've still got the tape, which has Pat in front of this bloody enormous picture of Jett and Baxter – and it was so windy Pat had to shout. Her hair was lifting, which made her look half-mad.

'Exclusive tonight on *A Current Affair*! Heartbroken granny fights for her grandchildren, and for YOURS!'

That was how they introduced the story on the program that night. The first shot was the reporter, facing the camera with the billboard behind him, saying, 'A Melbourne grandmother has taken her fight to see her two grandsons to the streets of Melbourne, erecting a giant billboard on the freeway near where they go to school to show them how much she loves them, even if their mum won't let them see her!'

Pat was in the next shot, yelling over the traffic: 'I love my grandchildren and I want them to know that. I realise some people might think this is a bit extreme, but when a couple breaks up, the children shouldn't be made to suffer. Why shouldn't my boys be allowed to see their nana?'

Next up was an interview with a lady from Relationships Australia, saying, 'This does seem extreme, and we can't comment on any individual cases, but certainly it's often the case that grandparents are the first ones to get cut out of the picture when a couple breaks up. But, you know, grandparents do have rights in court, and it seems to be that court might have been a better option here.'

Talkback radio was next to pick the story up. 'Who saw that story on *A Current Affair* last night?' said the bloke who does the morning shift on 3AW. 'I can't say I necessarily agree with this nana's methods, but I'm sure there's more than one grandparent out there who understands how upsetting it is when the family breaks up. Now, we've obviously got to be quite careful taking calls on this, but are you in a situation, or do you know of a situation, where the grandparents are fighting for access to children after a divorce? Give us a call now.'

Quite a few grandparents did phone, saying, 'We're in exactly that situation, and it's absolutely heartbreaking. We've been to that many lawyers and had that much advice, and we feel we can't get a good hearing. I just wish we'd thought to do what this lady's done.' Other people called saying, 'You can go to court if you want, but it won't get you anywhere. The only people who win in court are lawyers.'

I don't know whether Nerida saw the billboard, or the story on *A Current Affair*, or if she only heard about them. I do know that *she* wasn't at all shy about going to court. She was at the Family Court that same day. Her lawyer – how she could afford a lawyer, I don't know, but maybe she'd organised Legal Aid – told the judge that the children had been 'horribly embarrassed' by the billboard, so much so that they didn't want to go to school because everyone was laughing at them.

'The point of this exercise, in our submission, your Honour, was the public humiliation of the boys' mother,' the lawyer said. 'The song and dance – the story we're being told – is that this was all about the rights of grandparents, but what right does a grandmother have to embarrass her grandchildren, and their mother, in this very public way? There is a forum for this type of dispute, and it's this court, your Honour, not the city's freeways.'

The court agreed and, without even hearing from us, the judge made an order that the billboard had to come down, which was one thing. What was worse was that the judge said Pat had showed such poor judgement that she wouldn't be allowed to see the grandkids – not just Ethan, but also Jett and Baxter – without the express approval of Nerida, who was never going to give it.

It was about then that Frank got in touch.

'Barry Harrison,' he said down the phone into our old answering machine. 'Frank Brooks here. Why don't you and I have a couple of beers?'

Chapter Two

I've said that Frank and I were friends for more than sixty years, but that doesn't mean we saw each other every day. When we were kids living next door to each other, yes, but our paths split when Frank got a scholarship to Melbourne High. I stayed on at Footscray Tech. There were still weekends, obviously, but Frank's school was big on homework.

Then, at fifteen, I got apprenticed as a compositor, which is what they used to call the blokes who put letters down, so newspapers could get printed. Frank stayed on and did his HSC, and then went to uni. At some point – was it 1965? – he moved across the river. Two rivers, actually – the Maribyrnong and the Yarra – and that meant we saw less of each other again.

For the best part of fifty years, though, we managed to have a beer at least every other year, usually at a central location like Young and Jackson's. I'd have said that made us mates, although I do understand that a bloke's definition of what makes a mate is different to a woman's. Pat likes to say to me, 'How can this person be a friend, Barry, when you can't even tell me how many children they have, or what their names are?' But in my experience, those kind of details are pretty much lost on blokes.

We did, however, have our rituals. We'd meet up and have two beers – I'd buy the first round, and then Frank would say, 'I'll get the next one' – and we'd both give what Frank used to call a 'state of the nation' speech, which was a quick rundown of who in our family was doing what.

He was interested when I took retirement, aged fifty-five. Computers had come to newspapers. The old skills weren't needed. The camaraderie of work, I missed, but I was more concerned about being under Pat's feet than anything.

Frank would fill me in on his family, and on some of the cases he'd heard in the Family Court. It was never anything specific. He never told me anyone's name. It was more: I saw this bloke, an absolute drop-kick. A loser, a dead-beat. Won't pay a cent to put a roof over the head of his own children. Or: we had a mum, she won't give one inch. She's making the kids hate their own dad. It's a shame to see it.

I suppose that's why Pat thought Frank wasn't calling out of the blue when he rang that last time. And I had to agree, it was odd that he'd called then. It hadn't been long since we'd seen each other. Certainly not a year. Pat thought he must have heard about the billboard, and wanted to give us some advice on how to handle Nerida.

I said, 'He's a *judge*. Pat, believe me, there's no way he's coming to give us any special inside information. That would be totally out of order.'

Pat said, 'You're trying to tell me it's a coincidence that he's called up right when our case is all over the news? Hurry and get in touch with him, Barry. He must want to help.'

I wasn't convinced, but I called Frank. The first thing I noticed when he came to the phone was how weak his voice sounded.

'G'day, Frank,' I said. 'I was calling to take you up on that offer of a few beers, but maybe it can wait. You don't sound at all well.'

Frank insisted. 'No, no,' he said. 'Let's make it Wednesday. But let's give Chloe a miss this time, and meet downstairs.'

Now, if you know Young and Jackson's, you'll know Chloe. She's the nude who hangs in the upstairs bar, up the wooden staircase. For as long as I'd known Frank he'd thought that trip worthwhile, and now he was saying, let's have a beer downstairs, which told me everything I needed to know about how sick he must have been.

I rode a train into town, annoyed by the loud teenagers with their shiny tracksuit pants. I came out of the station under the clocks, crossed Flinders Street and ducked into the front bar of Young and Jackson's. Frank wasn't there, so I ordered a beer, and I'd barely got the froth off when the door opened, and there he was.

Now, Frank had always been tall, and when I say tall, I mean six foot six in the old language, so he had to duck under the doorway to get in, and even that small movement made him wince. He'd always been built like a beanpole, and now he was more like a skeleton. His cheekbones were sharp, like the corners of a building, and his skull was pretty much bare, except for a few grey strands combed over the top. He had what looked like bleeding sunspots on his head, too. As for his suit – well, it looked like he was wearing someone else's. The pants were belted so tightly they ballooned around his waist, and the jacket was loose around his shoulders, like a scarecrow's jacket.

He stopped at the door, breathing heavily and resting hard on a cane.

'Jesus, Frank,' I said. I'd got straight up from the bar and gone to him, and now I had him by a bony elbow.

'No need to say it,' he croaked. 'I look like the Grim Reaper.'

'Let me find you a chair.'

Frank waved his free hand.

'Where you were is fine,' he said, shuffling towards the bar. 'I'm not yet at the point where I can't sit at the bar.' I suppose that was meant to be a joke, given that Frank was a judge. I couldn't stop looking at him. As I say, it hadn't been a year since I'd last seen him, and yet Frank had lost so much weight it seemed to me that his feet were moving around in his shoes. I went to help him up onto a barstool, but he stopped me, saying, 'I'm fine, Harrison.'

'You're not well, Frank,' I said.

'No,' he agreed.

'It's more than a cold.'

'Cancer,' he said.

'Jesus,' I said. 'Where?'

'Everywhere.'

'How long have you known?'

'A fair while.'

'Christ.'

'Yes.'

I couldn't think what else to say, so I said, 'How's Betty?' meaning his wife, Elizabeth. I'd known Betty since our Footscray days, too.

Frank swallowed.

'Taking it worse than me,' he said. 'I'd rather not put her through this.'

'And the kids?'

'Ah, well. They're grown-ups now.'

'What does the doctor say?'

'Fast-moving. Ultimately incurable. We've both been surprised how fast it's got hold of me.'

Frank raised a hand and pointed at my beer. His finger was as crooked and bony as an old woman's.

'I'd like one of those,' he said.

'On me,' I said.

Being blokes, we didn't dwell for much longer on the state Frank was in. We sat in silence instead, waiting for the bar girl to bring a beer. When it came, Frank sipped the foam off the top.

'Damn it,' he said. 'The chemo kills the taste buds.

I thought, "Beer – at least I'll be able to taste beer." But no. Never mind. How are things, Barry?'

As is my habit, I opened the conversation with some observations about the Doggies – that's the Western Bulldogs – and it was only after we'd exhausted that line of conversation that I said, 'So, I take it you heard about the billboard?'

Frank looked a bit confused.

'I want you to know that I thought it was a bad idea, Frank, but Pat's pretty torn up about the whole thing with Brian and Nerida breaking up. She's crazy about the grandkids. She used to have them a few days a week, and now she doesn't see them at all.'

I can't say for sure how Frank was reacting to all this, mostly because I was keeping my eyes down on my beer, which is my way of getting out of a conversation when I want to keep it short.

'She's joined all these internet groups,' I said. 'People who've been to the Family Court and think they have an idea about how it works. They're telling her the law's changed. Fathers have got more rights these days, and grandparents have got rights too.'

I looked up. Frank appeared as confused as he had when I'd started.

'Are you asking my advice?' he said.

'I suppose I am.'

'Well then,' he said. 'Let me tell you the same thing I tell everyone: if you can avoid the Family Court, do.'

'You mean the cost? I heard it was expensive.'

'I mean because it's like rolling a hand grenade into your lounge room, with all your loved ones sitting there.'

'Right,' I said.

We sat for a bit longer. I'd finished my beer by this point. Frank had taken the froth off his, but that was about it. Then he closed his eyes and swayed on the barstool. For a second there, I thought he might have fallen asleep and was about to fall off the stool, but then his eyes opened and he looked at me. 'Harrison, there's something I need to speak to you about,' he said.

The way he said it, it was obviously something important. My immediate feeling was: 'Uh-oh, is he going to ask me to be executor of his will or something?' But it wasn't that.

'I've cocked something up,' he said. 'Not recently – it was a while ago. But I've only just found out how badly. And I want to put it right, if I can. But I'm at a bit of a loss as to how to do it.'

I wasn't sure how to react – or even what Frank was actually trying to say, so I kept quiet and let him go on.

'Not to be too dramatic, Harrison, I don't want to die leaving this thing out there,' he said. 'I've been turning it over in my head, trying to find a way to put things right. The only option, really, is the media . . . And, to be honest with you, I'm not sure they're capable of doing the job. It's a complicated story. It's going to take somebody with a bit of patience, and a bit of a way with words. And you're a wordsmith, after all.'

I've got to say, that absolutely floored me. Never once had I tried to present myself as a wordsmith. Okay, I worked for newspapers all my life, and maybe from time to time I'd take the mickey out of the journalists – they can't spell, or whatever – but I was never one myself. It's only since I've retired, really, that I've written a story when something has bugged me. Like the time a fire broke out at the old Barkly Street Picture Theatre, taking all the old picture equipment with it. I thought that was a shame. I wrote up some memories of Barkly Street for the *Footscray Mail*. I was pretty pleased when they printed it without changing a word. I'd said to Pat: 'Maybe there's not as much to this writing business as the journos like to make out.' Did I also say that to Frank? Maybe I did, and I'd forgotten.

I said, 'I'm pretty sure you've confused me with someone else, Frank.'

But Frank said, 'No. You've always had a way with words. I remember that from school. You got an A for that piece you wrote about the school holiday we had where we took two old bikes and turned them into one.'

I couldn't remember that. The bike, yes – it was a brilliant thing – but the school essay, no. Did Frank really remember that? And even if he did, what could it have to do with whatever trouble he'd got himself into? What could it be that I could help with? I carried on thinking he'd got me mixed up with somebody else. Maybe because of the morphine mixed with beer.

'You can't want me to write something for you, Frank.

43

You've got to have people who can do that,' I said, but Frank's eyes had closed again. Then they snapped open and he held up his arm – it was just a bone, really, with skin on it – and he tried to see what the time was but his watch had flipped around and was hanging loose on the underside of his wrist.

'It's four-thirty,' I said.

'Betty worries,' he said, and started getting down off the barstool.

'Alright,' I said. And I suppose I must have thought, 'Well, whatever this thing is that's bugging Frank, it can't be as important as him getting home.' He was shaking like children do in the freezer aisle at the supermarket.

'I'll walk you to the tram,' I said, and I took him by the elbow and helped him out the door. There's a green wooden bench at the tram stop at the corner of Flinders and Spencer. A young girl got up so Frank could sit down. The same thing happened when the tram came: a girl who had been sitting in the front seat got straight up and gave Frank her seat.

'Should I get you to your door, Frank?' I said. 'I'm not doing anything else. It's no trouble for me to ride with you.'

'Not on your life,' he replied. 'I'm not an invalid yet.'

He was holding his stick fast against his knee.

The driver had been watching us. I gave him a bit of a nod. Then, just before I got off, I leaned over and took Frank's hand. It was like holding a bird's nest – all sharp twigs.

'Next time,' I said, trying to smile.

'Next time,' he agreed, with something more like a grimace.

There wasn't a next time, obviously. Three weeks later Frank was dead. I found out like most of us Footscray boys did: we saw his name – *Brooks, Justice Francis (Frank) Belmont* – in the obituaries in the *Footscray Mail*.

'Ah, bugger,' I thought. He was only sixty-three.

I went to the funeral, both to pay my respects to Betty and, if I'm honest, to see who else might turn up. The Mass was at the church that had taken in Frank when he'd moved to Malvern to be closer to the courts. The pews were pretty much full. I noticed that the State Premier, Brumby, had taken time out to attend, and so had the Attorney-General from when Prime Minister John Howard was in office. Frank and Betty's eldest son gave the eulogy. There was a bit of a get-together afterwards. It wasn't as posh as I'd expected. Betty's friends brought cucumber sandwiches, and there was coffee and tea and little cakes. I counted seven Brooks grandchildren darting around the dining table, and getting scolded for pinching the little bags of sugar.

'I'm sorry, Betty,' I said.

'I am too, Barry,' she replied.

'She mustn't know what to do with herself,' said Pat as we got in the car to leave, and I could understand that. I wouldn't know what to do with myself if anything happened to Pat.

How long after that did I take the call from a lady who said she wanted to speak to 'Mr Barry Harrison of Barkly Street, Footscray'? I'm guessing that it wasn't more than a month.

'I'm Barry Harrison,' I said.

'Oh good,' said the girl on the phone. 'I've found you. My name's Lisa Olsen, and I'm from Melbourne City Chambers. If you're the Barry Harrison we've been looking for, I have some files here for you from the late Justice Brooks.'

I said, 'Files?'

The girl said, 'Yes. Not a small amount. You'll need to come and collect them. What size vehicle do you have?'

'I've got a station wagon,' I said.

'That's probably fine.'

I was that confused when I put the phone down, I went straight into the kitchen to speak to Pat.

I said, 'The lady on the phone, she reckons Frank has left a bunch of files for me – so many I need the station wagon to pick them up.'

Pat was rapt. 'It's got to be something that's going to help me. He must know about Nerida getting that order to stop me seeing the children. Didn't you mention that to him? Wasn't he interested in how we could fight that?'

I dismissed that out of hand. 'I told you before,' I said, 'if there was one thing that Frank made clear when I saw him that last time it was that he had no advice, other than to stay out of the Family Court, which is what our son wants as well, Pat.'

'Frank was a dying man,' said Pat. 'He must have known how out of our depth we are, that we need all the help we can get. What did he have to lose in the end by giving us a bit of help, in secret?'

To myself, I thought, 'No, Pat, you're wrong.' But what would have been the point of arguing about it? I'd made an appointment with the girl on the phone to pick up the files that Friday, and all would be revealed then.

Friday came around. Stupidly, I drove into town. I say stupidly because there was nowhere to park but at the $27-an-hour Secure Parking garage. That's big bucks when you're on the pension. I found Melbourne City Chambers easily enough. It was on the third floor of an old narrow Victorian building in Little Collins Street, near the Law Courts. There was a sign at the top of the stairs that said 'Watch Your Head!' I couldn't help wondering if that had been put there for Frank.

I made my way up and explained myself to the girl on reception. I got asked to sit and wait, so I did, and when I went to pick up a magazine from the table I had a bit of a laugh to myself. Every magazine on the table was an old copy of *National Geographic*. I thought, 'That's got to be Frank's influence.' Both of us liked to joke about how we had fond memories of *National Geographic*. It was where we saw our first boobs.

I suppose I'd been waiting for ten minutes when a young lady came out and shook my hand and took me down a corridor. She asked me to take a seat, and said, 'I'm sorry for your loss.'

'Thank you,' I said. 'Frank – Justice Brooks – and I were friends for sixty years. That said, I'm a bit surprised to find myself here.'

The girl who had called our house had told me to bring some ID, and now she wanted to know if I'd remembered to do that. I fished out my driver's licence from behind my Medicare card. The girl took it and photocopied it, but even that wasn't enough. She also got me to sign a legal document saying I was who I claimed to be. Then she left the room again and came back, pushing an upright steel trolley. It was three feet high, with black rubber handles, for holding and pushing. There were four shelves of lever-arch files loaded onto it, plus a bottom shelf loaded with cardboard boxes.

'Here you go,' the girl said, parking the thing next to me. 'Justice Brooks' personal assistant – his former personal assistant, Pam Harris – has signed off on it. Everything you need is here. I'm instructed to tell you that if you have any questions you're to direct them to her.'

The girl handed me a small card with the words 'Pam Harris' and a mobile telephone number on it. The hand-writing was the same as that on the files.

'I don't get what this is,' I said, looking at the trolley. 'I can't even guess.' But the girl just looked at me and smiled faintly, like she really couldn't have cared less but was too polite to say so.

'Well,' I said, 'thank you for tracking me down. Is there anything else I need to do?'

'No,' she said.

'In that case,' I said, 'I'll be off.'

It wasn't easy getting down the stairs with that trolley. I had to sort of bump it down, one step at a time, but before long I was back in the car park, trying to think how I was going to get it into the car. I'd assumed that when the girl said 'files' she meant manila folders, maybe in a cardboard box. This was something much more sophisticated, obviously. I'd been thinking, 'Maybe I'll open it when I get in the car, just have a quick squiz before I get it home and Pat rips into it.' Now I was thinking, 'Where would you start?'

Now, if you know my wife, Pat, you'll have guessed she was waiting for me when I pulled into the drive.

'Where are they?' she said, because she, too, had been thinking 'files' as in manila folders. I got out of the station wagon, opened the boot and pointed. The trolley was on its back, taking up every inch of space and then some.

'You're joking,' said Pat. 'What is that?'

'It could be court documents,' I said. 'But I haven't yet looked.'

Pat said, 'I told you! It's something to help me get the decision overturned.' Then she rushed inside to get the rubber-backed picnic blanket to lay down over the rear bumper, so I could get the trolley out without scratching the car.

'There's boxes as well!' she said. 'I can't wait to see.'

I told her straight, 'Listen, Pat. I've decided I'd rather do this on my own.'

'On your own?'

To say Pat was startled was to understate it. Ours is the kind of marriage where Pat has always opened the mail.

'I don't see what the big secret is, Barry,' she said, hands on hips.

'There's no big secret. I'd just like to be the one that goes through it.'

Miffed, Pat said, 'Well, Barry, if you want to be secretive, you go ahead. Take it down to Brian's room. You can have all the privacy you want there.'

I did exactly as I was told: pushed the trolley up into the house and down the hall to Brian's room and stood it near the wall. As I say, it had four shelves. The top three contained lever-arch files covered in white, with plastic overlay. The fourth had boxes with the same shiny white covers, and steel corners.

I took a lever-arch off the top shelf, and opened it. On the first page were the words *Monaghan v Hartshorn*, names that meant absolutely nothing to me. Well, okay, not absolutely nothing. I'm not a complete buffoon – I'm one of those few people who still reads the papers. The name Hartshorn – I knew that name. Most people do. But I didn't immediately remember where I knew it from. Anyway, the rest of the file was basically an index, with words like 'Appendix A (*i*) – Exford Police report, March 1964' and 'Appendix A (*ii*): Newspaper Clipping, *Melton Mail Express*,

April 1964' and so on, and I don't need to tell you it was all Greek to me. So I put that file back, and opened the next one. It was filled with what looked like transcripts from a court case, which again meant nothing to me, so I opened a box from the bottom shelf. It had a smaller box inside, thin cardboard, with those mini cassette tapes nobody uses any more, plus some newspaper clippings, a leather-bound blotter, and a couple of photographs of children I didn't recognise.

Every one of these items had a yellow Post-It note stuck to it, labelling it, and referring it back to the files. Confused, I left the box and went back into the kitchen. Pat must have heard me coming but she made a point of looking busy, chopping carrots.

'I'm not sure I really get it, love,' I said. 'It's court transcripts and old documents, none of which seem to have anything to do with us.'

Pat put down the knife and turned to me, wiping her hands on her apron.

'So, now you want my help?' she said.

'I can't work it out,' I said. 'Maybe you'll have more luck.'

'You should have let me open it,' Pat said, bustling in. I followed and found Pat opening the first of the files, with her brow creased up.

'These are court documents,' she said.

'That's what I thought,' I said.

'But they're not *our* court documents.'

'No.'

'They belong to somebody else,' Pat said. 'Are you even allowed to have these?'

'I don't think Frank would have given me something I wasn't allowed to have.'

'I need my glasses,' Pat said. 'Give me yours.'

I handed my reading glasses to Pat, who put them on her nose. Let me go off track for a minute and say I like it when she does that. Pat's reading glasses are rimless, with fine silver arms. Mine are big and black and bold, and when Pat wears them, they shrink her face, or soften it, and make her look like when she was a young girl on the production line at Kinnear's rope factory, agreeing to meet me after work in the Footscray Mall.

'This is to do with somebody's divorce,' Pat said. She had put down the first of the lever-arch files, and gone to the box I'd left open on Brian's old desk.

'And these photographs,' she said. 'Are these the children of a divorce? But whose divorce?'

I still had no idea. The first of the pictures was obviously quite old – it was colour, but faded colour, with a white border, like they used to put on photographs years and years ago, and it was of a small boy wearing long socks. It had the name 'Garry' written on the back. A second photograph was much newer – it was all colour – and it was of a little girl with pink cheeks and blonde curls and a happy, gappy smile. On the back it said, 'Matilda'.

'We don't know any Matilda, Barry.'

'No,' I agreed. 'There's no note. It looks like documents, from a court case. *Monaghan v Hartshorn.* That's the name on it.'

Pat's brow furrowed. 'Hartshorn?' she said. 'Like Rick Hartshorn, the car dealer?'

'I suppose,' I said. 'But we don't know them. We don't know any Hartshorns.'

'I remember something about a custody case with him,' Pat said. 'Something about a little girl?'

Now that she said it, it did ring a bell. Rick Hartshorn, the car king, he'd been in the papers. There was something about a child of his – a daughter? A granddaughter? – caught in some kind of drama. The details, they were lost to me, but yes, I remembered something.

'But why would Frank send the files from Rick Hartshorn's case to me?' I said.

'You're sure there's no note?' she said. 'There must be some kind of note.'

'No note,' I said, again. 'There's an index. But other than that, all I've got is the card with the number for Frank's personal assistant on it. I'm supposed to call her if there's anything we don't understand.'

'Well, Barry,' said Pat, 'you'll have to call. I mean, it's obvious what's happened. Frank wasn't well. He would have been on all kinds of medication. He's told his assistant to package up the wrong things.'

I have to admit that did make sense, and so, a day or so later, I got on the phone to Pam Harris.

'Excuse me, and I hope I'm not bothering you,' I said. 'My name is Barry Harrison, and I'm –'

Pam said, 'I know who you are. You're Barry Harrison of Barkly Street, Footscray. An old school friend of Justice Brooks.'

'Yes,' I said.

Pam said, 'I packaged up *Monaghan v Hartshorn* for you. The secretary from Justice Brooks' chambers called. She said you'd picked it up.'

I said, 'I have, Mrs Harris, but you'll have to excuse me. The truth is, I don't know the Hartshorns. I know of Rick Hartshorn, obviously, but don't know him personally – no, I don't. Nothing in the package means anything to me, and not to my wife, either.'

Pam said, 'You know the story, though?'

I said, 'I wish I could say I did. I've got the vaguest recollection of something involving a child of his, or a grandchild, caught in some kind of trouble. But it was never any of my business.'

Pam paused. Then she said, 'Maybe it would be best if we got together to talk about this?'

The next thing I knew, I was catching a tram from Footscray into the city, then another out to Glen Waverley, where Mrs Harris – Pam – lived. I raised the knocker but before I could bring it down, Pam opened the door. She looked exactly how I thought she would from her voice: she was about my age, maybe a year or two older, and she was wearing a tartan skirt, soft shoes that were like Hush Puppies, and a vest with a harlequin pattern down the front. A cat was winding around her ankles.

'Barry Harrison,' she said. 'Come on in. Meet my husband, Ron.'

I followed her down the hall to a sitting room. Ron was sitting in an armchair, reading a book. He had slippers on his feet and glasses on his nose. He rose to shake my hand and then said, 'I'll leave you two.' He put the book under his arm and went into what I assume was the main bedroom. He didn't close the door behind him, which made me think he was a bit like me, meaning old-fashioned: he would leave Pam alone to talk to this strange bloke, but only if he could keep an eye on things. I saw him settle back against a European pillow, and open up his book again. His feet were in socks, and his legs were crossed at the ankle.

Pam said, 'You're a friend of Justice Brooks, aren't you, Barry, from when he was a schoolboy?'

I said, 'We were next-door neighbours. We lost touch for a while with him being at uni and then at the Bar and the Bench, but there was always a friendship there.'

'I liked him very much,' said Pam. 'But I didn't know him for anywhere near that long.'

'How long did you work for him?'

Pam said, 'Almost twenty years. People used to say I was the only one who had the patience. I was forever telling new girls, "I'll deal with Justice Brooks; he's set in his ways."'

I said, 'I used to joke: "You never actually got old, Frank, because you were born an old man." At thirteen he was exactly as he was at sixty-three.'

Pam said, 'Even twenty years ago he had old-fashioned habits. He used to bring a boiled egg into chambers every day. A boiled egg, with a pinch of salt twisted into Glad Wrap. He'd leave the bits of shell wherever he happened to be when he peeled it, then complain loudly about bits of shell everywhere.'

I said, 'He used to do that at school. The egg part, I mean. Not the complaining.'

Pam said, 'He scolded a woman once for wearing pants in court. All the women lawyers threatened some kind of boycott. Of course, it never happened. But it did make the papers.'

'I remember that,' I said. 'He joked about it. He said, "They say I don't like women. All my life, I've loved women!"'

'He was a character.'

We smiled at each other and then I said, 'In his defence, it can't have been much fun, being a judge on the Family Court.'

Pam said, 'I can't count the number of times Justice Brooks said to me, "What did we do to deserve this, Ms Harris?" One case I remember, the wife came in saying she wanted to drive around town in a car with a bumper sticker saying "All Men Are Bastards". Justice Brooks had to say,

"And what lessons do you think your children are learning, while you carry on like this?"'

I said, 'Some people called him the Fathers' Rights judge.'

Pam said, 'They did. And that was unfair. He didn't like the way men got cut out of their children's lives after divorce, especially now, with men more involved in their children's lives, changing nappies et cetera. But people took what he said and twisted it.'

I paused a bit, waiting for the moment where I could raise the problem of the documents Pam had put together for me.

'Pam,' I said. 'The files Frank left for me – the folders and photographs and so forth . . . My wife, Pat, she's wondering if Frank wasn't a bit confused . . . Is it possible he made a mistake?'

Pam straightened up in her chair, even though she had already been sitting pretty straight. 'There's no mistake from my end,' she said. 'Justice Brooks wanted you to have every file we had from *Monaghan v Hartshorn*. He trusted you to handle things.'

I said, 'Can you tell me what it was he wanted me to do, exactly? Because Rick Hartshorn's dead, isn't he? I read somewhere that he died.'

Pam said, 'He's dead. Yes, he died not that long ago, actually. And when he did, well . . . It's all very upsetting, Barry. But Frank said you'd know what to do.'

She paused again. I would have had to be made of stone, not to see how distressed she was getting.

'Look, it's okay,' I said, a bit panicked to find myself in a lady's house, with her getting close to tears.

'No, I'm sorry,' she said. 'I don't mean to get upset. But I don't really want to go into the details. It's . . . well, it's just a mess, is the best way to put it. Justice Brooks, he made a mistake. He said some wrong things. Did some wrong things, or was about to, anyway. And it wasn't clear to him at the time how badly wrong . . . and then, when he found out, he was already so sick . . . And now he's gone, and there's been a great injustice done . . .'

I said, 'But do you have any idea what Frank wanted *me* to do about it?'

'Well,' said Pam. 'You're a newspaper man, aren't you?'

I said, 'I'm not a newspaper man . . . I mean, yes, I worked for newspapers, but I was on the printing side.'

'Well,' said Pam, and again, I could see her getting upset. 'That's odd. Very odd. Justice Brooks said you worked for newspapers. I assumed he meant as a reporter. His idea was that somebody needed to tell the story. To get the truth out there, and try to undo the wrong that's been done.'

Pam was by now wringing her hands, and her husband must have been able to either see or sense it, because it was at about this point that he came out of the bedroom, still in his socks.

'Could I interest either of you in a cup of tea?' he said.

I rose and said, 'Thanks, Ron, but no. My wife's at home. She'll be waiting on me, to tell her what I've found out.'

Pam said, 'I'm not sure I've been much help in that regard.'

I said, 'You've settled one thing: there's no mistake about the files. They're definitely for me.'

'Oh, they're definitely for you,' said Pam. 'Justice Brooks was quite clear about that. "Hand the matter to Barry Harrison," he said. "He'll know exactly what to do."'

Chapter Three

It won't surprise you to hear that I left Pam's place feeling no more confident about the job I had ahead of me. I thought to myself, well, Barry, at least you know Frank's files are meant for you, which was a start. As to what Frank wanted me to do with them, I was still uncertain.

If Frank had made a mistake in a custody hearing, wasn't that a matter for another court, or another judge? What did Pam mean when she said nobody seemed to know what to do about it?

I told Pat, 'Frank's assistant is lovely, but if she knows what this is about, she didn't let on. She basically said it's over to me. I can't think what to do, other than maybe get stuck into it and see what pops up. Maybe if we took a few files each . . . ?'

But Pat announced that she'd lost interest in the project.

'You know my view, Barry,' she said. 'Not to disrespect

the dead, but Frank was very ill towards the end there, and it's difficult to believe he hasn't made a mistake. Even if that isn't true, I don't want to be reading about somebody else's divorce when I've got Brian's to contend with. No. You take the files, and you read through them, and if, on the off-chance, something comes up, I'm sure you'll come and let me know.'

I wasn't that dismayed to have Pat wipe her hands of it. Part of me wished I could do the same. So I said, 'Okay, well, if that's the way you think I should play it, I'll take the files out to the shed. I can concentrate out there, stay out of your way.'

'Just don't be hours,' Pat said. 'We're due at Scott's for tea.'

'I'm not going to be hours. I'll have a quick go through and see if I can figure out what it's about. If not, I'll let Pam Harris know.'

I wheeled the trolley across the lawn. My shed's fairly standard: green tin with grey tin roof. Workbench with vice. Plastic shelves with nails in one drawer; nuts, bolts and screws in another.

There was space on the workbench under the holey Masonite where the tools hang. I put the first of the glossy white boxes there.

Pam had labelled pretty much everything in it, and obviously those things were more appealing to me than the reams of court documents. I took out the item marked 'Appendix A (i)'. It was a thing of beauty: an old police notebook with a bound leather cover, creamy pages, and the insignia of the Victoria Police faded on the front page. It had a pencil date – 1964 – on the inside. It smelled like old cigarettes. It was filled with cursive script.

I started to read it, but parts of the pencil writing had faded away, and it wasn't actually that easy to follow. I picked up the next item: it was a police report, done on an old typewriter. Some letters were faint; some had been smashed down so hard they nearly went through the paper. Where there were mistakes, a line of XXXX went through them. Between the two things, I was able to figure out that in the Victorian town of Exford, in March of 1964, police had been called out to a property by a sheep farmer called Kelly (Banjo) Patterson who was concerned about a woman who had taken a lease on one of his vacant weatherboard houses. In Patterson's statement he said:

A young lady rolled up here in an old Datsun a month or so ago, saying she needed a place to stay. She was skinny as a rake and there were two little kids with her.

Someone at the pub had told her about the house we've got, up over on the other paddock, the vacant one. It used to belong to my brother, but he's gone off the land.

I wanted to know her name, and she just said Anne, and she didn't want to say more. She had some money in her pocket, and she offered that to me, saying she wouldn't want to stay long.

There was no sense of her being shifty, just a bit scared, so I agreed to drive her and the kids up to the old house. She said no, that was fine, if I'd drive she'd follow me.

Nobody had been inside the place for a while, so it wasn't that clean.

My wife, Dallas, said she'd run the broom through, but this lady, Anne, said, no, no, it's fine the way it is.

She got the kids out of the car. She didn't tell us their names. We noticed they were skinny. Dallas tried to get them to say hello but it was like they'd jump out of their skin if she went their way.

Dallas had sweeties in her apron pocket. She took out two, and the kids near fell over themselves to get to them.

Anyway, this Anne said she'd like to take the place, and I said fine, and left her to it.

I don't say we never checked up on her after that, we did. Two weeks ago – that's a guess – I took the jeep up that way, and there was Anne, ankle deep in the dry grasses, which you don't want to do unless you're immune to those March flies.

I hollered, but she didn't say much.

Then, about a week ago my Dallas took the jeep up there, to see if Anne needed anything, but nobody was about. Then this morning Dallas went up there again, and straight away got a bad feeling, got back in the jeep and drove over to the paddock where I was working.

'Banjo,' she said. 'You better come and look.'

I drove back over with Dallas, and went up to knock on the front door. Right away I could see that things weren't right. The front door was locked up, and there was something like black plastic nailed down over the windows.

I thought, 'That's not on. I never gave anyone permission to make any modifications to the property.'

I thought, 'I'm in my rights to break the door down.' But on reflection I thought I'd call the constabulary instead.

That was the end of Banjo's statement. The police sergeant took up where he left off:

Senior Constable Paul McEwan and I attended a property owned by farmer Mr Kelly (Banjo) Patterson at 12.05 hours, on 9 March 1964.

The house in question was constructed of timber, set well back from the main road. The grass was overgrown, and there was a fair amount of jumble on the front lawn.

Senior Constable McEwen attempted entry via the front door, but it appeared to have been sealed shut.

It was not possible to see through the front windows. A black plastic sheet had been fitted across the glass.

Senior Constable McEwan and I proceeded to the rear of the property to attempt access via the rear door.

The rear door was also sealed shut.

Access was gained via a back window, with the permission of, and in the presence of, property owner Mr Kelly (Banjo) Patterson.

The property was in a state of considerable decay. Debris was piled throughout the property, including in the hallway.

Garbage had been strewn about, including items of clothing in rubbish bags, unwashed cooking utensils, food scraps and empty tin cans.

The property appeared unoccupied. There was nothing to suggest the presence of children, but for a soiled cloth nappy on the kitchen floor.

Senior Constable McEwen and I were preparing to vacate the property when a small cry was heard. To my mind it was a cat's cry, but the owner of the property, Mr Patterson, appeared convinced that the cry was not that of a cat but of a child.

Together with Mr Patterson, Senior Constable McEwan and I began a thorough search of the property and its surrounds. We entered a shed, which housed a derelict vehicle owned by Mr Patterson. The car the tenant Anne had driven to the property was not sighted.

A second shed housed a tin boat on a trailer.

Shortly after 13.00 hours, Senior Constable McEwan shined a torch under the foundations of the house and called out, 'Hello?'

There was a response, but it appeared not to come from under the house, but rather from a distant structure described by Mr Patterson as 'the chicken coop'.

Senior Constable McEwan was first upon the chicken coop, and it was there that two children were located, locked in behind a secure wire gate and fence.

Both children were in a degraded, neglected condition. Their hair was matted, their faces covered in sores, their clothes sealed to their skin.

There was an empty pail in the shed: it appears that the children's mother, the lady known as Anne, had been bringing that pail down from the kitchen, filled with food scraps.

It may have been some time since the pail had come down. The children had begun tearing at the plasterboard with their hands, and gnawing on it.

Senior Constable McEwan lifted the boy from the chook shed and placed him on the ground. The child proceeded to run across the paddock. Senior Constable McEwan chased the boy down, and carried him, hay-bale style, across the paddock to the divisional van.

I myself carried the girl.

Both children were transported back to Exford police station. We have, at this point, been unable to ascertain the identity of either child.

Now that's the kind of thing you can't imagine happening until it does, isn't it? The kind of thing you hear about or read about and can hardly believe. But what did it have to do with Frank?

There seemed to be only one way to find out: keep reading. So I kept reading. It seems that police did what they could to locate Anne. It was an uphill job. Nobody could remember the licence plate on her car. She hadn't left any trace of herself around the farm house. So police did something they hardly ever do now. They put in a call to the local newspaper, *The Melton Mail Express*, which sent a reporter to the police station to get the story. They must also have sent a photographer because the article, when I found it, came with a picture of the children, and it was a shocker: the two bald kids are standing there, little and skinny and, by the look of it, terrified. From what I could tell, police had put them briefly in the care of nuns at the Sisters of Mercy, who did what nuns did with orphans in the early sixties: peeled off their clothes, gave them a good, hard scrub with a brush, hacked off their hair with shears and doused them with insecticide.

They had them dressed in cream shirts that were far too long – longer even than the skirts and shorts or whatever they had underneath – so their white legs were sticking out like sticks. To my mind, asking the public if they recognised them was a bit ambitious: if they looked like anything, it was like survivors from a concentration camp.

Anyway, the headline on the story was: 'Coop Children Now in Christian Care'.

The article said the nuns had given the girl the name 'Anne', after the mother. They had put her age at around three, but as to whether she was actually three, no one could say for certain because there was no record of her birth, or none that anyone could find.

As to the boy, the nuns put his age at around two, guessing he must have been born around 1962. And as for his name, well, when the nuns asked him what he was called, he said, 'Gary.'

When they said, 'Alright, Gary, and what is your last name?' he again said, 'Gary,' and so they said, 'Alright then, you're Garry Gary.'

Garry Gary. It's not the kind of name you forget, is it?

Anyway, from what I could tell from the rest of the documents in that box, six weeks went by without a peep from the mother and so the children were declared abandoned. That was a pretty rare thing to be in 1964 but still, the nuns took both of them in (not together: Anne went to a girls' home, and Garry Gary to a boys' home) and, pretty soon after that, they became available for adoption. So far so good. But then, for reasons I've never been able to figure out, it seems that nobody wanted Anne.

Her file from the orphanage made it clear that she stayed with the Sisters of Mercy for thirteen years, probably learning how to sew up a hole in a sock, or how to wash and peel potatoes, and then, when she was around sixteen, she was turned out, to become a live-in helper for an elderly widow, but she didn't live long. Her death certificate – Appendix A (*iv*) – was in the box. 'Death By Misadventure', it said. But I dug a bit further and found out she got run over by a goods train on the Melton–Bacchus Marsh line.

As to Garry Gary, well, I suppose he had something of an easier time of it. His file from the Christian Brothers orphanage shows that he got adopted at about age four by a couple called John and Joan Cooper. Like the Pattersons, they were sheep people from Exford and they already had one child, known to them, and I suppose to everyone, as Beam. How did he get that name? Well, I hope I'm not offending anyone here – but apparently everyone knew, from the day he was born, that there was something wrong with Beam. The Coopers told the orphanage, 'He hasn't been right since he was born.' Water on the brain – that's what was on their application file. 'One child, water on the brain.' Today, we'd say: *hydrocephalus*. I've looked it up on the internet. The word itself, it comes from the Greek: *hydro*, for water, and *kephalos*, for head. So, literally, *water head*. There's a treatment for it these days, a thing called a shunt. They drain the fluid from the brain down to the stomach, but in 1958, when Beam was born, there weren't any shunts. You could drill a hole in the baby's head, but people thought that was a bit radical and not every hospital did it. They didn't do it for Beam, whose name was actually Dean, but Beam was all he could manage, and so everybody used it.

It was because Beam was born damaged that his parents – Joan and John – decided to adopt their next baby. John

Cooper told the orphanage they had a property, and things that needed doing: a fence to upkeep, or a gravel driveway to put down. John Cooper also told the orphanage he wanted to pass his name on, and since Beam wasn't likely to give the Coopers a grandson, they'd need to find some other way of getting one.

As to whether the Coopers knew Garry Gary was one of the Coop Children, the documents Frank left for me didn't say. They said only that the Coopers wanted a boy, and preferably one that was a bit younger than Beam. Garry was described as 'sturdy', with no lice or nervous conditions. He was 'progressing well' in Bible studies and was 'dry at night'.

The Christian Brothers provided a photograph of Garry, I suppose so the Coopers could inspect it. It's hard not to feel sorry for the kid in that picture. He's got long grey socks on with grey shorts. He's got a white shirt and small tie, and what I call the Christian Brothers haircut: short back and sides, like the military. He's holding a hard brown case, like a schoolboy's lunchbox. I couldn't imagine what would be in it. Maybe an apple? Because what else did he have?

The photograph is dated November 1966, which means Garry was about four when it was taken, when the Coopers came for him. You'd have to be cold as ice not to feel for him – mother gone, separated from his sister, about to be adopted into a family of people he'd never met before.

Do you reckon he would have been scared? I know I would have been.

Chapter Four

I've told you already about how Frank and I had a tradition, while he was alive, to get together for precisely two beers every year or two. One of the things we – or he – often talked about was how divorce had got more common. Anyone reading this who's about my age will know what I mean.

Back when I got married, and when Frank got married, people who wanted to get a divorce needed to have a reason. Adultery, maybe, or abandonment. But not any more. When a couple wants to get divorced these days, they have to go see a Family Court counsellor first. 'The counsellor's not there to save the marriage,' Frank would say. 'The counsellor's there to help the couple get *divorced*. And they don't need a reason.'

I thought it was funny, the way he put it. But Frank was actually in favour of counselling. He was in favour of anyone who could bang a couple's heads together before they tore each other apart in court, anyone who could help them to come to some kind of agreement over houses, kids, super, whatever the sticking point was; anyone who might be able to make things a bit cheaper, or easier for everyone.

Now, by law, I'm not allowed to tell you the name of the counsellor that dealt with our Brian when he was divorcing Nerida and, likewise, I'm not allowed to tell you the name of the counsellor that dealt with Garry Gary, when he grew up, got married and then divorced, and found himself in the Family Court, arguing over his little girl, Matilda. I'm going to call him Dr Ian Bell. It's a made-up name – for no reason other than I like the sound of it. You're going to get used to hearing it, because by my count, Dr Bell sat in on twelve sessions with Garry Gary. He taped those sessions and the sessions with Matilda's mum, and those tapes had been transcribed, plus there were dozens of other documents directly related to the case, and together these made up the files that Frank had left for me. In putting this story together, you should know that I've read through every one of those files, and I've listened to each tape. That last bit was more difficult than you might think, because like I said, the tapes were those miniature ones. I had to go to Tandy and get the right size recorder, and then the bloke in the shop didn't want to sell me one.

'What do you want a tape recorder for? Go digital!' he said.

I had to explain: 'I've got old tapes I have to play.'

'You'll want to transfer those to disk!' he said. 'Then go digital, and you'll never have to buy another cassette tape again!'

In the end, he agreed to sell me a tape recorder. I took it out to the shed, found a power point for it, pressed play. I wasn't entirely sure what I was going to hear, or how things would play out, but I quickly got the hang of it. There were two voices on the tape. One was Garry Gary, who was talking to a counsellor about his collapsed marriage. And do you want to know what was the first thing he said? He said, 'Right, let's get this over with.'

Dr Bell said, 'Hold up, there. Why don't you sit down?'

Garry said, 'So you can begin telling me how I'm not entitled to see my own daughter? How I should give up the custody case and leave her mum to it?'

Dr Bell was used to that kind of talk, obviously. He said, 'Well, Garry, you're booked in for forty-five minutes, and I can see already that you're keen to get out of here, so the sooner we get started, the sooner we'll be finished.'

There's a rustling sound on the tape at this point, which must have meant that Garry was agreeing to sit down. Then he said, 'I don't see why I should be here.'

Dr Bell replied, 'I hear that quite a bit.'

Garry said, 'But this is such bullshit. I've never needed a psychiatrist in my life.'

Dr Bell seemed unperturbed. 'I'm not actually a psychiatrist. I'm a psychologist. But most of the people who sit in that chair feel the same: they don't want to be here.'

Garry wouldn't let it drop. 'But I feel like I'm on trial.'

'Let me assure you, you're not on trial.'

Garry said, 'But I am on trial, aren't I? On trial for the right to see my own daughter.'

Dr Bell said patiently, 'Your wife will have to go through the same process. Whatever you may think, Garry, I'm not on anyone's side. I'm very much independent. Nobody is going to tell you to give up your custody battle. In fact, this being our first session, why don't we put aside Matilda for a moment and talk about you.'

Garry said, 'Whatever.'

Dr Bell said, 'I need your full name, and how old you are, how many brothers and sisters you have, that kind of thing. So, to begin: your parents. Where are they?'

Garry snorted, by which I mean he made one of those sounds that blokes make when they think they're being conned.

'Here we go!' he said. 'Here we bloody go!'

Dr Bell said, 'I beg your pardon?'

Garry said, 'Here we bloody go!'

'I'm not sure what you mean?'

'Well, I'm adopted, aren't I? I'm adopted, which you probably already know, and now that's going to be used against me, am I right?'

Dr Bell didn't sound surprised, exactly, but he set Garry quite straight.

'I didn't know you were adopted,' he said.

Garry snorted again. 'Of course you did.'

Dr Bell said, 'You don't have to believe me, Garry, but I'm coming to this with a clean slate. Whatever you say to me here today, you can be sure it's the first time I've heard it.'

Garry said, 'And yet you start with the fact that I'm adopted?'

Dr Bell said, 'If you recall, I didn't start with anything. *You* told me you were adopted.'

Garry's response to that was not recorded. Maybe he rolled his eyes or looked up at the ceiling or down at the floor. There's a bit of silence on the tape but you can feel the tension. Then Dr Bell says, 'But since you've raised it, let's start with that. You were adopted. Why was that? What happened to your biological parents?'

Garry didn't immediately answer. Then he said, 'I'm told my natural mum did a runner when I was a little kid. I went to the Christian Brothers, and they adopted me out.'

Dr Bell said, 'When you say your mother did a runner . . . ?'

Garry said, 'All I know is what the orphanage told me, which is that Mum was renting out near Exford. There was no bloke around so I can't say who my real dad is, and then one day, Mum wasn't around either. The cops knocked down the door to our house, but we weren't in the house, we were locked outside, in, like, a hen house. The cops took us to the orphanage, and then we went into homes for a while and, in the end, I got adopted out, and my sister didn't.'

Dr Bell said, 'And where is your sister now?'

Garry said, 'She's dead.' Just like that: 'She's dead.'

Dr Bell said, 'I'm sorry to hear that. When did she die, Garry?'

'Twenty years ago. More. When she was eighteen, nineteen. Run over by a train, or so they reckon. Sounds dodgy to me. But in any case, I hadn't seen her since I was two. None of which has anything to do with what's at stake here, which is Matilda.'

Dr Bell said, 'I understand that. But I need your help to build up a picture of you, Garry. From what you've said so far, you didn't have the easiest childhood.'

Garry said, 'Right. And once you've built up your picture of me, and my lousy childhood, you'll be able to use it against me in the court.'

Dr Bell said, 'That's not correct. I'm not for or against you, Garry. My role is to examine both parents, so the court can make a decision as to what is in Matilda's best interests.'

Garry said, 'And it's not going to be in her interests to see her father?'

Dr Bell said, 'In most cases it certainly *is* in a child's best interests to see their father. But we're getting way ahead of ourselves. Why don't you tell me what happened when you got adopted?'

Now there's a sigh from Garry.

'I don't know more than I've already told you,' he said. 'My sister and me, we were abandoned. We got put into a home – into two homes, actually, because they had one for boys and one for girls – and then I got adopted out. When I was eighteen I got a telegram saying Anne – that was my sister's name, or at least what they called her – was dead, which was a bit odd to hear. I was like: why are you telling me this? I wouldn't know her if I fell over her in the street.'

Dr Bell said, 'Did you go to Anne's funeral?'

Garry said, 'No. She'd already been dead a year when they told me about it.'

'Do you know why there was a delay?'

Garry said, 'I asked about that. They said I had no right to know until I was eighteen.'

'Alright. Well then, you've said that you got adopted out, even if Anne didn't. What can you tell me about the family that raised you?'

Garry hesitated before answering. 'What do you want to know?'

Dr Bell said, 'Well, how many of them were there? Were you their only child? If there were any other children, were they adopted?'

Garry said, 'I've got one brother. Beam.'

'Beam?'

'Beam. Yeah, well, his real name's Dean, but we call him Beam. That's what he says when you ask him what his name is. He's retarded. He still lives with Mum.'

'By Mum, you mean your *adopted* mum?'

'That's right.'

Dr Bell softened his voice. 'You're close to her?'

'Yes.'

'And to . . . Beam?'

'Yes.'

'Although he's older than you?'

'He is.'

You can't quite hear what Dr Bell says next, but I'm guessing he must be asking how much older Beam was than Garry.

Garry said, 'Two years, I think. So he was, yeah, maybe seven when I arrived. He's just had his fiftieth. Not that it matters. With the condition he's got – water on the brain – it's like he's fifteen.'

Dr Bell said, 'Do you have any memory of the years before you were adopted?'

'Only what I've told you.'

'About being abandoned by your natural mother?'

'About being left in a chicken coop.'

'Did you ever speak to your adopted parents about any of that?'

'No.'

'And you've never thought to find out whether your real mother is still alive?'

'To be honest with you, Doc, the only time I've ever thought about her was when Matilda was born.'

'Meaning . . . you wished that she was alive to see Matilda?'

'Are you joking? I wouldn't let her within a bull's roar of Matilda. No. I thought, "How could you dump a child that's your own?" What kind of bitch must she have been?'

There's real anger in Garry's voice when he says this, which to my mind is completely understandable. Dr Bell certainly seems to get it. He says 'Alright. And . . . Garry? Is that your real name?'

'It's the name they gave me in the orphanage.'

'And from what I see here, they gave it to you twice: you're Garry Gary Hartshorn?'

'I was Garry Gary in the orphanage. When I got adopted out, I became Garry Gary Cooper. Now I'm Garry Gary Hartshorn. But Garry's fine.'

Dr Bell pauses a bit here, and there's a scratchy sound on the tape, like he's opening a manila folder, or shuffling through some paperwork.

'And how did you become Garry Gary Hartshorn, from Garry Gary Cooper?'

Garry said, 'Well, the Coopers adopted me, and then old John Cooper died, and when Mum got remarried I took the new bloke's name, which, I'm sure you know, was Hartshorn.'

Dr Bell said, 'Wait . . . your adopted father died?'

'Yep.'

'When you were how old?'

'I don't know. Maybe ten? But we're going over some pretty ancient ground here, Doc. This was more than thirty years ago. It's got nothing to do with Matilda.'

Dr Bell said, 'As I've said, it all helps build up a picture of you.'

Garry said, 'A picture of me that you can put in a report that will go to Softie's lawyers.'

Dr Bell said, 'My report does not go to Softie – to your wife's – lawyers. My report will go to the judge in the Family Court. It helps me understand where you're coming from, that's all.'

Garry said, 'Right, and you'll compare my report with Softie's and say, "Oh, she's from a good home, and she's not adopted, and she's got the better family," and you'll recommend that Minty – Matilda – go and live with her, and I can see her on weekends and half the school holidays, just like in the good old days.'

Dr Bell said, 'Garry, believe it or not, a lot of people who come into these offices have been adopted. It doesn't make them bad parents. I'm interested only in knowing what effect your adoption had on you. For all I know it's made you a better parent, more determined than most to stay in your daughter's life, even if you and your wife aren't going to be together.'

Garry said, 'If it was up to me, we'd still *be* together. That's got to count for something, that I didn't choose this situation.'

Dr Bell said, 'Again, I'm wondering what effect you think being adopted had on you?'

Garry seemed irritated. 'And like I said, it had no effect on me.'

'Okay. Well then, Garry, let's talk about the family that took you in, the Coopers. You've said you're close to your mum. What about your adopted dad, John Cooper? Did you like him, Garry?'

'He was good to me. They both were.'

'And did they make you feel like you were part of the family?'

'Sure. Of course.'

'Both of them?'

'Sure. Why not?'

'And your relationship with Beam?'

'No problems there.'

'And how were things at school?'

At this point in the tape it sounds a bit like Garry is shifting in his seat. 'The kids at school might have wanted to pick on Beam, but they were going to have to get through me first,' he said.

'I meant, how was school for you, Garry?'

'For me, what? School was school.'

Dr Bell persisted. 'Did the other students know that you were adopted? I don't imagine you were the only one, in the sixties?'

'They knew.'

'And did any of them make an issue of that? Or was it mostly Beam you were standing up for?'

'It was mostly Beam. They might have tried to have a crack at me, but then I clonked one of them, and that kind of put a stop to it.'

'And in more general terms, Garry, your childhood with the Coopers, was it a happy one?'

'Sure. I mean, it was normal.'

Dr Bell said, 'Normal?'

'It was normal. I don't know what you want, Doc. We had a house in Exford, like a farm property, but it made no money. We had to shoot some sheep one year, because of the drought. After that, old man Cooper got a job at some factory in Footscray. Mum stayed home. She had to, because of Beam. I went to Exford primary. What else is there?'

'You weren't poor, then? Despite the drought, and being out on a farm?'

'We weren't poor, no. Because John Cooper worked.'

'And in terms of childhood memories, what do you recall?'

Garry seems genuinely confused. 'Memories? Like, of Christmas or whatever?'

Dr Bell said, 'Yes, that kind of thing.'

'I got a pushbike when I was eight. Mum made me wear an ice-cream bucket on my head when I rode it. She had this idea that magpies would go for a kid on a bike, peck him through the soft spot on his head. So I had to wear this helmet with black eyes painted on it. That was pretty embarrassing.'

I can imagine Dr Bell smiling at this point. He says, 'Anything else?'

'There was a creek at the bottom of the property. I'd get tadpoles there, and put them in Mum's old Nescafé jars. And then, like I said, when I was about ten, the old man,

John Cooper, he died, and a new bloke moved in.'

Dr Bell said, 'You're moving a bit fast there, Garry. How did your father die?'

'Keeled over at work. Just dropped dead. Durries did him in.'

'You mean he smoked?'

'Yeah. But everybody did.'

'Do you smoke, Garry?'

Quick as a flash Garry said, 'No. Softie does though.'

Dr Bell said, 'We'll get to Softie. Tell me more about your old man. It must have been a shock, the way you've described it, him just keeling over. I mean, the two of you were close, were you?'

Garry said, 'I don't know about close. We got on pretty good. He was a Doggies fan. AFL. Footscray. Now called the Western Bulldogs. We'd get a train, then a tram to Doggie Park on Saturdays in the freezing cold. He got me a duffle coat, one of those with numbers on the back. Wanted me to be Doggies too.'

'And were you?'

'Still am.'

'What else did the two of you do together?'

'Not much. When the Doggies played away he'd sit up in the tool shed with the radio on, listening to the cricket. This was the "bowled Lillee, caught Marsh" era, so it was good times. You weren't allowed to talk much, in case he missed a ball. He'd smoke and mess around with paint cans. And his smokes were Camels. He'd smoke a pack a day. He had yellow fingers. Yellow, near the joint, with brown nails. You don't see that much any more.'

Dr Bell said, 'He can't have been that old when he died?'

'I've never thought about how old he was. But yeah, maybe forty? Obviously that doesn't seem that young when you're ten.'

'Did you love him, Garry?'

Garry snorted. '*Love* him?' he said.

'Did you love him like a father, I mean? He was like a father to you, wasn't he?'

Garry said, 'Come on, Doc. He adopted me, so yeah, he was like a dad, but I mean we're talking the 1970s now. Blokes then, they didn't have much to do with kids, adopted or otherwise. You didn't see them changing the dirty nappies, all the stuff that I've done with Matilda. You wouldn't go to your old man to play games. If I'd said to old man Cooper, "Oh, I'm bored," he would have said, "Go play in the traffic." Or, "Go bang your head on a brick wall."'

Dr Bell said, 'I take it that's not the way you are, with Matilda?'

'Shit, no. I mean, no. I've put effort in. Minty – Matilda – loves her dad.'

Dr Bell said, 'So what happened after old man Cooper died?'

Garry said, 'Things were pretty rough for a bit. But then Mum got married again and I suppose they got better.'

'When you say you "suppose" they got better, you mean, financially? Or in terms of your happiness?'

Garry said, 'I mean, financially.'

Dr Bell said, 'And who did your mother marry? Was it someone you knew?'

Garry snorted again. 'Like you don't know.' And again, Dr Bell had to say: 'I assure you, Garry, I don't know. Why should I know?'

'She married Rick Hartshorn.'

Dr Bell said, 'Rick Hartshorn, the car salesman?'

Garry said, 'That's right.'

'The one from the ads?'

'You got it.'

'Well, there you go, Garry. I didn't know that he was married. But how old were you when your mother married him?'

'Eleven, maybe twelve.'

'So not too long after John Cooper died?'

'That's right.'

'I'm assuming, at the age of eleven – maybe twelve – you had an opinion about that? About your mum marrying Rick Hartshorn, I mean?'

Garry said, 'Well, first up, he wasn't famous then. Not like he is now. He might have had just the one car yard on Footscray Road, the one he started with. This was years ago so, you know, I suppose he had some money, but not the empire. But by contrast, we'd been doing it tough. I mean, Mum couldn't work because of Beam, and so once John

Cooper died we had no money coming in, except for what the government gave Mum, which I take it wasn't a lot. So, where we'd always had just enough, things were suddenly a bit tight and Mum was starting to go without at teatime. Like, putting down chops and peas for Beam and me and saying, "Oh, you boys go on. I'm not hungry. Grown-ups don't really get hungry. I've done my growing." Beam was fooled, obviously, but I wasn't because, you know, when the bills came in, she'd cry.'

Dr Bell said, 'And then your mother married Rick Hartshorn, and things improved?'

Garry said, 'Yeah, well, in a way they improved. Like I say, he wasn't absolutely loaded then, like now. He was just starting out. This was, what, the early seventies, so Franco Cozzo had gone on TV and started with his ads – *Come on down to Franco Cozzo* – and I kind of remember Hartshorn saying, that's bloody genius, and making up his own version, shouting and waving his arms around, you know: *Come and break my heart at Hartshorn Motors*. And it was only after that – that, and the arrival of all the Jap cars – that his business kind of took off. So it wasn't all the luxury cars, the sponsorship of the Grand Prix and owning racehorses and all the stuff he does now, not when I was a kid.'

Dr Bell said, 'Do you recall how your mother met Rick Hartshorn, Garry?'

Garry paused for a minute. 'The way they tell it, Mum went to him to get a new car. The old man – John Cooper – had a big car, a Holden I think, pretty heavy for a lady to drive. So after he died, Mum went up to Hartshorn's – that's what everyone called it, Hartshorn's – hoping to trade the big car in for a little Gemini or something, and Rick Hartshorn himself was there, to do the deal.'

Dr Bell said, 'And did he sell your mother a car, or did he ask her out, or what happened?'

'He sold her a car. A blue one. The Ga-Mini, we called it.'

'And then he married her?'

'That's the story,' Garry said.

Dr Bell said, 'And how was that for you, Garry? Was it unsettling, having a new man in the house so soon after John Cooper's death?'

Garry said, 'You're talking like I had a say in things. Like I could have put a stop to it, even if I'd wanted to.'

Dr Bell said, 'And did you?'

'Did I what?'

'Want to put a stop to it?'

Garry said, 'It wouldn't have mattered if I had. I mean, before it actually happened Mum made a big fuss of sitting us down – me and Beam, I mean – and saying this is really lucky, because Rick Hartshorn's a good man, he's got a good business, and not everyone would be interested in taking on a woman with two kids.'

Dr Bell said, 'And how did that make you feel, Garry? The idea that you – and Beam – might be a burden to your mum, as she set out to get remarried?'

Garry said, 'I never thought of it like that.'

'Never?'

'No.'

'Alright. Well I'm guessing things must have worked out quite well, given that you took Rick Hartshorn's name?'

Garry's voice was pretty sharp when he said, 'That was Mum's idea. She goes: "It'll be better if we all have the same name. It'll be better for you at school. We don't want people gossiping: are they married or not?" Which is why Beam took the name too. I mean, unlike me he was actually a Cooper. A real Cooper. John Cooper's son. But he's Dean Hartshorn now. Not that it matters.'

Dr Bell said, 'Why do you say that? Why doesn't it matter?'

'I'm not sure how much he actually knows about what his last name is, or isn't.'

Dr Bell said, 'And after your mother married Rick Hartshorn, did you stay in the same house, or move into his house, or what?'

'We stayed put for a while in that little house we had in Exford. It's probably fallen down now. But they've moved on, anyway. They're in Williamstown now, in that place that's always on the news when they do a property story, the one with the boat ramp that goes all the way out. Rick's got an interest in the boat races, obviously. He's got boats and cars, and horses. His big thing is to run a horse in the Melbourne Cup. Whether that will happen, I don't know.'

Dr Bell said, 'I notice you don't refer to Rick Hartshorn as Dad, Garry. You say Rick?'

Garry said, 'Well, that's his name.'

'And your relationship with him, is it good?'

Garry pauses here, as if he's thinking about how to phrase his response. 'Ah, well, it's alright,' he says. 'He's not the bloke you see on the ads, you know. He's not actually like that, waving his arms around and cheerful all the time. That's just the character.'

Dr Bell said, 'And, as I say, you don't talk about him as though he's your father.'

Garry said, 'Well, he's not, is he?'

'But your adopted mum – Joan Cooper – she's Mum, isn't she?'

'She is. But she's been on the scene a lot longer, remember.'

'And that's why Rick Hartshorn isn't Dad?'

'That's one reason.'

'There are others?'

'Look, Doc,' he said. 'If you're asking if I'm close to him, I'll say: not particularly. Rick Hartshorn is alright. We're not best mates, but he's okay. There's a part of me that thinks, you know, if people knew him like I knew him, maybe they wouldn't think he was such a funny character. But then, Mum is obviously fond of him. They've been married a long time. So there's the fact that he's done the right thing by her and by Beam. I've got to respect that.'

Dr Bell said, 'So, then, you respect him?'

Garry said, 'I respect what he's done. For Mum. For Beam. Sure. But the main thing you should know about Rick Hartshorn, Doc, is that Softie thinks the sun shines out of him. And Rick just loves Softie. Right from the start, and especially when she was pregnant with Matilda, I can't count the number of times he told me, "She's the best thing that's ever happened to you, Garry. Make sure you don't muck this up." Like it was all up to me whether it went pear-shaped or not.'

Dr Bell said, 'He was looking forward to being a grand-father, I suppose. Because he has no other children, does he, besides you and Beam?'

Garry said, 'Well, that's right. And he was, what, in his seventies when Matilda was born? So she's probably the only real baby he's ever been around. And he spoils her rotten. He got her a guinea pig and all that. He puts her up to ride on his ponies.'

Dr Bell said, 'Well, that sounds positive, Garry. Yet you sound quite negative about it. Don't you think it's good for Matilda to have a strong relationship with her grand-father?'

Garry said, 'But he's not her grandfather. Rick Harts-horn's not. He's got no blood ties to her at all. He's married to my mother, who adopted me. I've always thought it was a bit rich, actually, Softie getting Matilda to call him Grandpa.'

'And why do you think she does that, Garry?'

Garry said, 'Who the hell knows what Softie's thinking? Maybe she's got her eye on the Hartshorn fortune. That wouldn't surprise me. And what you should know, Doc, is that she was absolutely rapt when she found out who he was. That we were related, I mean. That he was married to my mother. I went right up in her eyes when she found out about that.'

Dr Bell said, 'Maybe she wants Matilda to have a relationship with him because she sees herself as his daughter-in-law, and therefore he is Matilda's grand-father. And maybe she thinks it's good for Matilda to stay in touch with her family, on her father's side?'

Garry said, 'Yeah, well, that would be okay if he was family. But he isn't family. He's a blow-in. *I'm* actually Matilda's father, and that's actually what we're here to talk about, isn't it?'

'Alright,' Dr Bell said. 'Fair enough. But, looking at the time, that is unfortunately all we have time for today, Garry. How was it in the end? I find that some people, despite their initial reluctance to be here, turn around during the process, and actually enjoy it.'

I was interested to hear what Garry thought about the whole thing too, but there's no answer from him on the tape.

Whether that's because he had nothing to say or because Dr Bell reached over at just that moment and pressed the off button, I can't tell you.

Chapter Five

If I had to say how long I sat listening to that first tape, well, it was probably much longer than it's just taken you to read it, and that's because I went over it more than once. To my mind, there's quite a bit to absorb. The fact that this little boy, Garry, from the hen shed had grown up to be related, in a way, to Rick Hartshorn, well, that was obviously interesting. And I could see what Garry was trying to do, which was not to lose his little girl just because his wife had pulled the pin on his marriage. I had a similar situation unfolding in my house at the time, remember. Brian and Nerida were split up, and Pat had been banned from seeing the grandkids, which meant I couldn't see them either, not without breaking her heart. And Pat was taking it hard – who wouldn't?

Whenever I put my head up from the files or walked in the house, I'd find Pat on the blower to Grandparents United (basically a group of people in the same boat as

Pat – meaning, estranged from their grandkids); or she'd be on the internet, trying to find out if there was a way she could get the court order reversed, without having to go to the Family Court. She wasn't actually getting anywhere – we still weren't seeing the grandkids – and there were only so many conversations I could have with Pat about how frustrating it was, and why wouldn't Brian let her go to court? And so, was I grateful to have a diversion, to be digging into Garry's case and pretending to Pat that my work out there in the shed might help her? Of course I was. Back to the shed and the tapes I went, and what did I find? Not another session between Dr Bell and Garry, but the first of the sessions Dr Bell had with Softie, who was, of course, Garry's wife.

To be honest, that startled me. I pressed down on the 'play' button and there was Dr Bell's voice, saying, 'Well, hello,' and then a woman's voice, saying, 'Hello,' and, 'How do you do?'

Dr Bell says, 'I'm fine, thank you. Come in. Please sit down,' and then, 'I've got your name here as *Softest Sound* – but you're Softie Monaghan, is that right?' And there was Softie's voice again, clear and crisp as a bell.

'Yes, that's right. I was christened Softest Sound. I'm known as Softie.'

Dr Bell said, 'I'm sure you've heard this before, but Softest Sound? That's obviously an unusual name.'

Softie said, 'My parents are to blame. They were hippies in the 1960s. I suppose they thought it was cute.'

'Hippies! I remember that,' Dr Bell said, I suppose because he was trying to put her at ease.

Softie didn't respond, so Dr Bell said, 'What year were you born, Softie?'

'Nineteen sixty-eight.'

'And where was that?'

'Inland of Byron Bay. A little village near Mullum-bimby.'

'In the hospital?' Dr Bell hesitated. '*Is* there a hospital?'

'There isn't a hospital. Or, if there is, I wasn't born there. I was born on the . . . on the commune, I suppose you'd call it, where we lived.'

'A home birth?'

'You could say that. My parents were slightly ahead of the hippie craze. They went up north in the late sixties, just before it became so fashionable.'

'And where did the name *Softest Sound* come from?'

Softie said, 'It was my father's idea. His philosophy then, or so my mother says, was for people to tread softly, not to make so great a mark on the earth.'

'That's not his philosophy now?'

'His philosophy now is take what you can get.'

Dr Bell said, 'I see.'

'They – my parents – they weren't hippies for very long. They became disillusioned when so many people started to join. I came to Melbourne for school when I was, what, seven? And the school wanted a proper last name, and over time I suppose I did too. I mean, *Softest*

Sound – I work in a bank, Dr Bell, it's not really . . .' She trails off a bit here. 'Anyway, Monaghan was my mother's surname, so she gave me that to use at school, and it's also what I use at work.'

Dr Bell said, 'Okay, Softie Monaghan it is. And do you have siblings?'

'Yes.'

'And what are their names?'

'Heavenly Sky, and Come The Dawn.'

'Goodness.'

'Yes. But they're now Heaven and Dawn.'

'And the three of you – you all live in Melbourne?'

'Heaven's in London – she's working in visual art. Dawn is here. Like me, she's not the imagine-no-possessions type. Not that we're greedy, but we both enjoy a hot running shower.'

Dr Bell said, 'Where in Melbourne do you live?'

'At Edgewater Towers. In St Kilda. Or I did, before I moved out. I'm hoping to get back in there, once all this is over. On the other hand, I wouldn't mind getting a place where Matilda can run around. I've owned the place at Edgewater Towers since before I was married and it's probably not suitable for Minty, now she's getting older. I probably need a place with a garden now.'

Dr Bell said, 'Edgewater Towers . . . is that the tall building, the one on the foreshore?'

'That's the one. I'm in 3A, front of the building. You can see the pier – St Kilda pier – from the balcony.'

'That's obviously quite different to how your parents lived.'

'When we were in Mullumbimby? Yes. But I mean, I don't really remember the barefoot, flowers in the hair stuff. We moved to Melbourne when I was seven. We lived pretty normally in Melbourne. I do remember feeling fantastic, moving away from Mullumbimby. Civilisation! I got a new pair of shoes. I couldn't remember having a new pair of shoes before. I was so happy about it, I wanted to wear them to bed. I thought it was a product of Mullumbimby. But now with Minty, when she gets new shoes, she won't take them off, so maybe that's just kids.'

Dr Bell said, 'How did your parents afford to move to Victoria like that, Softie, after what, six or seven years on the commune?'

'The commune was always a choice. I mean, Mum had money, because she'd inherited money when she was a little girl from an aunt. I don't know how much. Maybe not enough to buy a house these days, but enough to buy a house in Malvern when we moved here and enough to put us into a private school.'

Dr Bell said, 'Life obviously changed quite radically, once you got here, from Mullumbimby?'

Softie paused. 'It was different, in that it was better.'

'Are you still close to your parents?'

'To my mum, yes. My parents are divorced.'

'How old were you when that happened?'

'I think I was fifteen.'

Dr Bell said, 'Do you know why the marriage broke up?'

Softie said, 'My dad moved out because he'd met someone else.'

'You sound fairly sure about that.'

'It's not a secret. Dad had set up a business, selling car radios and then portable CD players, and he was making fairly decent money, and I suppose he decided he deserved a reward for all his hard work. Mum said he had an affair. I don't know if that's true. But I do know that he moved out to move in with somebody else.'

Dr Bell said, 'Have you ever asked him whether it's true?'

'No. I mean, we're not that close.'

Dr Bell said, 'And is your father still with that other woman now?'

'No. He has a new model.'

Dr Bell clarified: 'A third wife?'

'Right. He was on the start of the curve when mobile phones came in. You remember the first ones, big bricks that had to be charged from a suitcase? Well, he got in on the ground floor, so obviously he made a lot of money. And he's got a new model girlfriend, too. This one is, I think, younger than me and she actually has a baby, younger than Matilda.'

Dr Bell said, 'A lot of girls, they feel betrayed when their father moves out. That's especially true for girls in adolescence. How did it make you feel?'

'I'm not one of those people who think divorce is necessarily a bad thing. Obviously, given the path I've chosen for myself, and Matilda.'

Dr Bell said, 'Okay, we'll get to Matilda. But first, what happened to your mum after your father moved out? Did she remarry, for example?'

'No.'

'Do you recall rebelling at all, in the years after the divorce?'

Softie said, 'No,' but then corrected herself. 'Oh, okay, once. Once when Mum wanted to stop me from going somewhere I wanted to go. A slumber party, I think. I said, "Okay, if you won't let me go, I'll leave and live with Dad and he'll let me go." I picked up the phone to talk to him, and he said, "Put your mother on." They yelled at each other, and it ended with Mum handing the phone back to me so Dad could say: "Oh, look, Softie, I know you're not getting on with your mum right now, but she is your mum and she makes the rules." I said, "Fine, I'll come and live with you." And he got all shifty and said, "Oh, look Softie, I've only just got married again. And what about school? You don't want to start a whole new school."'

Dr Bell said, 'He left you with the impression he didn't want you around, then?'

Softie said, 'That's right.'

'And from there?'

'I buckled down, finished my HSC, went to university, studied, had my twenty-first. I invited Dad to it but he wasn't able to make it. He sent down $500 to cover the cost of the DJ and the punch. Like it was all about the money.'

Dr Bell said, 'It's difficult for me not to hear the bitterness in your voice, Softie.'

'It was a long time ago, Dr Bell.'

'It can be a long time ago and still be raw.'

There's no answer from Softie on the tape. There's just silence. Then Dr Bell says, 'And what about after university?'

Softie says, 'I got a job in the marketing department at Westpac.'

'Do you recall what you did with your first pay cheque?'

'My first pay cheque? I would have put some of it away. I was saving up for a car. I bought one later that year – a Daihatsu Charade. I called her Daisy.'

'It sounds like you were fairly keen to establish your independence, Softie?'

'Yes.'

'Did you take the opportunity to move out of home as well, once you had a regular income?'

Softie said, 'I moved into a flat in Elwood with some other girls from work. That was pretty soon after I started. But it didn't really work out.'

'And why was that?'

'Oh, flat-sharing. I'd get up in the morning and I'd open the fridge and the orange juice I'd bought – orange juice I'd *specifically* bought because I wanted to have orange juice in the morning – would be gone. The electricity bill would come and the other girls would say: "Oh, Softie, we're broke! Can you just cover it until payday?" Like, they didn't know the electricity bill was coming?'

Dr Bell said, 'I take it you didn't stay long?'

'Not long, no. I rented a one-bedroom flat for a while. And I was twenty-seven when I bought the apartment in Edgewater Towers.'

Dr Bell said, 'And what about relationships? Was there anything serious around that time, or even when you were younger?'

'Not really. I was concentrating on my career. I also wanted to travel. The Contiki tour was quite a big thing back then. Girls at work said to me, "Oh, you don't need to do that," meaning, go on an organised tour. "You don't want to be stuck with a group of people you might not like, in a bus, like cattle." But I liked being bussed about, and we weren't treated like cattle. It was more convenient, knowing where you'd be staying at night, somewhere safe.'

Dr Bell said, 'Did you go on that tour on your own, Softie?'

'No. I went with a girl from accounts. From Westpac. I'm at NAB now. It didn't work out, though. We had a falling out.'

'Do you recall what it was about?'

Softie said, 'It was towards the end. We were in Amsterdam, preparing to fly back to London to board the flights to Bangkok, then Melbourne. We had a free night, and this girl peeled off to go to a bar. She met up with some backpackers. She got very drunk and she didn't come back to the hotel until the morning. I was beside myself, thinking she'd been abducted. She didn't even apologise. But she was pleading with me, "Forget about Australia! Let's stay here and party and get stoned." She seemed to have forgotten that we both had return tickets that we'd lose if we didn't use them.'

Dr Bell said, 'Did she fly home with you in the end?'

'No. She went back to the bar and I flew home, like we were supposed to.'

Dr Bell said, 'I wonder what became of her?'

Softie said, 'Oh, I know what became of her. She got stoned in Amsterdam every day for a year, then went to London, then to Berlin, one love affair to the next, one backpacker joint to the next. Last I heard, she was in Bali.'

'That sounds like quite an adventure!'

'Not to me. But, you know, that's her choice.'

Dr Bell said, 'Your choices have obviously been different.'

'Of course they have. I have an apartment in St Kilda, which may not have been that affluent an area when I bought it, but it's now gone up quite a lot. I'm earning decent money. I've got my own office. I have a car space. I'm doing very well.'

Dr Bell said, 'I can see that. And you have a daughter.'

Softie said softly, 'Yes, I do. And she means the world to me.'

Dr Bell said, 'Some of my questions can sound rude, Softie, but do you mind telling me how old you were when Matilda came along?'

Softie said, 'I hadn't yet turned forty. I was thirty-nine. I turned forty shortly afterwards – that's not considered old these days.'

Dr Bell said, 'And your daughter, she's Matilda . . . although both you and your husband sometimes refer to her as Minty?'

'Yes. Well. That came from me. Matilda. Tilda. Tilda Swinton. Minton. Minty. I don't know. It happened.'

Dr Bell said, 'When you had Matilda, was it with the idea that she'd probably be your only child?'

Softie said, 'There's absolutely no reason why I couldn't have another. But that's obviously not going to happen now, or not with *him*, anyway.'

Dr Bell said, 'Why did you wait until you were nearly forty to have a child, Softie?'

'It wasn't by choice, Dr Bell. I couldn't find a decent man.'

'You didn't have any relationships at all before Garry?'

Softie paused. When she finally spoke she said, 'I don't doubt that Garry will tell you all about this so you might as well hear it from me: I actually *wasted* quite a lot of time on an affair.'

'An affair . . . with a married man?'

'Yes.'

Dr Bell said, 'And your lover, did you know he was married when you started with him?'

'Yes I did, Dr Bell. But it was the same old story. He told me he was unhappy. His wife didn't understand him. All that rubbish. I thought I was in love with him. He said he was in love with me. But it was all bullshit.'

Dr Bell said, 'Did your family – your mum, your sisters – know about that relationship, Softie?'

Softie said, 'I had no reason to hide it. *I* wasn't married. And if I hadn't told my mother about it, she would have kept at me with the, "When are you going to get married, Softie?" So I told her, "I have a man. It's complicated." It's complicated! I said, "He's married but he's really unhappy." I can hardly believe I'm repeating this. It sounds like bullshit, even to me. I said, "He wants to leave his wife but it's hard because he has children."'

Dr Bell asked, 'You said you wasted a lot of time on him?'

'Oh, it went on for years! *Years*. From when I was, what, thirty, basically until I met Garry.'

Dr Bell said, 'You left him for Garry?'

'No!' Softie exclaimed. 'No, no. We got caught, basically. Me and Mr Married. Found out. Bound to happen. And I never heard boo from him again.'

Dr Bell said, 'When you say you got caught . . . do you mean literally?'

Softie said, 'Not in the act! No! No, I mean, we got caught on the mobile. Text messages on the mobile. That's how we communicated – on the mobile. I obviously couldn't call him at home. We used to text each other a lot.'

Dr Bell said, 'And I take it *Mrs* Married Man picked up your text messages?'

'That's what he told me.'

'You don't believe him?'

'I don't believe a word that comes out of his mouth any more.'

Dr Bell asked, 'Why is that? Because he lied to you about being in love?'

'Because he lied to me full stop. But, you know, it's like my mother always told me, you make your bed, you lie in it.'

'That's a bit harsh, from your own mum.'

'Well. She tried to warn me.'

'And, Softie, you said that you met Garry pretty soon after this relationship – the one with the married man – ended?'

'Yes. Classic rebound. Which, again, everyone warned me about and I – again, I didn't listen.'

'And in terms of age, you were, by then . . . ?'

Softie said, 'I was thirty-eight.'

'Some women, at around that age, start to hear a clock ticking, Softie. Did you have the sense that you were running out of time?'

'Oh, look, yes, I suppose I did. I was thinking, "How am I going to find a man that isn't married or gay while I've still got time to have a baby?" Some of my friends said, "Go on the internet. Go on RSVP." But I had a look, and

I thought, "No. I don't want to put my face up there, advertising myself." And maybe I was starting to think, "What exactly is wrong with me? I'm smart. I'm not unattractive. I take care of myself. I have my own income. How come I can't meet anyone?"'

Dr Bell said, 'And then Garry came along.'

'And then Garry came along,' Softie repeated, without any enthusiasm at all.

Dr Bell said, 'Could you explain how you met?'

'Well, it was something different. A girl at work told me about this new thing, a Pop-up Restaurant. Basically a young chef, a talented guy, used to open his terrace place up and get people to come over and try his dishes. I don't mean his friends – he'd get strangers to come, and bring a bottle of wine, and sit at a big table in his hallway, and eat, and contribute a bit to the cost of the ingredients. People were raving about it, saying the food's so fresh and he's so talented. I said to this girl in accounts, "But how do you find it? And how do you get invited?" And she said, "Oh, you have to send an email and wait to get invited." So I went online and I found what looked like the email address, sent off an email, and bang, they sent one back, saying yep – we've got two free seats this Monday night. My colleague was supposed to come with me. I'm not the type to turn up to things alone. But at the last minute, she had to pull out. She called me at home and said, "Oh, the babysitter has called up sick, and Jared" – her husband – "has been kept back at work and I just can't leave." And, I don't know, it was quite out of character for me, but I thought, "Whatever, I'm going to go."'

Dr Bell said, 'And Garry was there?'

'He was there. I can hardly believe that now. I mean, you know him, Dr Bell. It wasn't really his scene, that kind of place. Big table, tea lights all down it, fancy food. He's not into that kind of thing at all. But one of the women he used to drive around, back when he was working as a taxi driver, she told him about it. And Garry being Garry, he probably thought, "Good place to meet chicks." Because that's how he thinks.'

Dr Bell said, 'Do you recall what you thought, when you were first introduced to Garry?'

'We weren't really introduced. Garry was already there when I arrived, in a chair halfway down the long table, with some of the share plates already in front of him. I walked in and took one of the vacant chairs, close to the door. Then seconds later, Garry got up and came and sat beside me, saying, "Oh, do you mind if I sit here? I like to be near the front door." It was so obvious. He was trying to pick me up. I mean, who wants to be near the door? Nobody!'

Dr Bell said, 'And was Garry attractive to you, Softie?'

'Oh no! Not *at all*. He was too short for one thing, and he was . . . I don't know, I don't like to use the word bogan, but there was something a bit bogan about him. He had a Triple M bomber jacket. He had a thick neck, like he worked too much. He had pock-marks on his neck, from boils. So, no, *absolutely not* attractive, or not to me. And then there was his name, which he told me was Garry Gary. I realise I'm not one to talk here – *Softie* – but Garry Gary sounded like something you might say if you had a stutter.'

Dr Bell said, 'Garry didn't introduce himself as Garry Hartshorn?'

'He didn't. He introduced himself as Garry Gary. And I know that, because that's also what was written on his business card: Garry Gary.'

Dr Bell said, 'Okay. But, Softie, if that first dinner didn't go all that well, how did you come to have a date with Garry and indeed to marry him?'

'Oh, I don't know, Dr Bell. How did it happen? It just kind of happened. At the end of the night, he gave me his business card. I gave it straight back to him. I said, "If you want to see me again, I'm sure you can find me."'

Dr Bell said, 'That sounds like something of a challenge, Softie. Were you flirting?'

'I wasn't flirting. I was sick of dead-end dates with blokes who weren't interested in anything serious. I thought, "If he wants to see me again, let him find me."'

'Although you weren't yourself that interested?'

'That's right, Dr Bell. I was just past caring.'

Chapter Six

Who amongst the blokes out there would argue with the proposition that women are a mystery? I'm not talking solely about Softie here. I'm actually thinking back to when I was a young man on the dating scene.

There were a range of girls around Footscray – at the Catholic school, and the local State school; at church; at the dance hall – and pretty much all of them were good girls, meaning from good families, and we, meaning them girls and us blokes, all had the same idea, which was to get married, have a few kids, get a roof over our heads, pay off the mortgage and, maybe later, when the kids had left the nest, go for a bit of a travel around.

To illustrate that point let me tell you about my Pat. When I met her, I thought, 'Yep, she's for me.' I didn't think, 'She's good, but maybe I'll see if someone better comes along.' We were in love, and that was enough. Pat felt the same way about me: I was the first bloke that came along who she'd taken a shine to, and that was enough. But women these days, they don't want to marry the first bloke that comes along. They want to wait. They think they have plenty of time. Then, before they know it, time's run out. It's five minutes to midnight, clock ticking, all the good blokes have already been snapped up, and you've got women diving in with men who obviously aren't right, but are basically all that's left.

Which brings me back to Softie. Was she in love with Garry? As I say, women are a mystery to me, but it doesn't take a rocket scientist to work out that no, she was basically settling for Garry, meaning grabbing him, before her clock ran out. Anyone could have seen it. Anyone, that is, except Garry. Which might have been fine if Garry wasn't the kind of bloke he was, which, to my mind, was a bloke who'd already had one too many rough ends of the pineapple shoved in his direction, leaving him pretty bruised. Which brings me now to the second session he had with Dr Bell, which was not that long after Dr Bell had sat down with Softie. It was like pulling teeth.

'How old were you when you moved out of home, Garry?' That was the first question Dr Bell put to him, to which Garry said, 'Out of Mum's place, you mean?'

'Yes.'

'I was twenty-one.'

Dr Bell said, 'And where did you go?' And Garry said, 'I got married.'

You can tell from the tape here that Dr Bell's a bit surprised. The fact that Garry might have had a wife and maybe even kids before Softie hadn't ever occurred to him, which, when you think about it, gives you an idea of where his head was at regarding Garry's chances of getting custody of Matilda.

'You got married?' he said.

Garry said, 'I did.'

'At twenty-one?'

'Yes.'

'So . . . Softie Monaghan – she wasn't your first wife?'

'No.'

'Well then, how many wives have you had?'

Garry said, 'Two. And that's my limit. It's one more than enough, in fact.'

Dr Bell said, 'And how old were you when you got married the first time?'

'I just told you. I was twenty-one. But it didn't last long.'

'Your first wife, I take it she had a name?'

'She did.'

'And it was?'

'Lisa.'

'And she was . . . the same age? Younger?'

'Younger. Not by much. But listen, Doc, what's the relevance of all this? It's ancient bloody history.' So, again you can see Garry all clammed up there, like he'd rather be at the dentist.

Dr Bell said, 'Well, humour me: how did you meet your first wife . . . Lisa? And were there any children? You're not estranged from any other of your children, are you?'

Garry said, 'I'm not strange to Matilda.'

'Not strange. *Estranged.* Separated from.'

'I'm not separated from Matilda either. Her mother is separated from me and she's trying to estrange *me* from Matilda. But that's not going to happen.'

Dr Bell said, 'Okay, but let's back up a step. Where did you meet Lisa?'

'She had a brother in the same school as me – at the tech.'

'Lisa was at the tech?'

'Lisa, I just told you, was at the Catholic school. Girls didn't much go to tech. Her brother was at the tech.'

'And how long were you married?'

'Two years, although technically – officially – we were probably married for longer than that. We got married in '86 and separated around '88, but it was only later, when Lisa decided to get married again, that she got in touch and said, "Oh, do you mind getting divorced from me?"'

Dr Bell said, 'How did you feel about that?'

'I said okay, because by then who really gave a shit? And Lisa said she'd pay, but I said, "No, it's alright, we can split it."'

Dr Bell said, 'And why did the marriage end, Garry?'

'Because we never should have got married in the first place.'

Dr Bell said, 'Well then, why did you? Were you in love?'

Garry snorted. 'You and your love! I don't know about *love*!' he said. 'We were definitely horny. Or I was.'

Dr Bell said, 'Why get married then? Why not date?'

'I didn't have that choice.'

'Because Lisa wanted to get married?'

Garry said, 'Oh look, Doc, it was different then. You must know that. If you were a bloke and you found a girl and wanted to have sex with her, you got married. Rick Hartshorn made that plain. He said, "If you want to hang around with this girl, Garry, you can't just go and ruin her reputation, you've got to marry her as well."'

Dr Bell said, 'That seems like quite an old-fashioned idea for 1986, Garry.'

'Yeah, well, Hartshorn is a bit . . . and anyway, we were living in Exford, where a girl could still get a reputation. And you wouldn't want to ruin a girl like Lisa, or that's what Rick Hartshorn said.'

'Rick Hartshorn told you to marry Lisa?'

'He didn't tell me . . . Okay, look, Doc, if you want to know what happened, I'll tell you what happened. I'm laying in my bed one night when I would have been what, thirteen or maybe fourteen. Hartshorn comes into my room and says, "Get up, Garry. We're headed out." He hands me a pair of pants and I get into them, all zombie-like because I'd been asleep. I go to get into the front seat of Rick's car and he says, "Get in the back, somebody will be joining us."'

'I get in the back and we go around to one of his mate's houses. I don't really remember his name. But this bloke had teenage daughters that everyone said were "growing up fast", if you know what that means.

'So Rick and this bloke, they're in the front seat and I'm in the back, and I said, you know, "Where are we going?" And Rick said, "Sit quiet." So I sat quiet, and we drove around to another house, parked out front and Rick sounded the horn.

'Nobody came out so Rick got out and went up to the front door and knocked. A light came on and the door opened and there was a young bloke – a kid, basically – standing there. From memory, he was not that much older than me, maybe fifteen or sixteen, wearing a pair of those silky boxers with Tweety Bird or whatever, no shirt, bare feet, with his hair standing up, like he's been dragged out of bed too.

'Rick takes this kid by the ear and leads him down the path and puts him in the car. No argument – just puts him in next to me – and closes the door. So now I've got this kid sitting next to me, his hands between his knees, you know, to stop them banging together. He's looking at me, making a face like, what's going on? I'm trying not to look at him because I have no idea what's going on.

'He says, "Where are you taking me?" but there's no answer.

'We drove down to where the weir is at Melton, when Rick suddenly veers off the road, to where there's no street lights. The kid next to me is getting more scared. He's saying, "Just let me out. I know what this is about. I won't see her again."

'Rick's mate goes, "You're right about that."

'We pull up under this tree and Rick drags the kid onto the grass. He lands on his arse. Rick's mate opens the boot of the car and gets out a shovel.

'I'm still in the back seat. My eyes are out on stalks. Rick's mate throws this shovel at the young bloke. It lands on the ground. Rick picks it up and gives it to the kid and says, "Dig."

'The kid says, "You've got to be kidding." Rick's mate says, "Do we look like we're kidding?"

'The kid stands up, barefoot, chest as white as the moon, and he says, "But I didn't effing *do* anything!" His voice has gone high, like a girl's voice. But Rick says, "I said dig!" And the kid, he kind of falls down on his knees again, and he's near hysterical, saying, "But I didn't *do* anything!"

'Rick and his mate, they let him sook for a bit, and then they take the shovel off him and throw it back in the boot.

'Rick sort of shoves a thumb at his mate, and says, "You know this bloke's daughter, right? Well, you don't know her any more. You don't talk to her. You don't ring the house. You see her in the street, you go the other way. You understand that? You *comprendo*?"

'The kid doesn't say anything. He's crying too hard. Rick says, "I said *comprendo? Understand?*" The kid nods, and says, "I get it." And Rick sort of spits in his direction and says, "Right then, we understand each other."

'And you know, Doc, that should have been the end of it. The kid had got the message, loud and clear. But Rick wasn't done. He lit up one of his cigarettes, and then he said to this kid, "Take your shorts off."

'The kid was like, "What? What the hell?" And Rick was like, "I said, take your shorts off."

'Rick's mate said, "Come on, Rick. He's got the message." Rick didn't say anything. Then he said it again, "Take your bloody shorts off."

'Well, the kid was shaking and had started crying again, and he kind of got up off his knees, and he was saying, "Come on, what are you going to do to me?" But it seemed like Rick wasn't going to do anything. It seemed like he wanted to stand there while the kid jimmied his shorts down to his knees.

'The kid was: "Come on! What the hell?" And Rick was just standing there, smoking. So the kid pulls his daks down and his willy is all curled up, and Rick is standing looking at him, and then he says, "Give 'em to me. The shorts. Your daks." The kid is like, "What the?" But he does. He does, and then Rick flings the kid's jocks into the bushes and says, "Good luck finding those."

'Rick gets into the car, where me and his mate are dumbstruck because it was kind of totally *off*, what he's just done, but neither of us says anything. Rick gets back in behind the wheel and drives off, leaving the young bloke out there with bugger all way of getting back, and no pants on.'

Garry paused. Dr Bell did too. But then he said, 'And you took it from that . . . not to have sex with a girl you didn't intend to marry?'

'Yeah, I took it from that, if I wanted to be hanging around with a girl – by which I mean a girl from a good family, not a town bike – I'd better get married, or else I might find myself being asked to dig in the dirt by Lisa's old man.'

Dr Bell said, 'That's quite a harsh lesson, Garry. You must have been scared out of your mind.'

'Rick made his point, if that's what you mean.'

'Made it strongly enough to convince you to get married to a girl you hardly knew.'

'That's right. Not that I minded at the time. I mean, why not get married? Everyone was getting married. It wasn't like now, where everyone waits.'

Dr Bell said, 'And how did you get married that first time? In a church? The Catholic Church?'

'Yep.'

'But you're not yourself Catholic?'

'Not one bit of me, despite what those Christian Brothers tried to do, and despite Mum – Joan Cooper – being in the Church all her life. I don't know. It just never held with me. But Lisa was Catholic, and the Church wants to be sure they'll get the kids, don't they? So when we fronted up, they were all, "Oh, you'll be raising the children Catholic? You'll be getting them confirmed?" And I was all, "Yeah, yeah." And they were all, "You'll have to become Catholic." And I was, "Whatever." I mean, I didn't say whatever. I said, "Yes, sure, of course," and I did two sessions with them, got the basics drilled into me, and that was that. Lisa's folks didn't have any money so Rick said he'd pay for the party. He got a spit and a keg and I gave a bit of a speech, saying, you know, thanks to Lisa's parents for taking me in, and thanks Mum and Rick.'

Dr Bell said, 'I must say, Garry, getting married because it seemed like a good idea at the time, that doesn't sound like the most auspicious start to married life.'

'Not what?'

'An auspicious start. A positive start.'

'Right. And it was downhill from there too.'

'Because it didn't work out, obviously.'

'No, it didn't.'

Dr Bell said, 'And do you feel like going into why it didn't work? We've got about twenty minutes left.'

Garry said, 'It won't take that long, Doc. I can tell you in two seconds. She found someone else.'

'Lisa did?'

'That's right.'

'That doesn't seem like a very . . . well, Catholic thing to do.'

'No. And the weird thing was, as far as I could tell, things were okay with Lisa and me, at least at the start they were. We were at it like rabbits, just all over each other.

Rick had helped out with us getting our own place, so there was no problem with money. I'd finished up at the tech, obviously, and was well into the apprenticeship at the local body shop, getting pies and sauce and shit for the boss at lunch time but also actually learning some of the trade. Lisa had got on as an apprentice at Shimmer. That was the local hairdresser. She was cutting kids' hair, yeah, and putting on the ladies' perm solution that made her fingernails all flaky. So, we were doing okay for money, not that you needed much. The only thing Lisa could think of that she wanted was a cat – I can't stand cats, myself – so she got a cat, and me, well, the only thing I wanted was basically a Holden. I couldn't think of anything I wanted more than that, actually, and Rick helped me out getting one. Being in the car sales business he got me a good deal, and of course he's for Holden – that's the team he sponsors, I mean – at Bathurst. Lisa's folks were actually Ford. I remember that because it was very nearly a deal breaker, even more than me not being Catholic. Her dad – Mick, his name was – got right stuck into me about it one night, over a beer, saying, "You know what the letters in Ford stand for, don't you, Garry? First On Race Day. Ha ha. First On Race Day." I remember thinking, "I don't know how I go home and tell Rick my girlfriend is from a Ford family, but anyway."'

Dr Bell laughed at that and joked, 'I hope she didn't leave you for a Ford driver?'

Garry said, 'Yeah, well, she did actually! Now that you mention it, she did! Which was fine, you know. I mean, big deal. Whatever. More proof that she had no idea about anything, in my opinion! But no, it wasn't the Ford–Holden thing that did us in, obviously. I mean, women don't give a shit about that, do they?'

Dr Bell said, 'Not in my experience, Garry, no. So if it wasn't the Holden–Ford rivalry that did you in, what was it about the bloke Lisa found that was so much better than you?'

Garry said, 'Ah, well, I'm going to be honest here and say I probably wasn't the easiest person to be around when I was twenty-one.'

Dr Bell said, 'Why do you say that?'

'Ah, well, truth is, I was on the roids.'

'Roids?'

'Horse pills. I mean, everyone was, but still. See, there was this bloke that opened up a gym in one of the Police and Community Youth Club places. An all-bloke gym. Not aerobics or spin, not treadmills and shit – just barbells, bench presses, blokes bulking themselves up, and I kind of got into that.'

'Into body building?'

'Yeah, well, it was a big thing at that time. Now it's a bit, I don't know, not what everyone's doing, at least not around Exford, not this side of town. But back then, out west and in Melton, all the blokes were into building themselves up. It was like: how big can you get? That was the thing. How big can you get? Because people thought, "You can't get too big. Bigger is better. Can you get so big you can't get a shirt on?" We had blokes so big they couldn't walk straight. Had to walk like cowboys because their thighs were so massive. So it was, "How big do you reckon you could get, before you explode?" You know? And there were days when I felt like I was exploding, because of the gear, you know. The roids. People say, "Oh, you can do it natural," but you can't do it natural. We were all on the gear.'

Dr Bell said, 'And the gear, the steroids, they affected your mood?'

Garry said, 'They affect everything! That thing you hear about how they shrink your nuts, that's actually true. They do shrink your nuts. They give you boils. These marks here, around my neck, that's all roids. I had boils on my back. They'd fill up with this, like, green-yellow pus. It was rank. But you wanted to be big. Or I did. So you took this stuff that the gym gave you, under the counter. The rumour was the pills were actually for racehorses, but it could have been that they were called horse pills because of the size of them. And then there was the roid rage. That's actually real. You do go a bit mental. But I was so into the scene, you know, thinking maybe I could get big enough for competition, I just put up with the boils and the feeling, some days, like my head was so, you know, purple, and pus-filled and swollen, it might blow off.'

Dr Bell said, 'And what part of that scene was it that Lisa objected to? The time away from home, the boils, the money it cost, the mood swings, the tiny balls?'

Garry said, 'Give over, Doc! It was my tiny balls! Nah, nah, nah. It was definitely the mood swings. Definitely. Roids basically make you behave like a dickhead, which is why I haven't taken them for years. I mean, not for years and years. Not, you know, since Matilda, and not even before that. Not for years. But back then, yeah, it was what I was doing and there were downsides to it, which was the temper.'

'And that's what broke you up?'

'Oh, look, Doc, I mean, yeah. There was a time where I would have said the roids had nothing to do with it. It was all Lisa's doing. She did the dirty, you know. But if you're asking me now, yeah, I can see I was too young to be married. I didn't get marriage. The point of being with a woman – supporting her, all that shit – I wasn't into it. Didn't know about it. I just did my own thing, and it was like Lisa was there, and that was good, but you know, who she really was – what did I care about that? I had no idea about that. And so, anyway, we had a bit of a ritual: Lisa and me and basically everyone we knew, we'd go to the pub on a Thursday night. Mac's Hotel, it was called. We'd have a counter meal, and then the blokes would have their beers, and the girls would have a few drinks too. Not wine, but a Fluffy Duck or something. A Fluffy Duck, a Tequila Sunrise, a Slippery Nipple. What those things were, I don't know. But that's what the sheilas wanted. The blokes might play some pool and when the music came on the sheilas would have a bit of a dance around their handbags, with the smoke machine going and a bit of coloured lights.

'And then one night, I was sitting there with the blokes, it was my round, and I went up to the bar, and I saw Lisa. She was with this bloke. She'd got a drink, and this bloke was taking a sip of it through her straw. And I thought, you know, that's a bit suss. Plus, I knew this bloke. He was the kind of bloke that's a bit "in like Flynn". You know, ask twenty sheilas, two might say yes. He'd have a go with the barmaids, the Saturday-afternoon strippers, whatever. He didn't care. A root rat, we used to say. He was a root rat. And I would have thought Lisa, being married, being Catholic, wouldn't have had much time for a root rat. But there she was, like, sharing a straw with him.

'I got my round, carried it over to where my mates were sitting, and they were all, "Hey, Garry, your missus there, she looks like she's having a good time." You know, nudge nudge, wink wink. And so I thought, "Well, I better do something about it."'

Dr Bell said, 'And so you confronted Lisa?'

'Fronted her? Like shirt-fronted her?'

'No, I mean, did you confront her? Did you go over to her, or over to Mr In Like Flynn, and have a word in his ear?'

Garry said, 'I actually didn't say a word to either of them at the pub. I just sort of went over and said, "Time to go." And Lisa goes, "Aw, why do we gotta go?" You know, all whiny. And I'm like, "Get your skinny arse in the car." And

I kind of got her by the elbow and shoved her out of there. Which nobody would have blamed me for. That's what a bloke should do.

'But then, when we got in the car, I let loose. It could have been that I'd had a few beers, but to be honest, Doc, I wasn't that drunk. It was mostly roids, I reckon, that was riling me up. Roids and the fact that Lisa was definitely flirting with this bloke. But yeah, I also had that Incredible Hulk feeling I'd get, like I was going to swell up and kind of burst out of my clothes. Because I was big, and when I got angry and pumped those muscles, it was like a shirt couldn't keep me in.'

Dr Bell said, 'Did you strike Lisa, Garry?'

Garry said, 'Strike her? Shit no. *Strike her?* No, Doc, no, no, no. I've never hit a woman. Never. Not ever. Not in my life. Whatever Softie might be saying right now . . . she's not saying that, is she? That's total crap. That would be a lie.'

Dr Bell said, 'We're not talking about Softie. This is about Lisa. You didn't strike her. So, what did happen?'

Garry's voice had got louder. 'Is that what Softie's saying? Is she saying I hit her? I never hit her.'

Dr Bell said, 'This isn't about Softie, Garry. It's about you. Go on, you're doing well. I'm not holding anything against you. As you say, it was twenty years ago. You're not on roids any more. I am interested in knowing how it turned out. That's all. Nothing more than that: I want to see how it turns out.'

Garry said, 'Yeah, well, you're making me suspicious now. Like, what do you need to know all this for? Like, I see you there, taking it all down, like it's going to be used against me. I know you're taping me.'

Dr Bell said, 'I'm taping you in case there's anything I need to check. Nobody's setting you up, Garry. I'm not in the habit of using things against people. It's still as I said to you on the first day, that I'm trying to build up a picture of you. So, please go on.'

Garry couldn't let it go. 'You say nothing will be held against me, but how do I know what you're doing with all this stuff? I mean, what are you writing down there?'

'I'm taking notes. I'm not making judgements. I'm taking notes. And I'm impressed with your candour – your honesty. Your honesty is going to count for a lot.'

Garry said, 'Right, well.'

'So go on.'

'Well, I didn't bloody hit her, or hit anyone. I drove her home. There was a bit of drama in the front yard. Lisa was like, "What's wrong with you?" I couldn't get my key in the lock for shaking, so Lisa took the keys off me. She goes, "Oh, you're drunk." I said, "I'm drunk, am I? Well, you're a slut." Or something like that. I said something like that.'

Dr Bell said, 'And when you got inside?'

'Oh, well, Lisa was furious. She was shouting, "I'm a slut, am I? I'm your wife and I'm a slut." I was yelling, "You're a married woman, and you're at the bar with some bloke, carrying on like a Malvern Star." Meaning like the town bike. And so then Lisa kind of shoved me, and, yeah, I might have shoved her back a bit.'

Dr Bell said, 'You were a body builder at the time, Garry. I take it Lisa was quite a bit smaller?'

Garry said, 'Yeah, yeah, she was a tiny thing. Tiny. Up to here on me. I mean, yeah, in retrospect, it was the wrong thing to do, shoving her, but I was just that angry.'

'And was that the end of the argument? Or did the argument end?'

Garry said, 'Ah, well, she called me every name under the sun. Went into the bedroom and said, you know, stay out. We had no lock. I could have gone in. But she shut the door and said, you know, you, out. Stay out. So I slept on the couch.'

'And that was the end of it?'

'Well, yes and no. It was the end of the drama that night. But I still had my suspicions. So when Lisa got up the next day, I, like, apologised and said, you know, I over-reacted, it was my fault, won't happen again. And she was like, "Okay. Okay. Let's forget about it." But to myself, I was thinking, "I'm going to be watching you from now on. You won't know it, but I'm going to be watching you." And it turned out I was right. I was one hundred per cent right. It wouldn't have been a week later that I drove past the house in the middle of the day and, bingo, there was this bloke's ute – a Ford ute, since you asked – on the street outside.'

Dr Bell said, 'This bloke . . . you mean Mr In Like Flynn?'

'Of course I do. Who else? And the bloke is obviously a sly bugger. He's not parked right outside the house. He's parked a few doors down. But I knew his car. Made a point of finding out what kind of car he had. And there was no reason for it to be there, in my street.'

Dr Bell said, 'I take it you went in?'

'You bet I went in. I went in. First, though, I parked my car right behind his shit box, and when I got out of my car and went around to his, I took the windscreen wipers and snapped them off. And then I looked around our front garden, like for a rake or a pole or a cricket bat, but all I could find was the junk mail, catalogues, you know, rolled up in the letterbox, so I took those and I went through the front door and there they were.'

'You walked in on them having sex?'

'Come off it, Doc. If I'd walked in on them having sex I wouldn't be sitting here talking to you, would I? I'd be in Pentridge, serving life for murder! Two murders. So, no, no, shit no. We had a bar in the lounge room, in a sunken area, with, you know, a dartboard and barstools and smoky mirror tiles, and the big bottle of Beam in the pouring stand. And they were at this bar, sitting there with two cups of coffee. I remember that because the bloke had my cup. Lisa had her cups when we moved in, like mugs that were done on some kind of pottery wheel. Glazed mugs, and I hated them. She was all, "Oh, they're hand-made." I was like, "They look to me like they're made of mud." And the coffee didn't stay hot in them. But I mean, big deal, because I'd brought my own cup to the marriage. A miner's mug, actually, white enamel with this blue rim, the kind of mug you could drop in the sink and the handle wouldn't fall off. And the coffee stayed hot. And there was this bloke, sitting there with my missus *and* my cup in the middle of the day.'

Dr Bell said, 'No chance that it was just a friendly neighbourhood call?'

Garry said, 'Right, Doc! Of course it was. A friendly neighbourhood call! No. I mean, a bloke walks into that situation, he knows what he's seeing.'

Dr Bell said, 'And what happened? I take it since you're not in Pentridge you didn't kill him?'

'Nah, I didn't kill him. I went for him, obviously. I had the junk mail in my hand and my idea was to belt him around the head with it.'

Dr Bell said, 'And Lisa? What did she do when you started hitting this bloke over the head with the Clark Rubber brochure?'

Garry said, 'Oh yeah, Doc, that's right. Take the piss. Take the piss. She was being a typical woman. She was all, "Stop, stop! What are you doing? Just stop!"'

Dr Bell said, 'And did you stop?'

'Well, yeah, I had to. He got out from under me. Bastard made it out the front door. My mistake not to close the door behind me.'

'And what did Lisa say after this bloke made it out, and it was just the two of you there?'

'Oh, you know, she was, "You're crazy, you're off your rocker, there's nothing going on."'

'But you didn't believe her?'

'Believe her? Why should I believe her? What you're forgetting, Doc, is they got married.'

This seemed to take Dr Bell by surprise. 'They got married?' he said. 'Lisa and Mr In Like Flynn?'

Garry said, 'Too right they got married! Of course they did.'

Dr Bell said, 'Well, Garry. I didn't expect that.'

'What did you expect?'

'Well, I thought perhaps with you being on steroids and so forth, that maybe it would turn out that your judgement was impaired. That nothing had been going on, and that in your temper you were too quick to judge. But it seems that you were vindicated.'

'I was what?'

'Vindicated. Proven right.'

'Well, yeah, if that's supposed to make me feel better.'

'And do you still feel angry about it, Garry, the fact that Lisa left you for another man?'

'I'm not saying she did that. She just left, you know, and he was there. Oh look, okay, maybe she did leave me for him. Whatever. But no, I'm not angry about it. How long is a bloke supposed to be angry for? But I mean, basically it led me to understand that women can't be trusted. Like

I didn't already know that, from what my own mother is supposed to have done to me. They'll tell you one thing and do another. Like: for better or worse, except if some "In Like Flynn" comes along, and then, you know, maybe I'll be off.'

Dr Bell paused a bit, then said, 'How often would you say you've seen Lisa since you broke up, Garry? Do you see her at all?'

Garry said, 'I can tell you exactly how often I've seen her since we broke up. I've seen her twice. Once when I ran into her at Highpoint, where she had two snot-nosed kids pulling on her and screaming; and once at the funeral of her brother, a few years back. He got cut up in some workplace accident – fell into a crusher of some kind – and I heard about it, and I went to the funeral, and Lisa was there, obviously. Not with Mr Flynn, because after waiting ten years to give her a baby, he then got tired of her and shoved off. So we had a chat, and that was that. So if what you're trying to find out, Doc, is whether I hold a grudge against a woman who might do the dirty on me, the answer is no. I figure karma gets them in the end.'

Chapter Seven

A week or so after I first started reading through Frank's files and listening to Garry on tape, I arrived home from bowls to find a bunch of people sitting in our lounge room, with Pat at the helm. This group, they were the strangest bunch I'd seen in my life. Every one of them seemed agitated. Some had manila folders on their laps; others had bits of paper coming out of every pocket, and lever-arch files with even more documents in plastic sleeves. They were talking over each other. Not one of them was under the age of sixty.

'Barry!' said Pat, when I came in and put down the bowling balls. 'Come in, meet the group.'

Of course, it was Grandparents United – people like Pat, whose hearts had been shredded, who weren't thinking straight any more, either because they'd fallen out with their own kids over something and weren't allowed to see the grandkids, or because there had been a marriage break-up somewhere, and the kids had got lost in the divorce.

'We're thinking of staging some kind of protest,' Pat was saying. 'Something that will really catch the eye of politicians, and I was just saying that you with all your work at the newspapers, you must know some editors. What happened to that nice Roy Coleman, who used to be at the *Footscray Mail* with you?'

'Pat,' I said. 'Coleman's been dead fifteen years.'

'He died?'

'You know he died, Pat. We went to the funeral.'

'Well, who took over from him? Come and sit down, Barry. We're going to workshop this.'

Workshop? It wasn't a word Pat would have come up with herself. I looked at all the faces staring at me, faces of people who had been knocked sideways by what had happened to them, whose grief was so raw you could see it.

I excused myself. I said, 'I'm sorry, Pat. I've got to get back to this project I'm working on.'

Pat said, 'Not those files from Frank?' And then, to her group: 'He got a trolley laden with court documents, from a judge who was in the Family Court!'

When I heard Pat say that, I can tell you I was that cross with her. The faces of the people in the group, they all lit up and I could see what they were thinking, 'Maybe he's got the key to our problems! Some inside information!' But I had already figured out that things weren't as they seemed with Frank's files.

'Pat,' I said, 'please don't say that, like it's got anything to do with this. I did get some files, but it's got nothing to do with anyone here. It's . . . personal things.'

Nobody in the group bought it. I could tell just by looking that they badly wanted to believe there was some kind of key to the Family Law system and maybe I did have something that would help them unlock it. Hurriedly, I retreated from the lounge room, across the garden back into the shed. Not for the first time, I felt some gratitude toward whichever genius it was who decided that sheds were for men and women should stay out. I already knew which of the tapes I'd be listening to next. You might think it was Softie's, but it was actually Garry's third session with Dr Bell. Did that mean that Softie had dropped out of an appointment? Because surely Dr Bell would have seen one, and then the other. I can't be sure. I do know that when I pressed 'play' and Garry's voice first came on, from the sound of his voice – Garry's voice, I mean – his mood was much improved.

'Hey there, Doc,' he said, by way of opening. 'How they hanging today?'

Dr Bell said, 'Hello, Garry. It's good to see you again. I think we achieved quite a bit last time. I hope you feel the same?'

'I said a lot of things I probably shouldn't,' Garry said, 'but yeah, I mean, if this is what I've got to do to get my rights to Matilda, I can do it. It's not that bad.'

'Well then, why don't we take up from where we

left off?' Dr Bell said. 'If my notes are right, you've just confronted your first wife, Lisa, with her new boyfriend. What happened next? Did you move out?'

'Well, I didn't have much choice,' Garry said. 'It was either move out or throw her out, and I wasn't going to do that. I mean, what did I care about the house? We can't have had more than five grand in it. She was welcome to it.'

'And so where did you go, Garry?'

'Back to Mum's. Didn't want to, and if there'd been any other option I wouldn't have gone there, but yeah, I did. And things were different. Mum and Rick, they'd moved on from Exford by that time. They had a new place at Williamstown, and they had a caravan in the driveway.'

'Meaning you could live in the caravan?'

'Right. Away from Rick – away from Mum, too, but Mum's Mum. I get on good with Mum. But I mean, Rick . . . anyway. It doesn't matter. The caravan wasn't a bad option for a while. The Man in the Van, Mum called me. She'd bring tea out. Did my washing. But I wasn't there all that long. I was pretty soon out of there.'

Dr Bell said, 'Where did you go?'

'First to a place with a bloke from the gym, but, yeah, that didn't really work out. Like I've said, I wasn't the easiest bloke in the world to live with at that time, and now I was pissed off about Lisa too.'

'And all your money was in the house?'

'Yeah, and I was going to have to forget about getting

money out of the house. Lisa didn't want to sell it and, to be honest, I was that keen to see the back of her, I thought, you know, whatever.'

Dr Bell said, 'So you walked with nothing?'

'I took the big Beam bottle I'd gotten for my twenty-first, and my enamel cup. That's all I wanted. The rest of it – the crap we got at the wedding; Lisa's bloody ugly clay mugs – she was welcome to it.'

'And what did you do, in terms of setting yourself up again?'

'Well, I still had a job. I mean, I was still earning.'

'At the body shop, you mean?'

'Ah, no. No, I'd lost that job and started working on building sites, helping out a mate. To be honest with you, Doc, I jumped around different jobs quite a bit in those days. Sometimes I didn't work at all. I was that into lifting weights, I could do it all day, which didn't leave much time for work.'

'That sounds a bad situation, Garry. Not working. Lifting weights all day?'

'Yeah, well, it's what I wanted to do. I couldn't be bothered with much else for a while there. But, I mean, you get over it, don't you? A marriage break-up, I mean. It's not the end of the world, at least when you don't have kids.'

Dr Bell said, 'But you didn't get married again until you met Softie, from what you've said? So that's twenty years – two decades – between marriages?'

'Well, that's because I had no interest in women for a

while. Didn't want one, except, you know, for the obvious thing. I was interested in how much I could lift on the bench press.'

Dr Bell said, 'You're saying you had no relationships – or none worth mentioning – between your first marriage and your second?'

'I had a few hook-ups. I was pretty strict about who I'd go with. I wouldn't pick up girls at the pub. I couldn't stand the way they'd get pissed and be falling over. And other options for meeting girls when you're not working, they can be limited. Mostly I was left to my own devices. Which isn't as bad as it sounds, Doc, because like I say, those roids, they kind of take care of that. You don't have much desire or, if you do, it's not exactly for romance. It's more for wham, bam, thank you, ma'am.'

Dr Bell said, 'Was there any point at which you thought, well, it might be nice to have something more intimate, more serious than that?'

'I did meet a bird through the newspaper classifieds. But that turned out shit. I mean, she gave me her number, I called her up, we had a chat, and I go, alright, do you want to go out? So we meet up, and not only is she much older than she claimed to be – I'm not an idiot and I have two eyes in my head, I can see when you're thirty-five and not twenty-five – she has two kids that she failed to mention.'

Dr Bell said, 'Can I take it you didn't want a relationship with a woman who had children?'

Garry said, 'I wouldn't have cared less, Doc. But why lie?

Like that's a good footing for a relationship, to start with a lie? But that's not something that happens only to me. On RSVP, for example, everyone is lying. You turn up to meet a girl who says she's thirty-five, she'll be forty-five.'

Dr Bell said, 'I take it you've had a look at some of those sites since you've separated, Garry?'

'What am I supposed to do? I'm that bloody lonely. I had a wife and a kid, and now, nothing. I got used to having a bit of noise about the place. Now the flat is quiet like a tomb. So, yeah, I've been on RSVP. Why not? Softie's on the laptop half the night looking for divorce lawyers. I might as well be looking for women.'

Dr Bell said, 'Have you had any success?'

'Depends. When I drop the name Hartshorn, I have plenty of success. Straight away, women go, "Are you related to that car guy, Rick Hartshorn?" If I'm interested in them, I say, "No".'

'You say no?'

'That's right. My idea is: are they still interested if I'm *not* related to Rick Hartshorn? That's the way I play it.'

Dr Bell said, 'Well, that's interesting, Garry. And, out of interest, how long after you met Softie did you introduce her to your parents – to your mother and Rick Hartshorn?'

'Oh well, I introduced Softie pretty much straight away.'

'And was that because . . . I mean, were you still living in the caravan outside Rick's house when you met Softie? You can't have been.'

'Of course I wasn't. Shit. No. No. Like I said, I roomed

with some blokes but then, maybe ten years ago, Mum and Rick, they pulled down the whole back of the house, the bit facing the bay, and put that boatshed in, down near the water, and Mum asked me to move in there, to live in the boatshed. Because of Beam, mostly. Because she said if she was going out with Rick at night it was good for me to be there, to keep an eye on Beam. Not that he can't be left alone. He's alright. But Mum felt better, knowing I was there. And so for Mum I said yeah, I'll do it, and I moved into the boatshed and that's where I was living when I met Softie.'

Dr Bell said, 'I can see you wanted to help your mum out with Beam, Garry, but how did you feel, personally, to be living at home in your forties? Even if it was out in the boatshed?'

Garry said, 'Well, it wasn't like living at home. When people said, "Oh, that's a bit weird, bloke your age still living at home," what they didn't get was that I had an obligation to Beam. What they also didn't get was that the boatshed never was built to just put a boat in. It's set up – kitchen, dunny. It's not enormous. The bed is up on a mezzanine. But it's self-contained – it's got its own entry. I didn't have to go near the main house.'

Dr Bell said, 'And are you living there again, now you're separated?'

Garry said, 'No. I'm in the flat.'

'The flat you shared with Softie? The one in Edgewater Towers?'

'That's right. She moved out. I'm still there.'

'Forgive me if I'm mistaken, but I was under the impression that the flat in Edgewater Towers was Softie's flat . . . that she'd owned it for many years before the two of you got married?'

'Well, sure. But it was our marital home, if that's what they call it. And Softie moved out. Took Matilda and upped stumps. Her decision, not mine.'

Dr Bell said, 'How long do you intend to stay there?'

'Until I'm asked to move out.'

'By Softie?'

'By a court. But that might not happen. It'll depend on who gets Matilda.'

Dr Bell said, 'But how will you pay the mortgage? Are you working, Garry? What's your source of income?'

Garry said, 'Right. Again with this! It was bad enough Softie giving me shit about this. The fact of the matter is, I work when I can. And it hasn't been easy since Matilda arrived because it's . . . well, you're up in the night, aren't you? So I can't go out and do jobs at night.'

Dr Bell said, 'I'm sorry, Garry . . . I don't think we discussed this. What is your job these days, or what was it before Matilda arrived?'

'Me? I'm a driver.'

'A taxi driver?'

'Not a taxi driver. A private driver.'

'Like a chauffeur?'

'Kind of. I mean, yeah, I started out with taxis, but now I've got my own business.'

'Your own cab?'

Garry said, 'It's a private car. Driving cabs didn't suit me. Nights in the city, you've got drunks on every corner. You've got people wanting to smoke in the cab or else they're so pissed they throw up, and then it's all sorry, sorry, sorry. But not so sorry that they want to clean it up.'

Dr Bell said, 'The hire car is different?'

'Well, there's no drunks, or hardly any. I'll tell you what happened. It was Christmas 2004. I was in the cab. I saw this woman standing on the street corner – cream suit, spiked heels – going mad trying to get a cab. I pulled over and she piled into the back seat, saying, "Oh, I'm late, *again*." And while I was driving she was saying, "Oh, I'm so glad to see you! There were no cabs! There's a million things I've got to get to tonight, and I'm not going to get to any of them."

'I thought, "I can help you with that." And I made her an offer: "You give me a hundred bucks" – which is about what I was making a night, taking my chances with yobs on the street – "and I'll take you wherever you want to go." And she thought that was a fantastic idea. She was all, "Oh, you'll wait outside for me? You'll be there when I come out? We can go to a few places? That would be so great." I'm yeah, yeah, that's no problem, here's my mobile number, just call when you're coming out and I'll be there to pick you up.

'She was so rapt with the deal – the convenience of it – she tipped me fifty bucks. So I said, "Do you have this kind of night a lot, where you've got things to get to and you can't get a cab?" She goes, "Oh yes, all the time!" So I got one of the cab cards and I wrote my name and my mobile on it and I said, "Well, if you're going to have a night like that, you call me and I'll do you the same deal." So she became my first, like, private client. And it was really great for a while. She had an office in Collins Street, and I'd pick her up at, say, six o'clock, and we'd go to, I don't know, the art gallery there on St Kilda Road, or to some private party in Brighton. I'd sit and wait for her, however long it took, turning down other fares, until it was time to take her home. All for the flat rate, which was a good rate.

'Then I thought, "There's got to be a bunch of sheilas like this – professional ladies – that are sick of waiting around for cabs. Maybe I could set myself up, as like a premiere car hire service." But, you know, it was hard with somebody else's cab. So I went to Rick with the idea and put the business case to him. Six or eight clients. Six or eight hundred bucks a week, minus petrol. Minus rego. I'd clean the car myself, keep the overheads down. And he agreed to sell me a Holden Calais, a superior one, a demo model, hardly anything on the clock, nice leather seats, pretty much for cost. I polished it up and got some business cards printed, and yeah, that became my business.'

Dr Bell said, 'So, Rick Hartshorn to the rescue again?' I could hear in Garry's voice that he didn't like the way Dr Bell had said that.

'What?' he said. 'No! No. Come off it, Doc. I hardly needed his help. He offered up a car. It's not like it was a bloody big deal for him to help me. It wasn't like I went begging. He was offering.'

Dr Bell said, 'Well, go on.'

Garry said, 'Right. Well, before Matilda was born, the business was going gangbusters. From thinking I'd have six or eight, I had around twenty people on the books, private clients, professional people. I still had that first lady, who set me up. She actually stayed with me for ages until I let her go.'

Dr Bell said, 'You let *her* go?'

Garry said, 'Yeah, well, I didn't have much choice. In the beginning she was all: "You're amazing, Garry, you're like my best friend in the world!" Because, you know, I was never late, I never left her wondering where I was; I kept the car smelling nice. And we got on pretty good, or so I thought, but after a while, I got the feeling she didn't respect me that much.'

Dr Bell said, 'How did you come to that conclusion?'

Garry said, 'Ah, well . . . okay, if you must know, I fancied her a bit. I kind of thought she fancied me, too. Because she'd complain to me about there being no straight guys left, and the night clubs being full of woolly-woofters. I thought, alright, maybe she might even be a bit keen on me. So one night, I'm being a shoulder to cry on – not literally, but you know – after some date of hers had gone badly wrong, and she goes to me, "You're wasted being a cab driver, Garry." And I go, "I'm not a cab driver. In case you haven't noticed, I'm operating my own business here.

I make reasonable money. And I'd know how to treat a woman like you."'

Dr Bell said, 'How did she respond?'

Garry said, 'She was a cockteaser, wasn't she? Never mind the weeks of leading me on: "Oh, Garry, you're the best." She kind of laughed at me and goes, "Well, fair enough, Mr Private Driver." It was pretty obvious she didn't see me as being in her league. She didn't say much else. She kind of got out of the car and tottered into her next function, and later that night, she called me and said, "Oh, go on home, Garry. I think I might have found a straight one tonight!"'

Dr Bell said, 'You sound quite disappointed with how that turned out, Garry?'

'Ah, well, not really. I mean, I had other clients. It was no big deal. And the more of them I had – the more career women like that, I mean – the more I saw how they can be with blokes they don't see as good enough. That, more than anything, should have set the alarm bells ringing with Softie.'

Dr Bell said, 'I'm sorry, Garry. You've lost me a bit there. Could you explain what you mean?'

Garry said, 'They've got a way about them, haven't they? Career girls. They've got a bit of what I call the Princess Syndrome. It's like they're that much better than anyone else, like no bloke is ever going to be good enough, and if they do find one that's good enough, it'll only be for a while, and then they'll shit on him. Which is odd when you think about it, because, let's be honest, Doc, none of them have got anything that all the rest don't have.'

Dr Bell said, 'Again, you might have to explain that.'

Garry said, 'Oh, come on! They've all got the same thing between their legs. The only difference is how it's packaged. Because some of them are fat and some are old, and some just aren't your type. But you see one that's packaged nicely – long legs, or a nice arse – and we all know the game, don't we? How to get access to it. How to get the legs open. And you come up with your techniques. A bit of flattery. A bit of humour.'

Dr Bell paused here. There's some silence on the tape. Then he says, 'Is that how you regarded Softie?'

Garry didn't immediately answer. Or, if he did, it's not audible, so maybe he shrugged. Then he said, 'Let me give you another example of how those chicks can be. I had this other client, another woman with a big job. I started out driving her just to work functions, but then, after a while, she says to me, "You know I'm separated from my husband, don't you, Garry?"

'Well, I thought it was a come-on. I looked at her in the rear-vision mirror. She had her legs all crossed over, skirt up to here. But she wasn't giving me the come-on. Not good enough for her probably. She goes instead, "I have a son, Garry, and the Family Court says he has to spend all this time with his father. It's very inconvenient. I'm supposed to take him to his father's in Yarraville after school on Wednesday afternoons. But it's a hassle for me, driving out there."

'At first I couldn't see what she was getting at. Then she says, "Is that the kind of thing I could hire you to do, Garry? Pick up the boy and take him to his father? I'd pay a good rate."

'I'm thinking, "You want me to ferry your poor kid around, because you can't be bothered?" But then, you know, what did it matter to me? A job's a job. I could ferry the kid around, if that's what she wanted. So I go, "Alright. I can do that." And she was just rapt.

'She gives me the dad's address, and she tells me the boy will be waiting outside Wesley College. So I go and pick him up and he's, what, six or seven years old? He's got a striped tie and a real sad face. He gets in the back of the Calais, and I drive him around to his dad's house in Yarraville. The dad is standing outside, waiting for us. He comes out to the kerb and he helps the kid out of the car, and waits for him to go inside, then he says to me, "No offence, mate, but I don't think this is right. My ex-wife sending our son across town in a cab on his own, it's not the right thing to do. Why can't she bring him?"

'What could I say, Doc? I happened to agree with the bloke. But at that point, my loyalty wasn't to him. My loyalty was to the person paying my bills. I said, "Yeah, well, I'm not a cab, I operate a private car service. I can be trusted. Here, you have my card."

'The bloke, he says, "I'd be happy to pick him up from school myself. His mother won't let me."

'I was thinking, "Why are you telling me this?" Because,

you know, I wasn't going to get into an argument about it. I had a job to do, which was pick the kid up and drop him off. Whatever else was going on, it wasn't my business.

'But anyway, the next time I picked this kid up – his name was Ben, by the way, and he never said a word, just sat in the back and played his Nintendo thing – the dad called me while we were on the Westgate, and he says, "Everything alright, Garry? Is Ben okay?"

'I was pretty moved by that. I don't know, I thought that was good. I said, "Yeah, yeah, he's fine, good as gold. We're on the bridge. We're almost there." And again, when I got to the dad's place, the dad was standing there, waiting for us. And he says, "You go on inside, Ben. There's a Popper in the fridge." When Ben was inside he says, "Well, I've got to say thanks for doing this, mate. I can tell you for free, I wouldn't be able to see him at all without you dropping him off."

'And I thought, "Well, what kind of bullshit is that? Why couldn't he pick up his own kid from school?" And he told me, "She won't have me near her house. She won't have me near his school." I mean, I just didn't get that. Unless I was missing something, this bloke was perfectly normal. You couldn't imagine him smashing his wife or anything.

'So I said, "Well, I don't get that." And he says, "She's got court orders, hasn't she? Court went in her favour. It was actually me that went there. To court, I mean. Everyone said I'd be right. I'd do fine. I was a good dad. But she puts on a song and dance. She says, Oh, I don't want my husband to know where I live. The court said, Well, that's fine, but Ben's going to see his father, and you're going to have to make that happen. The father can pick him up from school. So she comes up with the story: Oh, he runs me down in front of the other mothers. That's embarrassing for me. So now Ben's still got a right to see me, but she's not going to drop him off, and I can't pick him up. And that's where you come into the picture."

'Now, obviously, Doc, I didn't yet have a kid then. All this was before Matilda was born. The full impact of what this bloke was saying, it didn't really sink in. But I did start to look at his ex-missus a bit differently. I'd see her coming out of her house, all glammed up for gallivanting around. And she'd get pissed. She'd get pissed and call me up and I'd have to go and get her, and she'd be falling around in the street. I said to her once: "You're somebody's mother. Should you really be writing yourself off like this?" That was the night she asked me to pull over, saying, "Uh-oh, I'm going to throw up."

'I pulled over. I didn't get out of the car to help her. I sat behind the wheel. She was crouched up in the gutter, chucking. Then she got back in the car and said, "Just drive on, will you, whatever you're called." Like she didn't know what I was called. And she slurred to me: "I've got enough problems in my life without you going on at me." She was looking at herself in a little purse mirror, saying, "Oh God, I look like a hag." And I had to agree with her. She did look like a hag.

'But that wasn't the worst of it. The worst of it was still to come. Not more than, what, two weeks later, I was driving Ben back to her place in Brighton after his visit with his dad – and nobody's home. Ben goes up to the gates and presses the intercom and it's all locked up. He comes back to the car. I call his mum on the mobile. She's not answering. So I have to call Ben's dad, who says, "I'll come and get him." I don't even consider that there might be anything wrong with that. What are we supposed to do? Sit there all night until Madam Gallivant decides to come home? So I give Ben's dad the address, and he comes and gets Ben, who's crying his heart out.

'The next day, I get a phone call and it's Ben's mother, and she's absolutely feral, saying, "You gave my ex-husband my home address! That's a breach of a Family Court order. I've got that order for a reason! My ex-husband's not allowed to know my place of residence!" And, "He's going to pay for this!"

'I was like, "Whoa, lady, you were the one that abandoned the kid outside your own front gate." But apparently that didn't matter. What mattered was that Ben's dad had turned up at his ex-wife's house to collect his son from standing in the gutter. That put him in breach of a Family Court order. So there were no more trips for Ben to see his dad.

'He called me – the dad, I mean – and told me, "It's not your fault. She went back to court and basically stitched me up. I should have known better. I should have sent my mum or somebody to get him. I was just that anxious not to have him standing there, poor kid, with no one." I felt lower than low. Like it was my fault, when it obviously wasn't.'

Dr Bell said, 'It's a sad story, Garry. I take it that woman is no longer a client of yours?'

Garry said, 'Forget that! But as a learning experience, it was a good one. It's kind of fired me up for my case. I mean, I can see now what crap Softie might throw my way. And I'm ready for it.'

Chapter Eight

I wish I could remember the first year that we got a computer at home. I'm thinking it was 1998 or maybe 1999, and it was a hand-me-down from Scott. It lasted quite a few years, but now we've got a new one. Almost new. Windows 7, I think it is. It's what they call a desktop: with a box for the hard drive, and a flatscreen on top. It sits on this Ikea computer desk: there's a shelf for the hard drive, another for the printer and one for the screen. You can close the doors around it and hide it all away when people come. It's supposed to be hidden, in other words, but when things were at their peak between my Pat and Nerida, well, she made me wheel it out of the spare room into our sitting room, so she could be in front of it at all hours, glasses on her nose, studying the Grandparents United website.

I wouldn't be telling the whole story if I didn't admit that Pat did go looking on the computer for Rick Hartshorn's name, in relation to a custody battle.

'Why do you need to go through all that material?' she asked me. 'I'll just Google it up and we'll see what happened.'

And so that's what she did, and what she found, it upset her. It would upset anyone. And she came right outside to tell me about it, saying, 'You might as well stop whatever reading you're doing. I've got the story. This is one case you don't want to get involved in. This involves nasty things. We should stay out of it.'

She could barely get out the words she needed to say, in relation to the case, and I've got to say, it startled me, and there was a moment there where I thought, okay, this is too much for me.

But then I thought, no. Frank left these files for a reason. He said he made a mistake. So don't just take what you've read or heard and jump to conclusions. Maybe too many people have already done that. Go through the material. Look at things the way Frank saw them, and not with hindsight, which is obviously a wonderful thing.

Pat, though, she shut herself off from it, at least for a while.

'No, Barry,' she'd say, if I tried to raise something of the case with her. 'That one is too ugly for me. I've got enough on my plate, with Grandparents United. Now look at this,' she'd say. 'Here's another couple more like us. Haven't seen the grandkids for three years! Three years! You wouldn't even know them. They've approached the minister. Why don't we approach the minister? Or at least the local member. That's what he's there for, isn't he? To help people. I should write him a letter. Someone's got to take a stand. Do you think I should write to the local member, Barry? Is he somebody we know?'

He wasn't somebody I knew. He was the local member: an ALP guy, put into the role after being a union steward. Probably a perfectly nice bloke, but what was he going to be able to do to help Pat? Nothing, except maybe encourage her. I didn't want anyone to encourage her. I wanted her to settle down and ride out the worst of it, and see if she could try to make peace with Nerida. But that put me on a hiding to nothing.

'What am I supposed to do about the fact that she's taken an order against me, Barry? What do you think she'd do, if I picked up the phone and tried to get in touch with her? Do you want to see me in jail?'

I said, 'Well, what about a letter? You could write a letter, maybe saying sorry?'

'Sorry! For what? For wanting the best for my grandchildren? For wanting to see them? I've got nothing to be sorry about, Barry. What I actually need is for the court to step in and see the injustice here, and give me permission to spend time with those boys. But I'm not allowed to do that, am I? Brian's *banned* me from the proper course of action. So all I can do is campaign.'

I had sympathy for the spot Pat was in. But in terms of court action, I was on side with Brian. He'd held off having flying rows with Nerida, held off dragging his kids through the court, and sure enough it had paid off. It had taken a few months, but they'd brokered some peace, avoided the lawyers and worked out a plan where Brian was seeing the kids, no dramas. I was certain that Pat and Nerida could get to that point, if only enough water was allowed to flow under the bridge.

The more I got stuck into Garry's case, I could see that was the approach Dr Bell was taking, too. He wasn't in there, boots and all, spraying his own opinion around, trying to force things in one direction or another. He listened respectfully, quietly, professionally, to what each of them had to say and reserved judgement. And the more I listened to the tapes the more I began to like that style, and to like him too. I got the feeling that what he was trying to do was let Garry and Softie vent a bit. Get it all out. Chew each other over. Have their say. And then hopefully find some compromise for their future with Matilda. There was no judgement in him, not even when Softie finally upped and admitted she was never going to have been able to stay married to Garry.

'What would you think of me, Dr Bell, if I told you that Garry was never what I had in mind for a life partner?' Softie said.

Dr Bell said, 'I'm not entirely sure what you mean, Softie. What should I think of you?'

Softie didn't answer straight away. To me, it sounded like she was crying, which shows you how much Dr Bell had been able to help her, in getting confident with him. 'I feel so stupid,' she said. 'I *knew* that he was wrong for me. I *knew*, and I went ahead and married him anyway. We were so badly matched. So ill-suited. How did we ever end up married?'

Dr Bell was obviously keen to find the answer to that question too. 'Well, why don't you start at the beginning of the relationship with Garry, and let's see if we can figure that out,' he said.

Softie said, 'But I'm not sure I'll ever work it out! I'm not sure I'll ever understand what I was thinking! And now I'm stuck with him. Stuck with him in my life – in my daughter's life – forever! I can hardly believe it. It's like I'm in chains.'

Dr Bell said, 'Was there ever a time when you felt differently? Or did you go into the marriage feeling that way?'

Softie said, 'I went in feeling like I could *fix* Garry, if you can believe that, Dr Bell. I could see as well as anyone that he was rough around the edges. I could see that he wasn't polished, wasn't sophisticated, wasn't, you know . . .'

Dr Bell said, 'A metrosexual?'

'Right! Exactly right!' said Softie. 'He wasn't a metrosexual. Not that I'm saying I necessarily wanted a metrosexual. I don't mind a man who's a man, if you know what I mean. But Garry . . . he's just . . . I don't know . . .'

Softie trailed off at that point, so Dr Bell said, 'You moved in together quite quickly after you met. How did that happen?'

Softie sniffed, like she'd stopped crying and was clearing her nose. She said, 'I don't know if I can explain it. I was getting fed up with the guys I was meeting. Guys that friends picked for me, they seemed to be all the same. Not ready to settle down. Not wanting to talk about children. And I could see, obviously, that some of them thought I was too old for them. Because of course a man can date down, can't he? A man at forty, he can date right down to a woman in her twenties. Nobody thinks that's strange. But a woman turning forty, she's scary. She's in a hurry. She's got a ticking clock. And so I suppose I scared off a few of the better men.'

Dr Bell said, 'Garry didn't want a twenty-year-old girl, though, did he?'

'Oh, Garry. I don't mean to be a snob or anything, but he was pretty lucky to get me! I earned more than him. I'd achieved more. He's not the world's most attractive bloke. He's got a big scar on his leg. He's got a tattoo, an ugly old blue tattoo. He's got those boil marks. He's even a bit shorter than me when I've got my heels on.'

Dr Bell said, 'And so, if you had to explain what you did see in him, it would be . . . ?'

Softie said, 'Well, it's the old thing, isn't it? I thought I could change him. I suppose you know his stepfather – the man who helped raise him – is Rick Hartshorn? The car salesman? The racehorse owner? And he and Garry's mother have that nice place in Williamstown, the one with the boat ramp going out? So it's not like Garry was from,

I don't know, some bogan family. Although, obviously, what his actual background is, we don't know. You know he was adopted? He was adopted out when he was four or five. Talk to him about it. I bet he doesn't tell you anything. He certainly never told me any of the details, just that his real parents were dead, and he got adopted by his mum – that's Joan Hartshorn – and by Rick Hartshorn.'

Dr Bell said, 'Garry told you that he was adopted by his mum, Joan, and by Rick Hartshorn?'

'Well, no. There was some other father. Beam's father. But he's long dead. So it was Rick Hartshorn, really, that raised him.'

Dr Bell said, 'Do you recall how far into the relationship with Garry you were when you became aware that he was a Hartshorn – as in, related to Rick Hartshorn?'

Softie said, 'I was very quickly made aware of it. By Garry. He made a point of telling me, after our first date. And, for the record, I believe he did that because we had a disastrous first date. I don't mean at the Pop-up Restaurant. I mean the real first date. It was an absolute disaster. He'd tracked down my phone number, which was something I was already regretting asking him to do, and he'd called me at work, and said he wanted to go *fishing*. Fishing! But I thought, "Well, okay, Softie, it's not like men are knocking down the door." And look, it could be worse: it's not like he's invited me to, I don't know, the greyhounds. Which wouldn't have surprised me actually. But anyway, I agreed to go. And it was a disaster.'

Dr Bell said, 'And why do you say that? Did you fall out of the boat or something?'

Softie said, 'Fall out? No! No, of course not. No, it was just that he came in his driver's car, because that's what he was doing for a living – driving people to and from the airport for money, basically – so he had this big Calais with leather seats and silver dials, and *ugh*, it was awful. Sitting in it, I felt like a chauffeur's wife. I felt like people were looking at us and thinking, "Oh, there goes a hire car, and that couple must own it. It must be their business." I found that embarrassing. But we got on to the river. Not the Yarra. The Maribyrnong, of which I was only vaguely aware. Then, instead of fishing, Garry wanted to pull up, have a picnic, with supermarket dip – French Onion, or something horrible – and sitting there, he wanted to kiss me, and there were March flies, and dogs, and *ugh*!'

Dr Bell said, 'But did things improve? Because you must have gone out with him again, Softie?'

'Yes, I did. But only because he had a cousin's wedding, or some such. I had been absolutely determined not to see him again. But then he called and said, "*Please* come with me. I always go to these things alone. My mum will be there." And that's when he said, "She's married to Rick Hartshorn."'

Dr Bell said, 'And that interested you?'

'Oh, I was interested to meet him. Of course I was. Not just because he's famous. Certainly not because he's rich. I was interested to know how he ended up married to Garry's mum. I'd seen stories about him in the paper, how he married a woman with a disabled son, and thought how good he must be, because of that. No dolly birds for him. So I was interested to meet him, yes. And that's when Garry told me he hadn't put "Hartshorn" on his business card because he didn't want people around who were only interested in his money. Not that there is any money, mind. Garry and Rick Hartshorn barely get along.'

Dr Bell said, 'Do you know why that is?'

Softie said, 'I know only that it drives Garry nuts that I've become quite close to Rick, and Matilda is . . . well, he adores Matilda.'

Dr Bell said, 'Let's slow down a bit. How did the second date go?'

'Well, it was after that date – the cousin's wedding – that I started to think maybe there was hope for Garry. After I'd met Rick and saw how lovely, how charming he was, and after I'd met Garry's mother, Joan Hartshorn, who is also lovely, I thought, "This *is* a good family. Garry's obviously the black sheep. Let's see if we can change that."'

Dr Bell said, 'You didn't know at that stage that Garry was adopted?'

'Had he told me that? Maybe he had. I remember that for a while there I did think he was Joan's boy, and that Rick had adopted him, but then he explained about Beam, and how Joan and her first husband had been worried about having another boy with a disability.'

'What did Garry tell you about his birth parents?'

'Nothing at all.'

'And what about his early relationships?'

Softie said, 'Oh, I knew he'd been married once before, if that's what you're asking. Yes, I knew that. But why are you bringing that up? He told me it lasted two years. Not even two years. And he was only twenty-one. And he'd never wanted to marry her, but Rick Hartshorn said he had to. Is that not right? Have I been lied to about that?'

Dr Bell said, 'You haven't been lied to about that. That's the way I understand it too. But go on: you thought you could change Garry?'

'Can you believe that? How ridiculous. Because he never changed! He never changed. He's stayed exactly the same! Never mind what I've tried to show him about . . . you know, being a bit more sophisticated. He just does not get it. One night, for example, we were out with colleagues of mine from work. It's important to me that I present myself in a certain way at work. I hadn't been seeing Garry all that long – three months maybe – and I didn't know how he could drink when he gets nervous. So he was drinking and drinking, far more than is appropriate, and suddenly I hear that he's telling the story of our first date! Telling the story of flies, and the dogs that we caught out mating near our picnic! I was so embarrassed. So, so embarrassed. And I kept looking at him, as if to say, Garry! But it was like he didn't get the cues. He doesn't understand how to behave. He was sitting over his empty plate, his cutlery all splayed, grinning at me and telling this story as if it were appropriate. And the next day, a girl who was there, she emailed me and she said, "Softie! Who was the caveman?!" Because of course everybody could see how badly matched we were. Nobody thought it was going anywhere. What this girl didn't know, what I didn't really even know yet, when this girl rang to have a laugh about Garry, was that I was already pregnant.'

It was around this point that Softie started crying again. Her sentences are all broken up – but Dr Bell persisted. In a soft voice, he said, 'Here, have a tissue. Can I get you a glass of water? You sure? Are you okay to go on? Let's go back a step. When did you get pregnant?'

Softie said, 'Oh, Dr Bell, I just want to turn the clock back! No, I mean, I don't. I definitely don't want to turn the clock back. Matilda means the world to me. I would never wish her away. But in terms of the choice I made for her father . . . it was bad. It was bad, bad, very bad . . .'

'Slow down, Softie. Slow down. Things are not that bad. You've said you were pregnant. Was the baby planned?'

Softie said, 'Matilda was planned! Of course she was planned. She was planned in the sense that I definitely wanted a baby, Dr Bell! I wanted a husband and children and a normal life, like everybody else had! And I was running out of time. Yes, my clock was ticking, if people want to put it that way. *Tick, tick!* More like: boom, boom, Big Ben! And that wasn't something I hid from Garry. I was absolutely upfront with him. I said, "Garry, I'm thirty-nine years old and I want a child. I don't want to waste time on any guy who isn't interested in having a family, and soon." And Garry said, "Well, I've always wanted children." And after what I'd been through, waiting and waiting for . . . for . . . for . . . that *idiot* to leave his wife and start a family with me, well, a man saying "I've always wanted children" was like music. So I went off the Pill. Not, like, that day, but pretty much straight after I'd met Garry's family and decided, alright, this might work out. And I'd never *been* pregnant, Dr Bell. I'd heard horror stories about how long it can take. I have half a dozen friends who've ended up on IVF because they've waited too long. So why not get started? And then it happened straight away. Straight away! Two months after we met, I was pregnant. I told Garry. I said, "You won't believe this. I think I might be pregnant." And do you know what he said, Dr Bell? He said, "You don't have to tell me you're pregnant, Softie. I can tell." And do you know what *I* thought, Dr Bell? I thought, "Isn't that sweet! Isn't that lovely! He means I'm glowing, or something like that." I said, "Aw, Garry, how can you tell?" And do you know what he said, Dr Bell? He said, "Your tits are rock hard."'

There was a long pause here. I could hear Softie crying. Dr Bell kept saying, 'Okay, okay, alright, it's okay,' and 'Are you sure I can't get you some water?' And then, without Softie saying anything, but presumably having composed herself, Dr Bell said, 'Okay . . . and you were indeed pregnant, were you, Softie?'

Softie said, 'I was. I was. I had a test and that confirmed it. I was six weeks along. And I suppose I just put that ahead of everything else. I suppose I kept my eyes closed to other realities – to what Garry was really like – because I was finally going to have a baby.'

Dr Bell said, 'But a bright girl like you, Softie – it's hard to believe you could fall into that situation? Of thinking that you could change a man, or that a baby would make things better?'

Softie said, 'Oh, I know! I know! And I knew pretty much immediately how idiotic those ideas were. Because it was quite clear, from very early on, that Garry wasn't going to change. He didn't think there was anything about him that needed changing! Let me give you another example, Dr Bell. One of my closest friends, Herbie, is gay. I've known him forever. Since university. There was a point there where he actually lived with me in my flat at Edgewater Towers, and acted like my man-bag, because of course my man was married. Herbie's the nicest guy. Flamboyant, funny, just the nicest guy. He really is one of my closest friends. But Garry doesn't like him. And when I say he doesn't like him, I mean, he can't *stand* him. He literally cannot stand to be in the same room with him. We had a few arguments about it, even before we got married. I'd say, "But I don't get what it is that you don't like about him, Garry. So he's gay. So what? Plenty of people are gay." Garry would say, "What I don't get is why you like him so much."

'I'd say, "Well, what's wrong with him?" Garry would say, "He's *strange* is what's wrong." I'd say, "What's strange about him?" and Garry would say, "You bloody well know what's strange about him. It's not like he's hiding it behind a bushel, waving his arms around and screaming like a girl."

'I'd say, "You mean you don't like him because he's gay?"

'Garry would say, "I couldn't care whether he's gay, so long as he doesn't try anything on with me."

'I'd say, "Oh, please, Garry. What makes you think he's interested in you? Gay men don't go hitting on every man they see. It's other gay men they're interested in." And he'd say, "Don't talk to me about it. I don't want to even talk about it."

'At first I thought, "Well, this is silly." And then I thought, "Well, maybe it's something to do with the time he spent in the orphanage." Because, I mean, I have heard stories about those places. So I asked Garry about that. And he didn't take at all kindly to me asking about it. He said, "That's got nothing to do with it." But the way he said it, I thought, "Maybe it *has* got something to do with it." But then, maybe not. Maybe he just hasn't met that many gay people in his life. He grew up in Exford. What's the population of Exford? Do they have any gay people in Exford? I don't know. But I thought, "Well, he's living in St Kilda with me now" – because of course once I was pregnant he moved out of Rick's boatshed and in with me – "and so soon he'll meet other gay people, and he'll get over it. He'll see they're no different from anyone else – they can be fun! – and he'll, I don't know, grow out of it."

'So for a while there, I'd tease him about it. I'd say, "You think Herbie's interested in you, don't you? Or maybe *you're* interested in him?" But he wouldn't joke about it, Dr Bell. He wouldn't joke. He'd say, "Stop it, Softie. I don't even want to joke about that shit." And I'd keep going. I'd say, "You think because he's gay he's going to crack onto you? That's what you think, isn't it?" And he'd say, "He comes near me and he won't have, you know, a dick to go donut-diving with."

'And then one afternoon we ran into Herbie in St Kilda. And by this time I was more than three months along, and I'd started to tell people that I was having a baby. I was delighted. A bit worried about Garry, but still thinking he'd come good, especially once the baby arrived, when surely he'd grow up. So, I was a bit wary, but mostly shocked, and thrilled, and happy. So we're walking down Acland Street, and I saw Herbie and walked straight into his arms for a big hug and a kiss. He was screaming, "A baby! I heard about the baby! Let's have a look at you, sister! Give us a bit of a twirl around, show me that gorgeous baby figure!" And then he went to shake Garry's hand, you know, to congratulate him on being the father-to-be, and Garry pulled his hand away. Deliberately took his hand away, and put it in his pocket. It was so awkward, Dr Bell! But Herbie's such a gentleman. He's just a polite, honourable gentleman. He pretended not to notice. He said, "Well, Garry, this is great news. Softie's going to be a great mum." But Garry couldn't come at it. He said, "Whatever", and turned away. I was so embarrassed! Just so, *so* embarrassed! Because it was obvious what he was doing. I said to Herbie, "I'm so sorry." And he said, "*You've* got nothing to be sorry about." Then he turned to Garry – because Herbie's not one to just stand there and take it – and he said, "But you're a sorry bastard, aren't you, mate?" And Garry didn't even bother to turn, just kept his back to Herbie and said, "Whatever," and strode away, leaving Herbie and me standing there. Herbie trilled after him, "*Whatever!*" And then he said to me: "I hope you know what you're doing." Because he was hurt. Terribly hurt.

'In the flat, afterwards, I said to Garry, "I can't believe you did that." And he said, "Yeah, well, he put his hand out. And I don't need to touch him. I don't think it's such a good idea for you to be touching him either, in your condition."

'Well, I was floored. Because, you know, Dr Bell, there was only one thing he could have meant by that. Only one thing. He thought I was going to catch AIDS or something, hugging Herbie in the street. So I said, "Garry, that's just outrageous. That's just so stupid, it's really beyond stupid." And Garry said, "He's a freak. Look at the way he behaves. Mincing all around the place. Behaving like a woman."

'I said, "He doesn't behave like a woman, Garry. He's *gay*." And Garry said, "He's a freak." And I said, "Well, that's just homophobic." And Garry said, "I'm not homo anything. He's the homo." I said, "You are *homophobic*, Garry. That means you don't like him because he's gay."

And Garry said, "You got that right. I don't like him because he's a poofter, and I don't like poofters. You might want to make out like that's not normal, but actually it's being a poofter that isn't normal."

'I said, "And you think what you did is normal, Garry? You think it's rational to cut somebody off in the street because they're *gay*?"

'Garry said, "I've got a right to my opinion." I said, "You actually don't, Garry. You actually don't have the right to discriminate against people because they're gay. That's . . . that's old-fashioned, or stupid, or something. It might even be illegal."

'And Garry said, "Alright, Softie. I'm old-fashioned. I'm stupid. Maybe they'll put me in jail because I don't want to hang around with a bloke who takes it up the date." I said, "Don't be an idiot, Garry. What has his sex life got to do with anything? Does he care what you do in the bedroom?" And Garry said, "What I do is normal."

'I said, "And what he does isn't normal?" And Garry said it was sick. "Have a think about it, Softie. Two blokes going at each other. Kissing. It grosses me out."

'I said, "I hope you're not telling me I can't be friends with a man I've known for fifteen years?"

'Garry said, "You can do what you want. But *I* don't have to touch him, and I don't have to be date-mates with him."

'I wanted to keep arguing about it, Dr Bell, because I had actually had in mind making Herbie the godfather of our child. Probably he won't have children of his own, but he'd be a marvellous godfather. He just loves children. But Garry wouldn't talk about that. He wouldn't talk about Herbie at all after that. He went into the spare room, the one we were planning to use as a nursery, and sat down at the computer and made himself look busy. And I was in despair. Because, I mean, it was dawning on me that the father of my baby might be some kind of, I don't know, some kind of neanderthal.'

There was more crying on the tape at this point. Then Dr Bell said, 'Softie, I need to ask you this . . . if you felt that way about Garry, why on earth did you marry him?'

Softie started crying again. 'Because I wanted a proper family! Because I wanted to be Mum, Dad, kids, dog. This is actually a nightmare for me, ending up a single mum. It's precisely what I *didn't* want. It happened to me – the family broke up, and we all had to deal with it, and it was bloody hard – and the last thing in the world I want is to do the same thing to Matilda! But can you tell me what choice I've got? How can I stay? I can't stay . . . Garry's just . . . I don't know, he's *awful*.'

Dr Bell said, 'Let's go back to you being pregnant, with Matilda. Obviously that's a very exciting time. Garry had no children either, so it was a first for him too. How were things between you, at that time?'

Softie said, 'Oh my God! They got worse, Dr Bell! And perhaps that was because the pregnancy wasn't at all easy for me, which Garry really did not appreciate. I was throwing up morning, noon and night. I called Dawn – that's my youngest sister – and I said, "This is unbelievable. Did you go through this? You never said anything. How long does this go on? Dawn said, "Oh, six months." I said, "Six months!" And it was true! I felt absolutely appalling for six months. And I was *absolutely enormous*. I was walking for thirty-five minutes on the treadmill, swimming when I could, not eating for two, and then I'd go into the toilets at work and scoff down a packet of potato chips. I couldn't sit with my legs together. It was really difficult for me, and Garry, well, he was no help at all. I'd be in front of the mirror saying, "Look at me, I'm like a beached whale!", hoping that Garry would say something like: "You look beautiful! You're glowing!" But he'd say, "Oh, you'll be back to where you were after you've had the baby." Like that was supposed to make me feel better – "*You'll get back to where you were*." Could he really not see how that was going to make me feel *worse*?'

There is more crying here, and then Dr Bell asked the question that had been bugging me too.

Dr Bell said, 'Softie, I need to ask you this. When did you marry? And *why*?'

'Dr Bell!' Softie said, and her voice here is quite desperate. 'You've got to understand . . . I got married *for Matilda*! Obviously that was madness. But I was desperate to make it work and I must have had too many pregnancy hormones going through my system or something. Because I actually asked him! I actually asked Garry to marry *me*!'

Dr Bell said, 'That's not . . . *completely* unheard of, Softie.'

'Oh, but it's so embarrassing! Imagine having to ask somebody like Garry to marry me? But what choice did I have? He was never going to ask. He was going to be quite happy, having Matilda born outside wedlock. He kept saying, "I've been married before, it's a stupid piece of paper." I was so upset. But Rick was very much on my side. He thought we should get married too. He couldn't believe what Garry was doing, making me upset while I was pregnant.'

Dr Bell said, 'You get along well with Rick Hartshorn, don't you?'

Softie said, 'We get on brilliantly! We're very close. He's been great through this whole thing.'

Dr Bell said, 'Softie, how did Garry react when you told him that Rick Hartshorn thought the two of you should get married before Matilda arrived?'

Softie said, 'That was when it dawned on me how poisonous that relationship is – the relationship between Garry and Rick, I mean. Because Garry went berserk. Just berserk. He got right into my face about it, saying, "What on God's green earth has this got to do with Rick Hartshorn?" I reminded him, "Rick Hartshorn did the right thing by your mum when she was left penniless, a widow with two boys." Honestly, Dr Bell, I thought Garry's head was going to explode when I said that. He said, "You think I'm going to take lessons from Rick Hartshorn in how to behave?"

I said, "You take his money." Garry said, "I don't take his money!" I said, "He bought your work car. You lived in his house." Honestly, I thought he would explode. He kept going on, "He *should* help me," like there was some reason Rick had to help us. I couldn't figure that out.'

Dr Bell said, 'And so, how soon was it, Softie, before Matilda was born that you got married?'

'I was eight months pregnant when we had the wedding. That's how long he made me wait. By that stage Mum was even counselling me against it. She said, "You don't want to be uncomfortable on your wedding day. Why not wait until after the baby arrives?" Dawn was the same: "Don't you want to look nice in your dress?" Looking back now I can see what they were really saying, which was, "Think about this, Softie! He's really not your type."'

Softie had started crying again, but this time Dr Bell urged her on, saying, 'None of this sounds like the sort of wedding – marriage – a girl usually has in mind?'

Softie said, 'Of course it wasn't! When *I* was a little girl, I dreamed of the marriage I would have – a man asking my father for my hand, getting down on bended knee with a ring. But what could I do, Dr Bell? I was thirty-nine years old, pregnant with my first child, and I didn't want to give birth to Matilda and not be married. I know that sounds old-fashioned. I know some people wouldn't care, but it was very, very important to me that I be married before she was born. And that's why any suggestion from Garry that I somehow trapped him – that I got pregnant deliberately, because I was running out of time, and that I always intended to treat the baby as my own property – that is a complete lie.'

Chapter Nine

When you get into your sixties and you've been married forty years, nobody asks you how you met your wife any more and I suppose that's because they figure there can't be much of a story to it. And probably they're right. Take me and Pat. We met in Footscray. Frank Brooks, he met his wife, Betty, in Footscray. My folks met in Footscray. I can't tell you what an exotic idea it would have been for me to meet a girl from the other side of town.

Things are different nowadays, that's obvious. You've got people getting married who met on the internet. People of different colours, from different cultures. Horses for courses, I suppose, and it seems to work out as often as not. I mean there's nothing to say that two people from a different background aren't going to work out. There are plenty of examples of it working out fine. Greeks and Italians – that was the thing when I was a kid after the war. You wouldn't get Greeks marrying Italians. That would never work out.

And further back, when my parents were getting married: Protestants and Catholics. How could that ever work? But it did, and it does. The trick is to share the same ideas about the big things. Don't go to bed on an argument. Put up a united front with the children. Those are the things that get you through.

Now, I don't pretend to be a marriage counsellor, but it seems to me, from listening to Garry and Softie, that no couple was ever so badly matched. They didn't share the same ideas about anything, let alone the big things. They didn't even agree what the big things were. They might have been around the same age. They might both have been what we used to call Australian. But chalk and cheese, they were. Never was that more apparent to me than when I got to the tape where Garry was talking about how he met Softie. I'd already heard Softie's version of it. How awful she thought he was. But what did Garry tell Dr Bell about it? That it was love at first sight basically.

'I was in the car, driving this lady around, and she was going on and on about this new thing, a Pop-up Restaurant,' he said. 'I had no idea what all that was about. Sounded like a lame idea to me. But she said, "Everyone's going, it's become quite a place for people to meet, so sophisticated!"

'Now at that time, I had in mind the idea of hooking up with a career girl. I'd driven a few around. I reckoned I knew what made them tick. The blokes they were meeting didn't seem to do it for them. I thought, "Okay, I'll give that a crack." And then I saw Softie walk in, and straight away, I thought, "She's not leaving without my phone number."'

Dr Bell said, 'How did she look to you?'

'The thing I liked about her was she looked natural. Like, the way she looked – brown hair, not too much make-up – it was obvious, you know, she was good-looking, but not one of those women that wants to shriek over shoes, and carry on about a handbag.

'She sat down near the door. She had a look about her, like she didn't feel comfortable being there on her own. I liked that – she wasn't on the prowl. Later she told me, "Yeah, a girl that was coming with me dropped out." I got up and sat next to her. It was a bit hard to warm her up, but when we got talking, we didn't stop.'

Dr Bell said, 'Do you recall what you talked about, Garry?'

'My name. I gave it as Garry Gary. I like to see how people react to that. I didn't say I was a Hartshorn. I kept that bit to myself. Then there was Softie's name – it's not exactly normal, is it? Softie, short for Softest, which makes her sound like a hippie, which she obviously isn't, with her bank job and that. And what you've got to understand, Doc, is Softie and me, we've had these conversations a hundred times before. And it's bloody boring: Garry Gary, your name is Garry Gary? Softie, did you say Softie? So it's a good vibe, when you meet somebody you don't mind explaining it to.

'So there was that, and there were other things. I'm not

sure I can remember them now. We talked about the food maybe, the wine. I don't know much about wine. Softie gets into it. I do remember we were that into each other the woman who was sitting on the other side of me sort of got up, after the entrée, and said, "Well, three's a crowd" and moved up the table, where she might get a word in edgewise.'

Dr Bell said, 'So, at least as far as you were concerned, there was a spark?'

'There was a spark. Not just on my side. And at the end of the night it was Softie who actually said, you know, call me. Like, I was going to call her anyway, but you know, she was all for it. I gave her my business card, and she . . . hang on, I remember! That's right! She actually gave the card back and said, "No, I won't be calling you, but if you want to call me that's fine." And I'm like, "Well, what's your number, then?" And she's like, "I'm sure you can find me if you want to badly enough." And I was pretty impressed by that. That was like her saying, "Well, you know what I do for a living, you've got my name and it's a weird one like yours, so how keen are you? Reckon you can track me down, or what?"'

Dr Bell said, 'And I take it you found her easily enough?'

'Took no time,' said Garry. 'No time at all. I mean, Softie Monaghan, who was working at the National Australia Bank. I just rang the switchboard. Head office. There she was.'

Dr Bell said, 'Was Softie surprised by your ability to find her so quickly?'

'Nah, I don't reckon. She knew I was keen. She was pretty keen herself. She would have been ropeable if I hadn't tracked her down. I'd been racking my brain, thinking where would be a good place to take her? And I'd just got into fishing again, which I hadn't done for years. I thought, "I'll take her out on the boat somewhere and threaten not to take her back until she agrees to see me again."

'So I said to Softie, "Want to come fishing out on the Maribyrnong?" Not her territory, obviously, but why not take her somewhere she might not have been? People say it's a dump out west, and that's absolute bullshit. What I didn't know was, Softie rowed at school. Who does that? Rows at school? Not us, at Exford primary. A tinny on the weir maybe. So anyway, I'm in the boat at the oars – the controls, as it were – and she's all, "One hand over the other" and, "Like this . . ." And I'm thinking, "Who's running this date? Me or you?" But anyway, I pulled up on the first bit of land I saw. It was just out past the racecourse there at Flemington where we pulled up. I had a blanket and I'd bought a good bottle, one the bloke at the wine shop in Williamstown recommended to me, and I laid it all out . . . and that's when I realised, "Holy crap, this isn't an island. This is like a swamp. This is mudflats." It was absolutely swarming with mozzies. Mozzies and March flies. I'd been thinking, "This'll be nice, this'll be romantic. I'll have her in the palm of my hand here." But actually, we were on a mudflat.

'I put the rug down. I put out all the things I'd brought – you know, the dip, the biscuits and all that crap – and just when we were getting into the first glass of wine, these dogs came up. Two dogs – one big hairy one, like an Airedale, and a scruffy little mutt thing, and they just started going at it! Going right at it, right next to us, if you see what I mean.

'I was on my feet, trying to shoo them off. You know, "Hey, get on, get out of here!" They separated and ran off a bit – and then they got straight back into it, pumping away like there was no tomorrow! I was chucking sticks, everything. Finally they bolted off into the bushes. I chased after them to make sure they were gone, and do you know what I thought when I got back to Softie on the blanket? I thought, "Well, that's got to be a good sign about where this date is headed!"'

Dr Bell said, 'The dogs mounting each other . . . you thought that was a good omen?' His voice here had a bit of humour in it.

Garry said, 'Ah well, you know. When you put it like that. And yeah, she was a bit cold after that first date, like she didn't think it was all that funny as me, and I thought, "Bugger, how can I put this right?" And one of my, like, distant cousins – a bloke I call a cousin who is actually related to Rick Hartshorn – was getting married that next weekend and it was going to be quite a posh do, and I thought, "Maybe that's more her speed?" I sort of let her know that it was going to be pretty nice and maybe she should come along and, you know, give me another chance.'

Dr Bell said, 'Until that point, you'd avoided telling Softie you were related to Rick Hartshorn.'

'Related is pushing it. He's married to Mum. But yeah, I was wary. I wanted to see what she thought of me, without knowing that. But it was fair enough for me to show Softie that side of things eventually, wasn't it? Like, she's all for Rick Hartshorn now, getting Matilda to call him Grandpa and all that. So, yeah, it must have worked, because not too long after that, Softie was saying, "Do you want to have a baby?"'

Dr Bell said, 'From what I understand, Garry, you didn't get married until Softie was eight months pregnant. Did you feel nervous about marriage? Maybe because of your first marriage?'

Garry said, 'For Christ's sake. You're bringing all that up again? I told Softie: having been married I couldn't see the big thrill. It's a piece of paper. Doesn't stop anyone from doing the dirty. But Softie wanted to get married. My idea was, okay, fine, let's wait until after the baby comes so she doesn't have to be fat in her dress. She was always going on about how fat she was – "I feel gross, blah, blah." I thought, "Get the baby out, get your figure back, and then we'll get married, maybe go on a honeymoon, leave the kid with my mum. Or her mum." But Softie couldn't wait. And so she went and got Rick Hartshorn to put the pressure on me. And I can't tell you how that pissed me off.'

Dr Bell said, 'You could have told Rick Hartshorn to mind his own business.'

Garry said, 'I could have. Except that he was going to have to help pay. Because the wedding Softie wanted was going to cost a bit. And her mum obviously couldn't afford it. She got that house in Malvern when she got divorced, so everyone thinks she's loaded, but what they forget is, she's had it thirty years. She's never earned an income from it. She doesn't have a job. She's cash poor.'

Dr Bell said, 'Traditions are going out the window, Garry, but traditionally it would be Softie's father who would pay for the wedding?'

Garry said, 'Yeah, well, things aren't good there. Hey, how about you take that into account when you write your report? Softie doesn't actually speak to her old man. Isn't that relevant to how, you know, she cuts men off? She says it's because he's got this new wife, a third wife, but it's actually because she's pissed off about him walking out on her mum. And now she's doing exactly the same thing to me.'

Dr Bell said, 'Softie being pregnant – that was clearly a motivator for her to get married. How about for you?'

'Well, she got pretty fat, and she didn't like that. Maybe she thought, "Get married now, in case I stay like this after."'

'Is that something you thought at the time, Garry, or something you think now?'

'Oh, I didn't see that she was fat. But like all women,

Softie was, "I'm so fat, I'm so fat." And that's a trap you don't want to walk into, isn't it? What do you say? "You're not fat." You can't win. So I'd go, "You're pregnant. You'll get back to where you were before," and that would send Softie berserk, crying. She cries all the time. At anything. She was like, "I'll never get back. I'll be fat forever. At least now I've got an excuse for being fat on my wedding day."'

Dr Bell said, 'And did you propose, Garry?'

'You know I didn't! You must know that! That's something she goes on and on about, that I never actually proposed! But anyway we still got married, so why she complains I do not know.'

Dr Bell said, 'And the wedding – it went off without a hitch, I hope?'

Garry said, 'It wasn't actually all that bad in the end. Maybe even pretty good. A big piss-up basically. Not for Softie. She couldn't drink. So she had to stay out of it – out of the fun bits of it. But yeah, everything else was okay. Her old man didn't show up.'

Dr Bell said, 'And then, a month after the wedding, along comes Matilda.'

'Along comes Matilda,' Garry agreed. 'And I've got to tell you, I was that rapt. I hadn't much wanted kids before, but I hadn't been with someone like Softie before. I'd been a bit – how will things change, after the baby comes? But she was a beauty. Was that rapt with her. Still am.'

Dr Bell said, 'Did you go to the birth of your daughter, Garry?'

'Of course I did.'

'And how was that?'

'How was that? You know. You can't do anything right. I got screamed at from start to finish. But yeah, it was pretty amazing.'

'And afterwards . . . did Softie breastfeed?'

'Yep.'

'And you were happy to see that?'

'Was *I* happy to see that?'

'Yes. Did you have a view on whether Softie should breastfeed or . . . ?'

'It wasn't up to *me*, Doc. I wasn't consulted. That was Softie's business. Myself, I don't like it much . . . looks a bit primitive to me. But if that's what she wanted, whatever.'

'But did you support Softie in that?'

'Support her? You mean help her do it?'

'Support her choice. Encourage her.'

'Ah, well, she wanted to give it a go. If she didn't want to give it a go, I would have been fine with that.'

'Okay. And those early months . . . the nappies, the feeding, the night-waking, how did that go?'

Garry said, 'Yeah, well, I did my best to stay out of the way, if that's what you mean. Softie had some pretty firm ideas on how things should be done. She had this routine. She had this book – *Contented Little Baby Book*, it was called – with all these strict routines . . . you're smiling.'

Dr Bell said, 'I know the book.'

'Well, you know it says you've got to do this and then

do that, and you can't go anywhere because the baby is the boss. It's pretty full-on.'

'How did you feel about it, Garry? That style of parenting – did you have a view on that model versus some of the other models?'

'Other models?'

'Other philosophies?'

'I don't really know what you mean, Doc . . . I mean, it didn't really seem to matter what I thought. I thought, "Look, I'm the bloke here, she's the mum, what do I know?" To myself I might have thought, "I'm sure people have raised kids without books before." But Softie was keen. All the women in her mothers' group were on this book. So the book, it was like the Bible. We had to do whatever it says. Never mind when it wasn't working – Matilda still cried a lot, when the book said she wouldn't – we had to keep doing it. Then, like, out of the blue, it wasn't that book any more. It was some other book that had Matilda out of her cot, where she was always supposed to be for nap time, and sleeping in the bed with us. As a bloke, you try to keep up, but it's not easy.

'I'd say, "First you were running the place like boot camp. Matilda's in the cot, crying the house down, and no one's allowed to touch her. Now you're all, pick up the baby, swaddle the baby, rock the baby, and whatever I do is wrong." So I decided to leave her to it. I thought, "Get back into the weights, keep your own fitness up, keep your own mind clear." Which didn't thrill Softie. She was, "You think you can take two or three hours out of the day to do weights? You're supposed to be helping me." I'm like, "But whatever I do is wrong." She's like, "Go on then, go to your beloved gym." But you could see she wasn't happy about it. Like one day, I went to the gym – an outdoor gym by the beach. I met up with some mates from the old lifting days. They said, "Hey, how's it going? It's fantastic, isn't it, being a dad?" Some of them were new dads too. They were asking, "Getting any sleep? How's the wife?" And it was a relief, I tell you, to be able to joke with a few mates about how tough it was at home. How tired Softie was, and how she was freaking out about every little thing.

'They said, "Come to the pub. Have a few beers." I called Softie from the mobile. I said, "I'm heading to the Esplanade, the pub there, to have a few beers. I'll be home around six." The mobile started going at five past. By seven, I had six text messages from Softie, one every ten minutes, the last one saying, "If you're not home in five minutes, don't bother."

'I made my way home. It's a walk to our place, from the Esplanade. Softie was in a foul mood. She was saying, "What kind of husband does that, goes off to the pub when their wife is at home with a crying baby?" I said, "Whatever you think, Softie, I can't sit around with the baby all day." She goes, "You could get a *job*, Garry. You could pick up some old clients, start bringing in some money. That would actually be helpful, instead of going to the pub, coming home stinking of beer." I couldn't believe she'd brought that up. I'd already told her I didn't want to go back to driving. I wanted to set up my own business. I said, "I'm working on a business plan," but Softie had no respect for that. She said, "You're not working on a business plan! You're surfing the internet. You're mucking around on Facebook." I said, "I'm researching." My idea was to set up an online fitness business, selling gym equipment. I said, "Softie, if I knew that having a baby would do this to you . . . you're acting like you're crazy." She goes, "I'll tell you what's crazy, Garry. Thinking your life can go on like before when you've got a new baby, when you've got responsibilities for the first time in your life." I said, "It would help if you'd let me do anything. It's your way or the highway." She goes, "That's not true. I want your help. But you don't do anything right."

'Her idea of not right, Doc . . . we had a jogging pram. I was allowed, sometimes, to put Matilda in the jogging pram and run along with her. Once, I decided to stop by the post office. That's all – stop by the post office. And I left Matilda on the street outside. I mean, it was perfectly safe, plenty of people around, I could see her from where I was standing in the queue. She was fast asleep. I figured it was better than waking her and I couldn't get the jogging pram inside the post office, so I would have had to wake her, to get her inside.

'I picked up a parcel for Softie. I thought, "That's one less errand for her to run. She'll be happy with me for once." But the first thing she says, when I hand the package to her, is, "How did you get the pram inside the post office?" I go: "Matilda was sleeping –" I don't even finish the sentence, and Softie's going nuts. "You left our baby on the street?" I go, "She was one metre away! Not even a metre. She was right outside the door. I didn't take my eyes off her." Softie goes, "What if somebody had walked off with her? I can't believe you left her on the street!" On and on.

'So, those were the kinds of fights we were having – I was crap at taking care of Matilda, or crap as a human being. One night she got stuck into me over how I eat. *How I eat!* She'd made some dinner: steak and salad with a bit of avocado, a bit of lettuce and then the tomato. Softie goes, "Who taught you to hold the knife and fork like that?" I said, "Like what?" Softie's like, "In your fists. You hold the knife and fork in your fists." I'm like, "You've got a licence on how I eat now? Tell me, Softie, is there anything I can do right? Or is everything about me wrong?" But you know, Doc, I already knew the answer to that question.'

Chapter Ten

You'll remember I told you that Pat and I were married in the early sixties. It was a bit of an odd time for marriage. Pretty much everyone was still doing it, and I suppose that's because the archbishop, Mannix, was still alive, but some of the old rules for church were falling by the wayside. Girls were turning up without the big white dress. Maybe even in a miniskirt wedding dress. And blokes would go in a skinny tie, with California Poppy in their hair, and after a while not even receiving Communion at all.

My Pat, I don't mind saying, had great legs, and if she'd wanted to be one of those who wanted to get married in the new miniskirt, I wouldn't have minded, but she was a traditional girl, and in the end she turned up in white, with a hat the size of a block of butter. Her sisters were in dresses that Pat and her mum sewed from the Butterick pattern. We did the full Catholic Mass and danced the waltz at the reception, and we did the Twist, which was Number 1 on the charts that year. I remember thinking as we headed out for the Windsor (just one night because, let me tell you, it costs a pretty penny) that we'd set off on the right foot, and we were really happy.

Forty years later, when the last of our kids – that would be Brian – finally made it to the altar, well, there wasn't even an altar. Nerida told Pat she wouldn't have minded getting married in a church, 'so the pictures look nice' – meaning, she'd have some bluestone in the background – but neither of them made a secret of the fact that they didn't believe all the stuff that used to get shoved down our throat in Sunday school. The wedding wasn't anything to do with anyone's religion. Brian and Nerida got married because they wanted a big party, basically, with booze and a DJ and dancing around, and everyone having a good time, and that's all that really matters, isn't it? That you start life together happy.

Garry and Softie's wedding . . . well, whatever Garry might have said, to my mind, and to Softie's, it was a fiasco from start to finish. I mean, it's not like she made a secret of that.

'The whole thing was a disaster,' she said, when Dr Bell asked her about it.

'How so?' said Dr Bell.

'For one thing, I had to organise *everything*. Never mind that I was eight months pregnant. I had to call Births, Deaths and Marriages to ask what we had to do legally to get married. The lady on the phone, she said, "Oh, you can't just get married in a fortnight!" Which was what I needed to do, because Matilda was well on her way.

'She said, "You have to wait three months. That's the law." I had to plead with her. I had to say: "I'm eight months pregnant!" Luckily she said, "Oh, well, there is a provision for that. If you write and explain the situation, and include a letter from your doctor, you can get special permission." Garry said, "That's what the war brides did, before their husbands went to sea." I said: "Oh, fantastic, Garry, that makes me feel fantastic." Then we had an argument about *where* we would get married. My mother would have liked the chapel where I went to school, but not in the condition I was in. So we settled on St Kilda beach. I thought, "Well, that'll be nice, both of us barefoot, maybe with some frangipani in my hair." But oh, Garry's friends! I mean, Dr Bell, he had all these friends from when he drove cabs. They came in these suits, suits that didn't fit them. Some of them were obviously body builders, taking God knows what. And Garry's feet! He refused to have a pedicure. He'd agreed to go barefoot, but he wouldn't have a pedicure. He said it was poofy. So his feet were all gnarly and hairy.'

I don't need to tell you that Softie had started crying again. Then Dr Bell said, 'Was the occasion at all joyful, Softie? Or is that a stupid question?'

Softie said, 'Well. Nothing's ever *all* awful, is it? It was great to have Mum there, and my sisters were so happy, you know, that I was going to have a baby. That I hadn't missed out. They knew I'd been worried about that. Mum wore a hat. My sisters, Heaven and Dawn, they both made it – they held hands, and they sang from under the rotunda. They have such lovely voices. They got their children all dressed up the way I wanted. And Rick Hartshorn – Rick Hartshorn was so, so amazing. He said he'd pay for whatever we wanted. He'd pay for the champagne, the flowers, the catering. And Garry's mum, Joan, she was there, and she's lovely. And Beam was there! I'd met Beam a few times and it was great that they brought him along. He actually wore a suit. I don't know if I've described him to you or if Garry has, Dr Bell, but he's got a large head, basically, and his stomach sticks out like a pregnant woman, and we were actually bouncing our stomachs together at one point because they were the exact same shape! Beam doesn't tend to do that kind of thing. He doesn't . . . well, he doesn't normally engage, or so Garry told me, and for him to do that kind of thing was kind of, I don't know, unusual for him.'

Dr Bell said, 'Has anyone ever told you what exactly is wrong with Beam, Softie?'

Softie said, 'No. I don't really know. I asked Garry about it once. He said, "He's retarded." I said, "That can't be the medical condition, Garry, *retarded*?" He said, "He had water on the brain. It made him retarded." But there are other things wrong. He has some kind of skin condition. He doesn't like too much fabric near his skin. So his suit was short pants, and short sleeves, like a sailor suit, but on a grown man. It makes him look stranger than he is. But he was perfectly lovely. He stayed close to his mum. He was smiling the whole time. And he's got a habit of taking photographs. I don't mean taking photographs of people the way . . . *normal* people do. He has a little digital camera that he takes everywhere. He took photographs of everything, just *click, click, click* all afternoon. What the photos were of, I cannot imagine. But Garry's mum – Joan – she was so patient, pulling him away from the cake, saying, "Come on, Beam, maybe not so up close with the icing." So, yes, there were some good things about the wedding.'

Dr Bell said, 'You haven't yet said that Garry was one of them, Softie.'

Softie said, 'Because he wasn't! I mean, Garry! What can I tell you, Dr Bell? I'm sure you know how it went. First there was the argument about what he was going to wear. He said, "I'll just wear my driver suit." I said, "Garry, you can't wear a work suit. It's your wedding day." He said, "Who needs to spend money on a suit to wear once? I'll be right in my driver's suit." I thought, "Okay, Softie, humour him. That's just him putting on his bogan act." Because he'd make the point from time to time that he was a bogan, and proud of it. One time when he was in the kitchen at our flat, for example, and he couldn't find the coffee, he called out to me in the bedroom, "Softie, where's the coffee?" And I said, "In the freezer, dozy." And he was quite amazed. Why would the coffee be in the freezer? I told him, "It's proper coffee. It's ground. The freezer keeps it fresh." He said, "Nescafé's fine with me." So that's sort of what I was dealing with. And it's not an act. That's actually how he is.'

Dr Bell said: 'And so, did you manage to get him into a new suit for the wedding?'

Softie said, 'I did. I did get him into a new suit. But it was a nightmare negotiating with him. Then, on the actual day of the wedding, his mates had this idea that he should have a beer before the ceremony. They were all: "Dutch courage!" So he'd had a few beers even before I walked onto the beach. In all the photographs you can see his mates there, holding up their VB cans. The differences between my guests and his – I mean, Rick and Joan were fine, obviously, but in general – it was embarrassing.'

Dr Bell said, 'It wasn't a religious ceremony, from what you're saying?'

Softie said, 'No. Oh no. We had a celebrant, a woman celebrant. Garry wasn't happy about that either. Not happy about the celebrant. Not happy that he had to get a new suit. Not happy that my friend, Herbie, was there. But I'd put my foot down about that. I'd said, "Herbie's one of my oldest friends. He'll be at the wedding." And he – Herbie, I mean – actually looked amazing, barefoot like all the guests, but in this amazing tuxedo, with his partner also gorgeous. They were actually the two best-dressed men there. But Garry and his mates, they wouldn't engage with them at all. Wouldn't have them at the buck's night. When I asked why Herbie wasn't on the guest list for the buck's night Garry actually said to me, "Wouldn't he rather be at the hen's night with the rest of the girls?" Which was just ridiculous. But Herbie didn't make a scene. He kept out of

Garry's way. He gave us the most beautiful wedding gift, vases from Villeroy & Boch, which I know cost a fortune. I'd felt guilty even putting them on the bridal register at David Jones. I'd actually thought no one would buy them. But Herbie did.

'So I walked onto the beach – or more accurately waddled – and the celebrant took us through our vows, just the basic ones, nothing written by us, which I might have liked to have done if Garry could have put, you know, a romantic sentence together. And then, once we'd exchanged vows and the celebrant had said, "You may kiss the bride," Garry's friends from the gym all cheered and lifted up their VB cans, and one of them shouted, "Stick the tongue in!"'

Dr Bell lets Softie cry a bit here. Then he says, 'Was there a reception, Softie? Given your condition at the time?'

'Oh, well, we had the pavilion near the pier there. I couldn't drink, obviously. I had one glass of champagne. Rick Hartshorn gave a lovely speech. Thanked everyone for coming. Then he and Garry's mum took Beam home. I wouldn't have minded leaving at that point myself, but Garry had organised a DJ. And his mates sort of took control of that, and were playing all this, I don't know, AC/DC and Meatloaf, singing at the tops of their voices. I could see my friends looking at each other. Just *looking* at each other. None of them were dancing. Which was fine with me. I couldn't stand for long periods, my feet were so swollen. I was tired. I had a headache. My head was killing me actually. There was supposed to be a dance, like a bridal waltz, not a formal one, but a nice one. I'd chosen INXS, "Never Tear Us Apart". And Garry announced to the whole room, "Never tear us apart! I can't get near my bride!" And then he made a big fuss of trying to get his arms around me, at which point I thought, "Okay, enough. I've done the right thing by my baby, I've got married, now I want to go home." But Garry was into the beer, and when he drinks beer he's like an alcoholic. He can't have just one. So he'd loosened his tie and was partying on, shouting, "Khe Sanh – *Last plane out of Sydney, almost go-o-on –*" over and over, and squabbling near the boom box with other people who wanted to choose different songs. So, you know, when you ask me, Dr Bell, how was the wedding? What can I say? It wasn't exactly a dream come true. And I don't need to tell you that the wedding night was more of the same. We had a room at Crown. Rick Hartshorn paid for that. But, you know, we were exhausted. Or I was. I was exhausted, and Garry was drunk. So there was a part of me that maybe would have wanted to snuggle up to my new husband – a different husband, maybe – and go over the details of the night, laugh and remember and maybe make love, but the truth is, Dr Bell, I just wanted to sleep. And I was intensely worried about that. I thought, "What kind of a start is it, if you don't even make love on your wedding night?"'

Dr Bell said, 'I can assure you, Softie, it's not at all unusual.'

Softie said, 'But I mean, shouldn't you do it? I thought maybe we should at least try. But then I was saying to myself,

"Oh, it's not like we've never done it!" We'd already been living together before we got married. I was pregnant, for heaven's sake! And to be honest with you, having sex when I was that pregnant . . . I didn't like it. Oh, I know, I know, there are women who say that's the best time! You're so full and ripe and sexy! I didn't feel sexy. I felt *fat*. Fat and tired and gross.'

Dr Bell said, 'You didn't get the feeling that Garry thought you were beautiful? Pregnant, and now his wife?'

'Oh, I don't know. I don't think so. Do you mean sexually? That he was turned on sexually? He had a bit of a go, if you know what I mean. I was lying on my side, and I could feel, you know, that he was ready, or half-ready in that drunk state, and he sort of pushed up behind me and said something like, "It's bad luck not to have sex on your wedding night, Softie." I said, "Oh don't, Garry. I feel awful." And he said, "You're just pregnant. You'll get back to normal." And that sort of hurt my feelings: "*You're just pregnant.*" And, "*You'll get back to normal.*" Like being pregnant wasn't special, and wasn't even actually normal. Like I was in some terrible temporary, horrible state. I said to Garry, "You've got no appreciation for what I'm going through. This is meant to be a really special time." And he said, "Come on, Softie, forget about the baby fat. Let's just root around a bit." And then he fell asleep.'

There's another pause at this point, and then Dr Bell said, 'You know, Softie, I hope you'll forgive me when I say this, but when you describe your wedding to me I can see that the marriage was already over.'

Softie didn't object.

'It was already over,' she agreed. 'It was over before Matilda was even born.'

Chapter Eleven

I told you before that women are pretty much a mystery to me, and because of that I'm not even going to pretend I know what it's like to be a woman who is expecting a baby. There are some things us blokes, well, we just won't ever know. I can say – I hope without being pelted too badly – that women today, Softie included, seem to make more of a fuss of being pregnant than my Pat did when she was having our kids. I mean, ten months after our wedding, Scott came along. Ten months after that, John came along, and so on, and so forth, four times in total, with one in between that Pat thought she might have lost, although we were never one hundred per cent sure, because maybe she'd just been late.

There was no announcing to people we were trying for a baby. You got on with things, and on the babies came. Blokes had very little to do with whatever planning there was associated with it, and as for the actual pregnancy, well, I found out when Pat decided to tell me, which was usually after she'd been to her doctor to make sure everything was going okay. There were no home pregnancy tests. You didn't make a big fuss about whether it had happened or not. Just, over the ironing maybe, Pat would say, 'We'll have another one by Christmas.' And I might say, 'Is that right? Well, that's beaut.' Then, some time later, it would be, 'Might be best to get ourselves to the hospital.' And, 'Where's that little bag of mine? I better put a nightie in.' Then, 'You've got another boy.'

From memory, the time in hospital was longer than it is today. Pat would stay in at least five days and then it was longer still after she had Brian, because she had a little op to make sure that was the end of it. Then she'd come home and the new arrival would go in the crib at the foot of the bed, and after a while we'd make space in one of the boys' rooms – two single beds in each room, we had, in the end, and on with the show, meaning nothing seemed to be that much of a big deal. And maybe that's because Pat was younger, with no other responsibilities in her life other than to take care of the kids and keep the house. Not that I'm saying that's easy. Believe me, I'm not silly enough to say that. But what she didn't have to do was worry about the job she had to get back to. She didn't have to worry about who would look after the kids if she went to work. The hundred dollars a day, or more, that it costs to put the baby into child care. You have to wonder if it's even worth women going to work, but of course they all want to say it's their right, or else mortgages being what they are these days, they've really got no choice.

The other thing that's changed is how much stuff babies seem to need. I don't say we didn't fuss over our babies. We fussed. Don't worry about that. Pat fussed about making sure they had their little bonnets, and grandmothers went mad, knitting little matinee jackets and so on. But the stuff babies seem to need these days – well, it's blown all out of proportion. Like, when our Brian and Nerida were first having Jett, Pat and I, we said, 'Well, what do you need?' Thinking, maybe, we could buy something sensible like some baby clothes, or one of those capsules for the car. But those weren't the kind of things Nerida wanted. Nerida wanted a baby change table – a $700 one to match the $900 crib for Jett – and everything else in the room she wanted to be the same pattern. And it all had to be new. Nothing could be secondhand.

Pat said to Nerida, 'Believe you me, you don't need a change table. You can change the baby on the floor.'

Nerida said, 'But we want things to be nice!'

Then, of course, Jett arrived. And he had to have this, and he had to have that. Pat told Nerida, 'A baby doesn't need much. When Brian was little, he had a bouncer – a crocheted bouncer on a metal frame – and I gave him pots and pans to play with. And he turned out fine.' But Nerida wasn't of that mind. She wanted a jungle gym for Jett. She wanted one of those red and yellow trucks for him to sit in before he could walk. She wanted a Thomas the Tank Engine set, with tracks and every kind of engine, and a tunnel and a bridge. Pat said, 'She's going to send Brian to the poor house. I don't want to think about their credit-card bills.' Because of course Pat knew they had credit cards. Didn't approve of them, but knew that they had them.

From what I gather, Softie was one of those who wanted everything that opens and closes too. From the day Matilda arrived, it was like everything she had would be invested in the child. And so, from the start, she was obviously one of those mums that hovers, and worries.

'The final few weeks of the pregnancy were difficult for me,' she told Dr Bell. 'The only way I could really get comfortable was in water. I'd drive myself to the hydrotherapy pool, the one they built at Albert Park, and I'd sit in there and float. It worked for a while, but then it started getting hard for me just to drive. I could hardly get behind the wheel. So Garry said to me one morning, "Don't worry, Softie. I'll drive you. You can sit in the back like a real Lady Muck." I said, "But don't you have clients?" because Garry was still working then and Garry said, "They can wait." And I thought it was lovely of him to be thinking of me, to be offering to drive. I thought, "Maybe he does understand how uncomfortable this is." But actually he didn't. He just wanted to get out of work.

'The pregnancy itself – the development, the growth of his first child, the miracle of it, was of no interest to him.

'I'd be in front of the TV at night, sitting with my

stomach up under my chin, and I'd see Matilda's foot, or an arm, or a knee, come up against the skin. I'd call to Garry, "The baby's kicking!" He'd take his time looking over, and then claim he couldn't see anything. Then he'd look back at the TV. I'd say, "You have to be patient. Look, look, look." And he'd say, "Softie, I don't know what you can see, but it's like a mountain of blubber to me!" Like, as a joke.'

Dr Bell said, 'You didn't find it funny?'

'Of course I didn't. No woman would. And then, as well, Garry didn't seem to understand how frustrating it was, to be waiting, waiting, waiting for the baby to come. I got to thirty-nine weeks. I was stunned because my doctor had said the baby would almost certainly come early because of my age. I said, "Can't we bring it on? I'm so over this." But he said, "You don't want to do that, Softie. However much we know about it, pregnancy is not a precise science. Your baby will come when she's ready." And of course my mother was the same: "I had you three girls out in the field at Mullumbimby, never did me any harm, tra-la-la." But then she was twenty-one! I was nearly forty. I said to my doctor, "I'm so uncomfortable. I can't sleep. I'm exhausted. More than anything in the world, I want to lie on my stomach. I've always slept on my stomach."

'To Garry's credit, when I told him that – that I'd do anything to be able to sleep on my stomach – he came up with an idea. He took me down to Elwood beach one evening, at dusk, and dug a hole in the sand for me.

'"Get on your knees," he said, and helped me down so

my stomach was in the hole. "Let me put this over you," he said, and he took a rug and put it over my back. "And here's a pillow for your head." So I was laying down flat, on my stomach for the first time in months. And it was bliss. *Bliss.* I just dozed off. And when I woke up, I was moved to tears. Besides driving me to the pool, it was the only bit of kindness Garry really showed me when I was pregnant. Other women I know, their partners were massaging their feet, rubbing the small of their back, pressing the perineum to bring on a strong labour. It might have been nice for Garry to heat up a wheat pack or something, to show he cared about the pain in the small of my back. But his approach was always: it'll soon be over.

'And then, when I actually went into labour – when my waters broke, the night before Matilda was born – Garry woke me and said, "The mattress is wet." I didn't understand what he meant. He said, "You've wet yourself." I thought it was entirely possible, Dr Bell. My body felt like it had a mind of its own, so I was thinking, maybe I am now wetting myself. But this was a large wet patch. I rose up and saw the size of it, and I said, "Oh, I think it's my waters," and Garry didn't know what that even meant. I had to tell him, "It means the baby's coming."

'He said, "What, here?" I said, "I don't know. I've never done this before. Maybe we should call the hospital. The number's on the fridge." We'd booked in to the Royal Women's. I had private health cover. Garry didn't, but that didn't matter: it was me that was having the baby. So Garry called the hospital. The night nurse on the telephone asked him: "Is your wife having any contractions?"

'Garry said, "I don't know."

'The night nurse said, "Well, trust me, if she's having contractions, she'll know." I didn't think I was. I said to Garry: "Ask them, is the baby going to be alright if all the water has come out?" And Garry said, "I'm not asking her that. You ask her." So I had to take the telephone. The nurse said, "If this is your first, you've probably got hours to go. Why don't you call back when the contractions are two minutes apart?"

'I said, "I'm sorry, but this is my first baby. I'm almost forty. I don't want to take any chances." The nurse said, "You'll be sitting around waiting here. Don't you want to be at home where it's comfortable?" I nearly burst into tears when she said that. Comfortable? I hadn't been comfortable for *weeks*. So I took my hospital bag and went into the foyer, and waited for the elevator, and Garry went and got the Calais and opened the door for me. And do you know what he said to me? He said, "Is that water that's coming out going to get on the seats?" I was so upset I could barely speak to him as we drove across town. Can you imagine that, Dr Bell? Driving across town to have your first baby, not even being able to speak to your husband?

'But anyway, we got there. Garry pulled up near the door. I was so hoping to see men in white coats waiting for me. I was so hoping to see a trolley, or a wheelchair, or some sign that they knew I was coming, and how nervous and frightened I was. Because Garry seemed to have no idea. But there wasn't anyone waiting for us. And Garry didn't seem to know that he'd need to help me out of the car. Didn't take me by the arm or anything. I was left to waddle up behind him, cramped over, because finally I was figuring out what a contraction felt like.

'In any case, they checked us in. They – the hospital staff – asked me if I was okay to walk to my room. I can't tell you . . . those little gestures of concern made me want to weep. A nurse came and asked if she could get me anything. I said, "Something's hurting my back." The nurse said, "That's okay, that's normal," and helped me onto the bed. She walked across the room and opened the door to the en suite, saying, "There's a shower in here, and a toilet." I said, "Where's the doctor?" And the nurse said, "We've paged him." I thought, "Oh, great, they've paged him. But how long will it take him to get here?" Then a midwife came in and helped me lie back and, you know, looked inside. She said, "Your waters have broken but you're hardly dilated. Maybe two centimetres." I said, "But it's agony." And the midwife, who was making notes on the clipboard, said, "Well, you've got a way to go." I said, "That can't be." The midwife said, "I'm afraid it is."

'The midwife left the room, saying she'd be back in an hour. I could hardly believe that. An hour! How was I going to last an hour? But Garry didn't seem to get it. Didn't seem to understand how much pain I was in. There was a TV in the room, suspended from the ceiling. Garry turned it on.

I asked him what he was doing. He said he was looking for *Rage*. Some rap guy was on, cavorting with these semi-naked women. And I was, by this stage, on all fours, my stomach against the mattress. I had to say, "Can you please, *please* turn that off?" And Garry got all shirty. I mean, shirty with *me*. Me, who was in agony. He turned the TV off and he said, "What can I do then?" I said, "Garry, it's so painful." He said, "I get that. What I don't get is what you want me to do. Tell me what to do, I'll do it."

'I couldn't think of anything to tell him. What I wanted, more than anything, was for him to step up, Dr Bell. To take control. To recognise that I was completely out of my mind with pain and worry. To comfort me. To soothe me. But it's not in his instincts. He doesn't know how to do that. I asked him, "Do you think it's okay if I get under the shower? It's really hurting my back." He said, "Well, how would I know, Softie? Don't we have to ask a doctor?" I said, "There is no doctor to ask, in case you haven't noticed. Can't you please step up? Turn on the shower at least?" So Garry got up from the easy chair, and helped me from the bed, and into the en suite and out of my clothes, like I was some kind of cripple, not the mother of his child, and he reached past the plastic curtain and turned the shower on, and I got down on all fours in the bottom of the shower. I stayed in there for what seemed like forever, Dr Bell. I was so grateful that the hot water didn't run out. And then the midwife came back and said, "Where's Mrs Monaghan? I'd like to have another look." And she – not Garry – helped me back onto the bed and had another peek and said, "No change, I'm afraid."

'I couldn't believe it, Dr Bell. I couldn't believe I was still no closer. Garry was sitting, reading an old newspaper. I told Garry, "I want to go back to the shower." He just said, "Okay." He didn't move to help me. I had to hobble in there by myself. And while I was in there, under the water, I heard him turn the TV back on. *Doof, doof, doof.* I was too tired to shout, "Turn it off." Just too tired, and in too much pain. And then, finally, I heard my doctor come in. The doctor I was paying a fortune to deliver Matilda. I staggered out from under the shower, looking like a drowned rat, wearing a towel that didn't close around my stomach, and there he was, in his suit, studying print-outs by the bed, saying, "Okay, Softie, I think we'd better get your baby out. That sound like a good idea to you?"

'I said, "Oh God, yes. Yes, yes!" He said, "I thought you might say that. See you down in delivery. You're doing great." Two men came – orderlies, I suppose – with blue sacks over their shoes. One of them said, "Can you hop on up onto the trolley?" and I said, "I'm not sure," so each of them had to take an elbow and sort of help me on, but you know, they were jovial. "Time for a ride," said one, and off we went down the corridor, with me flat on my back. And all around me, I could hear this howling noise – it was a woman, but she was making a noise like a wild animal. They certainly don't let you hear that when they're giving you the big tour, showing you how beautiful everything is –

and the one person I couldn't see, Dr Bell, was Garry.'

Dr Bell said, 'But why? Where had Garry gone?'

'I don't know. But then, you've got no idea, really, have you, what's going on, when you're in a state like that. No idea how a birth is going to be, before you have one. You have all your plans, and they go out the window. I must have been mad with pain because when I got to the birthing suite my doctor was there and I couldn't imagine how he'd got there from my room. I said, "Weren't you behind us?" He smiled and said, "No, I'm here." And then Garry was there too. And do you know what he was doing? He was holding up a CD. He was saying, "I've got the music" – meaning, the music we'd chosen for the birth! He was saying, "What track do you want to hear?" When all I wanted to hear was me stopping screaming.'

Dr Bell said, 'To be fair to Garry, he was probably trying to help, don't you think?'

'Maybe he was. But a CD wasn't going to help. Asking me about songs wasn't going to help. Pain relief – that would have helped. Getting the baby out. That would have helped. I was begging for pain relief, and then, thank God, my doctor said, "I think an epidural is probably in order, Softie," and although I'd sworn no pain relief, I nodded, yes please, *please*, and they were rolling me onto my side and putting the needle in until I couldn't really feel anything any more. I didn't know they'd put my feet into stirrups. I just sort of saw them there. There were a whole lot of things going on, actually, that I couldn't really understand. I felt like screaming, "This is me! Here I am! I'm a person, giving birth!" But then it turned out that I wasn't giving birth. My doctor was saying: "Softie? I think it's best that we go for the caesarean, don't you?" And a caesarean actually wasn't what I wanted. I'd wanted to give birth. I'd been adamant about that. I wanted to say, "But why?" But I'd been in so much pain, and I was sure the epidural wasn't working properly, because I was getting these pins and needles, and to be honest I was at that point where I was thinking, "Oh, I just don't care. I don't care. I want the baby out." And my doctor said, "Right, then." And then there was silence and more silence, and nobody said, "Okay, we've got you open now," or anything like that. Certainly Garry didn't say anything so I had no idea what was going on. A big curtain went up. I remember that. I heard my doctor saying, "Okay," and then, "You're doing great, Softie," and then, "We're almost there." And it was like it was happening to somebody else. And then they said, "Here we go, Softie. Here she is. Here's your girl." And that was that. Matilda had arrived.

'And they gave her to me, over the curtain, and she was all pink and smeared with white gunk, and her umbilical cord was trailing, and her mouth was open like a cat. I don't remember seeing Garry. I remember the anaesthetist leaning over and saying, "Do you feel like a little sleep?" And I don't know if I nodded or not, but the next thing I knew I was awake again, and alone, and shivering under one of those silver blankets they give you. And a midwife was saying, "You're in recovery. You lost a lot of blood." I said, "How much blood?" She said, "I was sliding around in it on the floor! Lucky I had the gumboots on!"

'I said, "My stomach hurts."

'The nurse said, "That won't be your stomach, love. Your womb's been in the wars! But you'll be alright." And then she said, "You'll want to see your baby!" And do you know what, Dr Bell? I'd actually forgotten about the baby! And the nurse must have seen the shock on my face. But she was as nice as can be. She said, "Oh, don't worry. That's the shame of that anaesthetic they give you, it wipes out the memory for a while. But you've got a beautiful little baby girl!"

'I said, "Is she alright?" And the nurse said, "Oh, she's perfect." I thought, "But where is she?" But then of course they brought her to me, and sort of held her up, all swaddled, and they said, "Can you see her?" But I couldn't really see her. They had to lift me up and hold her a bit higher, and she was tiny, obviously, pink and wrinkled, with a wise, wise face and no hair at all, and a shiny spit bubble where her lips were pursed, and I thought, "Oh! Oh!" And the nurse said, "What are you going to call her?" And I said, "She's Matilda." Because that was the name I'd chosen after we'd found out that we were having a girl.'

Dr Bell said, 'Did Garry like the name?'

Softie said, 'Oh, Garry wasn't bothered. Before we had the scan to find out whether it was a girl or a boy, I'd said, "If it's a boy, maybe we can call him Rick?" Like, homage to the man who married his mother. He said, "No way is a son of mine being called Rick." I said, "Well, what about if it's a girl? Do you have any girls' names you like?" And he said, "Oh, I can't say I'm that bothered. I don't want something stupid, is all." Nothing stupid. That was his contribution.'

Dr Bell said, 'I take it that when you woke up, you were in recovery, but did you get to have a little cuddle of Matilda?'

Softie said, 'Oh yes. They let me do that. That was very special. And I was holding her when I asked about Garry. They said he was out on the ward. I was pleased about that. He hadn't run off to the pub or anything. And then I must have slipped back into sleep because the next thing I knew, the midwife was back and she was telling me: "Your little girl needs a feed." And they helped me to sit up properly with my back straight, and although I was tired, I was looking forward to feeding my little girl. And I did think, maybe Garry should be here for this? But he couldn't be found. And Matilda needed to be fed. So I got on with things. And it wasn't easy. I so much wanted to do things right. I wanted to give my baby the best start, with breast milk. Not put formula into her. Because she was innocent and pure, and what do they make formula out of? I mean, it comes in a tin, like for tennis balls. It smells like chemicals. So I thought, "No, I really want to feed her myself."

'But you know, Dr Bell, people who say that breast-feeding comes naturally, they've obviously never tried it. Because it certainly didn't come naturally to me. Just sitting was proving difficult. My mid-section was extremely sore. I told the midwife: "I've got a lot of pain." She came and rearranged the pillows, saying: "It's okay, we'll prop you up. There you go. Feel okay? Think you can hold her?"

'I nodded, yes, so they gave Matilda to me. And then the midwife sort of opened my gown and my breasts fell out. And that was a shock. How swollen and purple and *ugly* they were. And they felt very hard: hard like rocks, and sore. I hadn't expected that. I'd expected them to feel soft, full of milk, warm. But they were throbbing and sort of hurting.

'The midwife said, "She won't take much but it's good to get it going. That first milk, the colostrum, it's vital to get it into her if you can." She was holding Matilda's head the way they do, gripping it and twisting it towards the nipple, pressing my baby's cheeks to make her open her mouth, and saying: "Latch on, Matilda. Latch on." And bringing my poor boob and the baby together.

'Then Matilda did latch on, and I cried out! It hurt so much! I'd thought she'd have a soft little suck, like a baby sucks on your finger! It was like being bitten. Like a nipple clamp! Like needles shooting through me. The nurse said, "It does hurt a bit, at first. Here, the angle's wrong." And she twisted Matilda's head some more, pulling her away from me and pressing her down again, really manipulating her. I was saying, "No, look, stop, this doesn't feel right." And my poor little girl, she was starting to cry. She was wailing. She was obviously so hungry. The nurse was pressing her face into me, saying, "Latch on, latch on." And I was saying, "Stop, it hurts, you're doing it wrong," and pulling away, and Matilda was crying so hard, and by this stage I was crying too.

'The nurse said, "Oh, let's try again, it takes a few goes. You'll get the hang of it." And she was really pressuring me. Really trying to force it, when it obviously wasn't working. And little Matilda, it was like she was fighting, blindly fighting, scratching me with her little nails. And the nurse said, "Here we go, here we go, she's on," and it was like a knife of pain went through my whole body. Something in my stomach, in my womb, just clenched up, and I had to say: "Oh, please, just stop!"

'But it was like the nurse didn't care. It was all about Matilda. It was: "Oh, it can be painful." I said, "It's not in my nipple! It's my stomach!" She said, "That's just your womb seizing up. The feeding is good for your body. It'll help get your womb back to shape. You'll get the hang of it. You've just got to get into the rhythm. You've got to make sure you keep the angle right. Sit up straighter, if you can." And her manner was so *businesslike*. I was saying, "It really hurts!" and pulling away, and Matilda was flailing and screaming. And then the nurse said, "Well, I think she got some," and sort of took her away. I said, "No, wait, let me have a go by myself," and the nurse said, "It's probably better if everybody takes a break, calms down a bit. She won't starve." I was so angry with her. Like, that's my baby daughter you're talking about! She needs me! I have to feed her! But the midwife was adamant, saying, "They don't take much the first day. They don't need much. We'll try again in an hour or so." I was just thinking, "Where is Garry? Why isn't he here helping me? Supporting me? Standing up for me?" But you know, by this stage Garry's mates *had* taken him off to the pub. I tried to call him but the phone went to voicemail.

'I was crying so hard, Dr Bell. Just feeling like such a failure. And then, the next day, the nurse brought an electric pump to try to bring on the milk. But it didn't seem to be working. Little drops would spurt out and the midwife would try to put Matilda on, but she'd shove me away with her sharp little hands, gnawing and scratching at me. And it was only when Dawn came, and she's so sensible, she held Matilda for me and said, "It's okay, Softie, it just takes practice. You'll get the hang of it." I said, "I love her so much, Dawn. I just wish I was better at it." And Dawn said, "You'll get better." And I knew that was true. I knew I would get better. But I was also thinking, where is Garry through all this? Because he was either at the flat, or at the pub. It was like he was trying to avoid us, actually. Like he knew he couldn't possibly be any help. He'd see me struggling and instead of doing, I don't know, something useful, he'd say, "It doesn't look like she wants to breastfeed. Why don't you ask the nurses to get her a bottle?" I had to say, "Because I don't want her to be bottle fed, Garry. I want her to have breast milk. Everybody says it's for the best." And he said, "Well then, I guess you're going to have to stick at it."

'Because I'd had the caesarean I had to stay five days in hospital. I was grateful – so grateful – because I was also terrified of being sent home with a baby that was fighting with me all the time. And yet I was so tired of being in a bed, in a gown. Then the nurses said they had a program for new mums to go for dinner! Me and Garry, I mean. A romantic dinner. Do you good. Last chance you'll have to be on your own for a while. Go celebrate the new arrival. But when I tried to get dressed, well, I couldn't believe I still had to wear maternity clothes. My body was just as it had been before I'd had the baby. And I had the stitches. And the bra! Oh my God, Dr Bell, the bra. Dawn had brought one in for me. A maternity bra! I'd never really had to wear a bra before I got pregnant. Now I had this contraption like my grand-mother's, with wide straps and clips and pads inside . . . So here we were at this dinner in this restaurant down the road from the hospital, and it was supposed to be romantic and I felt like a big cow – a milk cow – and Garry said, "Have a glass of wine." I said, "How can I have a glass of wine, Garry? It'll get into the milk." He said, "One won't hurt," but I said yes it will! So we were off to a bad start. And then all I wanted to talk about was Matilda: she was beautiful, she was amazing. And there were other couples there – couples like us, with the women a bit dazed, and their husbands all proud – all of them talking about how wonderful their new babies were. But all Garry wanted to talk about was having found a supplier for his gym equipment, and maybe going to New Zealand to look at the products.

'In the end I said, "Let's go back." I wanted to get back to Matilda. I couldn't bear the idea that she was hungry, or maybe wondering where I was and I certainly didn't want to be sitting listening to Garry give me a lecture about the bench press. But Garry was saying, "They're paying, Softie. We might as well make the most of it." But make the most of what? I wasn't interested in anything they had in the restaurant or in anything Garry had to say. I wanted to get back to my baby! So I got up and we left. I rushed straight into the nursery, and I couldn't immediately see Matilda. All the other babies were there, but I couldn't see Matilda. Garry said, "How do you even know which one she is?" But of course I knew which one she was! And when I found her, in the nursery, she was crying. I said to the nurse, "I shouldn't have gone out. She's hungry!" And the nurse said, "She's been like a lamb." Garry said, "You're carrying on, Softie." And that kind of set the scene. Whatever I did was "carrying on".

'When it was time to leave the hospital, for example, I told Garry, "Drive carefully!" And to be fair, he was good. He did try to drive carefully. But once or twice I had to say, "Take it easy" – you know, when he went around a roundabout too fast. I was in the back seat with Matilda in the capsule, and Garry was saying: "I've got a real back-seat driver now!" But you know, Dr Bell, I was still in pain. I had stitches. I wasn't myself. I was conscious of every other car on the road, I could see how close they were getting to us. I told Garry, "I want you to get one of those stickers –

the Baby on Board stickers. Make people think, at least." And Garry said, "Do you reckon your mum would have had one of those? Back when she was a hippie?"

'I said, "Things are different, Garry. That era is gone." He said, "It didn't seem to do you any harm." I said, "That's because I've put order into my life."'

Dr Bell said, 'How important would you say order is to you, Softie?'

'I don't think it's any more important to me than it is to most people. I mean, I wasn't asking for the world, Dr Bell. Just for people to be a bit more careful around us. And for maybe a bit more time with my new baby. Because the next thing I knew, we were having an argument about when I was going back to work. I said, "I know I always said that when I had a baby I would go straight back to work. But now Matilda's here, Garry, I don't actually think I can leave her." And Garry was saying: "But that was always the plan, Softie. You're the one with the good job." I was saying, "But things have changed, Garry. Can't you see they've changed? I can take a year's maternity leave – they'll hold my job. You could pick up some of the old clients. I'd be able to stay home with Matilda." But of course that didn't suit Garry. Meaning working full-time didn't suit Garry. He had this idea that he should stay home with the baby while I went to work. And I had encouraged that idea. But then when Matilda was actually born, and I could see her and hold her, I suddenly realised how hard it would be, to leave her. So all the way home we were arguing about that.

Arguing, with a five-day-old baby in the back seat. That's such a good start, isn't it?

'Then we got back to Edgewater Towers. We took Matilda up in the elevator, into the flat, and I put her capsule down on the floor. She was sleeping and Garry said, "So, what do we do now?" To be honest with you, Dr Bell, I had no idea. It was one o'clock in the afternoon and the apartment block was quiet. I said, "I think I'll make a cup of tea. The midwife said it's important to keep my fluids up, for the milk."

'Garry said, "Well, alright. Maybe I'll go to the gym." I said, "What, now?" And Garry said, "Why not?" And I said, "It's our first day at home with our daughter." And Garry said, "What are we supposed to do, sit and look at her?" I said no, she needed a nap. Garry said, "Well, put her in the pram and we'll take her out and she can nap in the pram." But I said, "No, she might get sunburnt. She hasn't got a proper hat."

'Garry said, "Do you want me to go and get her a hat?" But really, Dr Bell, what kind of hat would he buy? I said, "No, I'll get her the hat. Don't worry about it. Maybe I'll feed her." Garry said, "How do you know she's even hungry?" I said, "I don't know. But she needs to get into a routine." Because that's what everyone had told me: you have to get your new baby into a routine. One of my girl-friends from work had given me a book, to use as a guide. *The Contented Little Baby Book*. It had all these suggested routines: you feed the baby at this time, and put her back into the cot. After one hour, you put a load of washing on, and you get the baby and give her a bath, and give her another feed, and then it's back into the cot. And while she's in the cot, you take the washing out of the machine and hang it out, and so forth. And it seemed to me that the sooner Matilda was able to get into that routine, the smoother everything would be, and then I'd be able to make decisions about when to go back to work, and so forth.

'But of course, Matilda had no intention of sticking to the regime. Babies don't, do they? And Matilda wasn't an easy baby. All the other mothers at the baby clinic, they were saying, "Oh, my baby, she's sleeping twelve, thirteen hours. We have to wake her up!" Matilda wasn't sleeping at all. She wasn't sleeping and she wasn't feeding. And she cried and cried. I couldn't work out what was wrong. I thought maybe it was the wipes. Dawn told me some of the baby wipes you can buy have alcohol in them, and that can sting. So I sent Garry out for organic wipes. Or maybe it was the nappy cream that made her cry? Maybe we needed to use some other type of cream? Or maybe it was the baby wash? Or was the water in her bath too hot? Or too cold? Was she getting enough to eat? I felt like I didn't know anything. Those first few weeks, I was forever at the baby clinic, saying, "Could she be teething? Maybe I could get her a teething ring?" The baby nurse said, "Oh, I think it's unlikely that she'd be teething." I said, "What about dummies? Do you approve of dummies?" Because some mothers said they'd never use dummies. It ruins a baby's gums, and later on they'll need orthodontics. The nurse said, "She's just a baby,

Softie. Sometimes babies cry for no reason." And then she asked me how much I was crying. And did I feel depressed? Was I feeling defeated? Did I need to talk to somebody?

'I could see what she was getting at, Dr Bell. She was thinking: is this woman nuts? Has she got more than the baby blues? But it wasn't that. What I needed, obviously, was more support from Garry, but he was about as difficult, and stubborn, as a person could be. He'd say to me things like, "I think Matilda would be better if you were a little less in her face all the time. She's a baby. Babies cry. Everybody knows that." I said to him, "Well, thank you, Garry. That really is a big help." Then one night he actually said to me, "What about us, Softie?" I'd been walking Matilda up and down the hall in the flat for an hour, trying to soothe her, trying to get her to take some milk. She'd been inconsolable all day, and I was starting to wonder did she have reflux? Reflux or colic or some kind of allergy? I was near my wit's end. And Garry said, "Why don't you just put her down? Because it seems like there's no time for us any more."

'I said, "What do you mean, us?"

'He said, "I haven't had a boat out for weeks. I haven't been to the gym."

'I couldn't believe it. Our little girl was in such distress and he was worried about *fishing*. And then he said, "Why don't we get a babysitter one night? We'll go out, have a bite to eat, maybe a glass of wine."

'I said, "Garry! How can you think of leaving her with a stranger? She's a *baby*!"

'Garry said, "We'll go out after you've put her down. She won't even know you've gone."

'I said, "Of course she'll know! And what if she wakes up and I'm not here?"

'He said, "The babysitter can call us. We won't go far."

'I said, "I really can't believe this. I don't want a stranger picking my baby up to comfort her because I'm out having a glass of wine!"

'Garry said, "Well then, let's not get a stranger. Let's get Dawn. Dawn's always saying she'd be happy to do it. And how many times did you sit for Dawn, when she wanted to go out?"

'I said, "That's not the point. And I was single then. Dawn's not single. She's got her own kids to look after."

'Garry said, "She can leave them with her hubby. She's done that before. On your hen's night, for example."

'I said, "Just stop it, Garry. I don't want to do it." But he wouldn't stop. He said, "What about us, though, Softie? Are we supposed to spend every night of our lives inside, until Matilda's grown up?"

'I said, "Of course not! I'm just not ready to leave her yet. *Us* now includes our daughter, Garry." I mean, did he really not understand that, Dr Bell? That Matilda wasn't something we'd purchased, that we could take back? Did he not understand that if I had to choose between him and Matilda, I'd choose Matilda every time?'

Chapter Twelve

One thing I probably should have said at the outset is that I'm not opposed to divorce. It's not for me to say two people should stay together forever, just because they've got kids, or a big mortgage, or whatever. What I can say is that divorce never crossed my mind. Not that things have been perfect in my marriage every minute of every day. I'm sure there have been moments when I drove Pat up the wall, but never did she say she wanted me out, and I certainly never wanted to go. When I got married it was for life. Maybe there were times when Pat questioned that. Maybe she sometimes secretly thought I was a boring old fart. But if that happened, I didn't see it or sense it, and the fact that she's stuck with me, well, I think that shows that she's got the same idea as me.

Maybe it's for that reason that I was gutted when Brian and Nerida broke up. But I can see that it was fair enough that he wanted out. His wife had done the dirty.

That's not an easy thing for a man to deal with. Maybe he could have forgiven her. But he wasn't ever sure if he was seeing a pattern. And so he got out.

As for Softie . . . Well, nobody was going to convince her that their problems could be worked out either. So she wanted to get out too.

'I was looking at Garry one night, studying him as he ate – and I saw that he ate like a caveman.' That's how Softie started the conversation with Dr Bell about how she and Garry broke up. 'I asked him to perhaps eat more politely. He said, "Is there anything about me that you like, Softie?" And do you know what, Dr Bell? I actually heard a voice in my head, saying, "No, actually. No, there's nothing about you that I like. Nothing. And I think I knew then that it was over.'

Dr Bell said, 'Did you speak to anyone about the decision you were making, Softie?'

'I talked to Dawn. I drove over with Matilda in the back, and kind of collapsed into her arms one afternoon. I said to her: "I don't think I can do this any more. He's lived his whole life doing what he wants to do and he doesn't seem to have got his head around the idea that he's now got responsibilities. He's supposed to be supporting me – supporting both Matilda and me – but he just doesn't get it."'

Dr Bell said, 'And Matilda was how old?'

'When I spoke to Dawn? I'd say she was maybe four months. Maybe not even four months.'

'And did you tell Dawn you were thinking of leaving? Were you actually thinking of leaving?'

'I was thinking of leaving. Of course I was. But on the other hand, how could I leave? Garry's Matilda's father. I do understand that's important. I didn't want to raise Matilda in a broken home. And I had wanted more than one child. And after she was born, I became more convinced about that: Matilda would need a sibling. And yet, I was so unhappy. So that was my dilemma: here I was, with a husband and a baby, everything I'd thought I'd wanted, and I was so unhappy. Here I was, getting into my forties, the last chance to have a sibling for Matilda ticking away, and I could barely even look at Garry, let alone think of, you know, trying for another baby with him. It had actually got to the point where I couldn't be at home all day with Garry. I simply couldn't stand the sight of him. So I got in contact with the bank where I'd worked before Matilda was born. I told them I was going to come back early. That I needed to cut short my maternity leave. And they were fine with that. It's a bank. They've got good policies on women returning from maternity leave.'

Dr Bell said, 'What were you going to do about child-care? I hear it's not easy to find.'

Softie said, 'It's not easy to find. And it's expensive. But I was pretty desperate, so I called a few places and basically begged. And I got lucky. There was a place in the city with a spot for a baby. I grabbed it.'

Dr Bell said, 'Did you have reservations about putting

Matilda into childcare at such a young age, Softie?'

'Obviously I did. It actually broke my heart the first time. I sat in the car after I'd left her there, just crying. But what could I do? I had to go back to work.'

Dr Bell said, 'And you didn't feel you could leave Matilda with Garry?'

'No.'

'No?'

'No. I never would have left Matilda alone with him for eight, nine hours. Not when she was a little baby. There's just no way I'd trust Garry to take care of her for long periods of time. He's got no idea what he's doing.'

Dr Bell said, 'When you say he has no idea . . . ?'

'Well, he doesn't do things the way I do them, which means I have to redo everything. I mean, women joke about this: do men deliberately do things badly so they won't be asked to do them again? I think they might. One example: I'd ask Garry to do the washing, and he'd put whites in with the coloureds. Everybody knows you can't do that: the colours run, you have pink underwear. But he'd do it, and to my mind that's got to be deliberate. Another example: he knew what Matilda needed in her bag when we went out. But he still wouldn't pack it properly. He'd go out without a change of clothes for her. And Dawn said to me: "Oh, Dave" – that's her husband, Dave – "he's the same. All husbands are the same. They have no idea. I leave Dave to dress Imogen, and she'll come in with purple tights and a Superman suit. It's ridiculous. You can fight and argue

222

and carry on and in the end you end up doing it yourself anyway, and it's not worth the effort."

'And with Garry, it's worse than that. He's rough with Matilda. Like, if he had to carry her down the stairs if the lift was broken at the apartment, he'd grab her and sort of throw her over his shoulder like a rag doll, and grab the pram with the other hand, and lug the two of them down together, and never mind if she was struggling or crying and didn't want to go, he'd still pick her up and charge down with her. One time I thought he was actually going to bump her head on the wall, that's how rough he was being.'

Dr Bell said, 'How many times do you think you left Matilda alone with Garry when she was still a small baby, Softie?'

'Probably not more than once or twice. I did try. I did sometimes say to him: "Can't you take her out?" So I could catch up on some sleep or go and get a haircut or something. I was turning into one of those women who is never out of her dressing gown, with hair like a bird's nest. And he'd say: "Alright, I'll take her out." But I'd have to pack the bag. I'd have to make sure she had a clean nappy, and a nappy to change into. And her clothes. And milk from the pump. And then I'd jump in the shower and start getting myself ready to go out and Garry would come back! And I'd say: "You're back already? You've only been gone five minutes." And he'd say: "Half an hour. I think she's hungry." Because Matilda would be crying. And I'd say: "I expressed some milk. Why didn't you give her some milk?" And he'd say: "I forgot the milk." I'd think, "Of course you did. You forget *everything*." And so, when Matilda was about five months old, I told Garry: "I've found a place for her in the child-care centre." He wasn't happy about it. He wanted to know how much it was going to cost. I ignored him and went ahead and did it. And then, of course, Matilda got sick in child care. It happens to every child, in every child-care centre, for the first six months: they just get sick. And everybody says it's not all bad: a bit of sickness can build up immunity in a child. So in her first week Matilda got sick. The centre called me and said she was throwing up. I raced down there, and maybe I was overreacting, but I took her straight to the Royal Children's, the one on Park Parade.

'There was a junior doctor there, lovely young Indian guy. He stripped Matilda down and looked into her ears and eyes and said, "Oh, it's a virus. The best thing to do is let her fight it off. She'll need baby Panadol from a dropper three times a day. That'll bring her temperature down so she'll at least be able to sleep." Then Garry, who had come over to meet us there, piped up, saying, "Could it be the child-care centre?" And the doctor nodded, saying, "Oh, yes. Those places are like one big Petri dish." Garry said, "I didn't think it was a good idea for her to go when she was still so little." I thought, "Oh, you bastard. It's the child-care centre, is it? It's not the fact that you're an absolute failure as a provider? It's not the fact that if you actually had a job I'd be able to be home with my poor baby girl? No, it's the child-care centre that's to blame."'

Dr Bell said, 'Despite the difficulties you were having with Garry, Softie, you have said that you were also thinking of having another baby. Did you in fact try to get pregnant at any point?'

Softie started to cry. She said, 'Oh, Dr Bell. I did try. I didn't tell Garry I was trying, but I did try. And I did actually get pregnant a second time. That was about a year ago. And for a while, I actually kept it to myself. The fact that it had happened, I mean. Because I knew quite early. Don't ask me how but I knew. It could have been that I have a scar from Matilda – a short one – across, you know, the pubic area. The C-section scar. And it's usually quite soft there, I suppose because they cut through the muscle. And then it went hard. I thought, "That's odd. I'm sure that's odd. Could I be pregnant?" But things were so bad in the house I felt I couldn't even raise it with Garry.

'I didn't want to go to our regular chemist, the one I used to take Matilda for weighing and Bonjela and so on. I wanted a place where I was anonymous, where I could buy a testing kit without the girl saying, "Oh! I see! You're off again!" So I actually got in the car and drove across the Westgate, just went where the road took me, and pulled over somewhere, I don't know, in Yarraville, to a chemist on the side of the road and bought a testing kit and took it to the public toilets at the railway station. And there was a blue line. A faint one, but it was there. At first, I thought, "What does that mean?" Because you see the line but it still means you have to see a doctor.

'I went back to work and Googled "medical centre" and "South Melbourne". I wanted somebody I'd never seen before. There were five or six places – anonymous chain medical centres like they have these days. I called the first two. They didn't take appointments. You went in and you waited. I called a third place. They said they could see me. I'd have to leave work early. It would be a bit of a juggle, fitting the appointment in and picking up Matilda. There was no parking. I had to park illegally.

'My mind was racing as to what Garry was going to say about this. I'm sitting there – horrible cream waiting room, horrible prints on the walls – thinking, "My life is about to get very complicated." Because I was half-out of the marriage, Dr Bell. I had been making up my mind to go. And yet I did want another child, a brother or a sister for Matilda, and now it seemed that I was going to have one, and that I'd have to suffer for it, meaning have to stay with Garry for it.

'The doctor's computer was open to a new file. He said, "What can I do for you today . . . Mrs? . . . Monaghan?" I said, "I think I'm pregnant."

'He said, "Is your period late?"

'I said, "Not yet. I took a home test."

'He said, "They aren't always reliable."

'I said, "I'm pretty sure."

'He said, "Well, when was your last period?"

'I said, "Four weeks ago."

'He said, "You're not strictly late. But okay. Let's have a look at you." And he got up from behind the desk and gave me one of those little plastic jars with a yellow lid, and white sticker on the side. He said, "There's a toilet down the hall, first on the right. We need the middle section of urine if you can."

'I went down the hall and peed again, took the jar back to the doctor's room. The doctor dipped the paper in, and straight away it changed colour. It was instant, just instant. It flared up, bright blue.

'The doctor said, "That's a definite positive, Mrs Monaghan. You are certainly pregnant. Your last period was four weeks ago? You're about six weeks along."

'He was tapping at the keyboard, not really looking at me. And then he said, "Is this a good-news story for you, Mrs Monaghan?" Like, he could *sense* how worried I was.

'I said, "Oh, yes."

'He said, "Do you have a regular doctor?"

'I said, "I do."

'He said, "And will you be going back there or staying here with us?"

'I said, "Probably going back. I work near here. I just came in because I wanted to know."

'He said, "That's fine. I'll make out a letter for you, for your own GP, with this pregnancy noted. Is there anything else you need?"

'I said, "No." And when I left there, Dr Bell, do you know what I was thinking? I wasn't thinking, "I can't wait to tell my husband!" I was thinking, "This is wonderful for Matilda." She was . . . well, she had started walking, so she wasn't a baby any more. She was a toddler, and just so sweet, with little dresses and little shoes, and a doll's pram she pushed around, and lots of new little words – Mama, and boat, and heli-chopter, and bird. And now if anything did happen with me and Garry, she would have a brother or a sister. And who knows? Maybe this would help things. Garry and I were both new to the baby thing. Maybe it would be better second time around. Garry would understand more. He'd help more."'

Dr Bell said, 'And so did you run home and tell Garry the news?'

'Not straight away, no. I thought, "I'll wait a bit. Wait until things settle." It was early days. Then I started throwing up, like I'd done with Matilda, and that's hard to hide in a small flat. At first I just said, "Oh, there's something going around at work." But then of course you start showing so much earlier the second time. It's like your stomach muscles are already stretched out, and they just give way.

'So I suppose when I was eight weeks, after I'd told my GP, and I'd put Matilda down for the night, I just blurted it out. I said, "I'm pregnant." I said it to the back of Garry's head. He was watching some kind of motor racing. He said, "What?" I said, "I'm pregnant." And Garry's not totally stupid. He said, "How long have you known?" And I said, "A couple of weeks." He said, "You've been to a doctor, I take it?" And I said, "Yes." I saw him looking down at my stomach. There wasn't that much to see, but if you were looking you could notice a swelling. So he said, "And why didn't you tell me before now?" I said, "I wanted to be sure." And he said, "You wanted to be sure?" I said, "Yes, because I didn't want it to be a false alarm."

'And then Garry said, "Are you sure you know what you're doing?"

'I said, "Well, that's an interesting thing to say, Garry: you ask me what *I'm* doing, not what *we're* doing."

'Garry said, "I haven't really had a say in it, have I?"

'I said, "I didn't exactly do it without you, did I?"

'Garry said, "You actually have done it without me." Meaning, he hadn't been consulted. And I didn't want an argument, Dr Bell. I could see one coming and I didn't want it. Matilda was stirring in her cot. So I went to her. Her forehead was damp. She had only a nappy on, and she was slippery. I went back in to where Garry was sitting, carrying Matilda on my hip. I said, "I think she's got a fever." And he said, "She's been sick ever since you put her in child care. And now we'll have two of them there, both sick as dogs." So that was how he greeted the news.'

Dr Bell said, 'I know from your file that Matilda is in fact your only child, Softie. Can you tell me what happened with that second pregnancy?'

Softie cried again. 'I went for a scan at thirteen weeks. I was all ready to see the first pictures of my new baby. The screen started off black, like it had with Matilda, then lit up with stars, the way it does. The technician said, "There's your baby." She pushed the probe, moved downwards. "Here's the head. Here's a hand."

'And then she went quiet. She was quiet for a long time, and then she said, "I'm just going to shift position here, Mrs Monaghan. I'm sorry, it might be a bit uncomfortable." And I was trying to joke with her, saying, "I'm used to it, don't worry!" But she wasn't smiling at all.

'She said, "I need to get a good look." She was moving the probe and staring at the screen and, well, I just knew. I just knew there was something wrong. She wasn't saying, "Look here, she's waving," or anything like that, like they normally say. She was saying, "Tip your hips forward for me. Now back. See if you can lie still." And I was getting more and more nervous.

'I started to say, "Is everything alright?" And she said, "See if you can lie still." And then, "Okay, make fists for me and pop them under your bottom. Lift yourself up. That's right."

'I was trying as hard as I could to see what she was seeing, but of course, it's all shadows, isn't it? All I knew was that the technician's face was full of concern. And then she said, "Just stay there for me, Mrs Monaghan. I'm going to step out for a minute. You can put your knees down."

'I was shaking so hard while she was gone. And then she came back in, but not alone. She had another person with her. They looked at the machine together. They were saying, "If you could tilt your hips a little higher, Mrs Monaghan? Like this, yes. Okay. Now lie still." And then they were staring and staring and sort of making points on the screen with a little computer dot, and measuring between them.

'I was nearly out of my mind with worry. I said, "Something's wrong, isn't it?" The technician said, "I'm just trying to get a better look." And then she said, "There's not as much fluid as we'd like to see."

'I said, "What does that mean?" And she said, "I'm not entirely sure." She was pressing buttons on the machine. It seemed to me that she was taking still shots of what was on the screen. There was a whirring sound and the ultrasound pictures rolled out, and they tore them off and looked at them, but they still weren't saying that much to me. And then they said, "You can get dressed, Mrs Monaghan. Pop your clothes back on and we'll see you in the consulting room."

'I got dressed. I could hardly get my feet into my shoes I was trembling that much. I put my suit back on. I was trying so hard to make things normal. I was smoothing my skirt. I was looking in my bag, trying to find a comb for my hair, but I couldn't find anything.

'I went back into the consulting room. I sat down and they just blurted it out. I mean, not in a mean way, but they just said, "I'm sorry, Mrs Monaghan, things aren't as we'd like to see them at this stage." I said, "There's something wrong with the baby?" And they said, "The pregnancy isn't proceeding in what we might call a normal way." And I said, "But I don't understand that. Is something wrong?" And they said, "It's really not looking good. The fluid isn't at the level we'd like to see."

'They just kept saying that, Dr Bell. "The fluid, the fluid." Not "the baby". And I said, "Is the baby alright?"

But it was like they were trying to deny there was a baby. It was "the fluid", and "the pregnancy", and how "the pregnancy might not continue", and no talk of the baby at all.

'And so I said, "The baby's in there, isn't she?" Because, I mean, I'd seen her on the screen. And they said, "Look, there's definitely a fetus there, but we're not sure at this point that the pregnancy will continue. Have you had any bleeding?"

'I said, "I've had spotting. But I had spotting the first time."

'They said, "It might have been something different the first time." And then they said, "Have you had any loss of fluid, like a splash, anything like that?" And I said, "No, not really."

'And they said, "Alright then, all we can do is wait." And I said, "Wait for what?" And they said, "To see what happens." And I said, "Well, is there anything I can do? Anything I can take to increase the level of fluid, or something like that?" And they said, "I'm afraid it doesn't work like that. When there isn't the fluid we'd like to see it's not a matter of increasing the amount of fluid. It's more that things aren't as we'd like to see them, and it may be a sign that the pregnancy isn't viable. We just have to see what happens."

'I went out to the car, Dr Bell, and I was just crying. I had my head down on the steering wheel and I was just crying. And there was nobody to call. I couldn't call Garry. I didn't want to call Mum, or even Dawn, because they would have wanted to know: What are you doing trying to have another baby? They knew how bad things had been. So there was nothing to do but go back to the office and wait.

'And then, that afternoon . . . well, I started to lose her. There was so much blood. Blood and fluid. I called my GP and he said, "You've got to go into the hospital." I called Garry and said, "You'll need to get Matilda from child care." I didn't say why. And they put me straight into a bed in emergency, and they said, "You're going to need a scan." So there was another scan. And that's when they said, "There's no heartbeat." And at first I couldn't quite understand it. I couldn't quite get my head around it. I said, "No heartbeat?" And they said, "We're sorry." I said, "You mean the baby has died?" And they said, "That's how it looks." I said, "But what happened?" And they just said, "Well, sometimes we don't know. We just don't know."

'And then, worst of all, they said, "Sometimes it's for the best. Sometimes it means there was something wrong." I thought, "How can you say that? Say it's for the best?" Because I'd pinned all my hopes on that baby. That baby, and Matilda, they were the only things I really had to be happy about.

'I said to the nurses, "This can't be right. There must be something you can do." But they said, "No, there's nothing." And I said, "But what happens to me now?" Because the baby was still inside me. And they said, "You're going to need a curette." And I said, "What's that?" They said, "It's a surgical procedure. You'll have a general anaesthetic. You're going to be in hospital for a day or two. Is there somebody you'd like us to call?"

'And do you know what I thought, Dr Bell? I thought, "No, there's nobody I want you to call." Certainly not Garry. Because it wasn't like he'd been with me, for the pregnancy. It wasn't like he'd come around and was pleased. But I could hardly say to them, "No, I have nobody I want to call." So I gave them his number. I said, "Could you call him?" Because I didn't want to call him. I wanted them to tell him. I wanted him to get the message: your wife is in hospital, and it's serious.'

Dr Bell said, 'How did Garry respond when he heard the news, Softie?'

'Oh, well. He wasn't a complete bastard. He came in. Didn't bring Matilda, who was the one person I really wanted to see. He dropped her at Dawn's, and then came in, alone. I said, "Where's my baby?" Because you'd have thought that a husband would know that I really needed to hold my baby. But he said, "I didn't think it was a good idea to bring her in. It's the middle of the night." And he said, "I'm sorry," and all that, but I knew he wasn't really sorry. Not that sorry.

'I said to him, "You're sorry but it kind of suits you, doesn't it?" And he said, "No, that's not true. I'm really sad about it. I'm sad for you. I'm worried about you."

'And then the nurse came in through the curtains, with the blood-pressure machine. She was asking, "When was the last time you ate anything?"

'I said, "I didn't have breakfast. I've been so sick. I've had morning sickness." To kind of remind them, I'm *pregnant*. And the nurse said, "I'm so sorry." I said, "Am I going to have the operation today? Now?" And the nurse said, "You're third on the list. So probably around 4 pm."

'And I thought, "Well, that's when my life ends. Because I just couldn't stand that they were going to go in there and take my baby out. I said, "What'll they do with her?" And the nurse said, "With the baby?" And I said, "Yes, my baby." The nurse looked down at her clipboard and she said, "You're thirteen weeks along?" and I said, "Yes." She said, "That isn't really . . . I mean, the baby isn't . . ."

'I knew what she was saying: there wouldn't be anything there. She was so small that they were just planning to scrape her out and throw her in the bin. So I said, "I want to see her." And the nurse said, "Mrs Monaghan, I'm not sure . . ." And Garry said, "Softie." I said, "I don't care how big she is. I want to see her."

'The nurse said, "I'll have the doctor come and see you." I said, "I don't care what the doctor says. I want to see my baby." When my doctor came he said, "There won't be anything to see, Softie." I told him the same thing. I said, "I don't care. It's my baby, and you're not throwing her in the rubbish bin."

'By that stage, I'd had Garry call Mum. But Mum, for all her hippie history, was no good. She came right into the hospital and said, "Be reasonable, Softie. It's a miscarriage.

We've all had one. You just need to have this operation and put it behind you."

'I said, "You've had one?" Because I hadn't known that. She said, "Most women have had one, Softie. It usually means there's something wrong." And my head felt like it might explode. All these people telling me: it's nothing, it's nothing, just get it scraped out, she must have been retarded or something.

'That's not the way I felt about her. Because I'd seen her on the screen. I'd felt her. She wasn't nothing to me. And thank God, there was a midwife on the ward who had a bit of sympathy. A bit of compassion.

'She told my doctor, "She wants to bury the baby." The doctor said, "There isn't likely to be all that much to bury. It's very early days." And I said, "She's my child." And so he agreed to give her to me. He said he'd save what he could. And he did. He saved what he could and put it in a sealed bag, and packed it with the gauze cloths into a box and he gave it to me, saying, "I want you to know there isn't all that much there, Mrs Monaghan. It probably isn't a good idea to open the box. But it's your baby, and you can bury her." But when I mentioned that to Garry, Dr Bell, he thought it was macabre. I had in mind a proper ceremony, maybe with the two of us and Matilda releasing a balloon. I saw that once, on a program about stillbirth and miscarriage, on television. It looked really lovely. But Garry wanted no part of it. He could not see the point of that at all. And I suppose that was about when I thought, "I really have to leave him. I just can't stand it any more."'

Dr Bell said, 'It's a difficult time for a woman after a miscarriage . . .'

Softie said, 'Of course it is. At times I felt like I was going completely mad. My mind would spin around and around. But I knew it wasn't only that I'd lost a baby. I knew I had to get out of the relationship. And I thought, "This is a tragedy for Matilda. Her whole little world" – which was basically bath toys and her silky blanket and her squishy books for bath time – "it's just going to be blown apart." But I had no choice. I had to go. And at the same time, I had to plan my moment. I didn't want to just up and storm out, and then have to come back. I wanted to get everything in order. I wanted to be ready.'

Chapter Thirteen

I read somewhere once, in *The Age*, maybe, that most blokes don't know that their marriage is about to end. It comes at them, out of the blue. The women, they know, mainly because they are the ones most likely to pull the plug. Most of them have been plotting it for years, putting money away, getting ready to shoot through. They'll say to their mates, oh, things were rotten for ages. I was waiting for the right time to go: when the kids had left school, or as soon as I'd found a place to live.

Talk to the blokes, they'll say: I had no idea anything was wrong. We had the odd argument. But that's marriage, right?

I can't say I didn't feel for Garry as he described the end of his marriage to Softie. Listening to what he told Dr Bell, you can tell he didn't see it coming.

'The main problem in our marriage was that Softie

changed so much, after Matilda came along,' he said. 'It was like having a baby changed her whole personality. She'd been an interesting person to be around when we met, and suddenly it was no going out, just a lot of complaining about how she had no life. How I never did this, and I never did that. I mean, what do babies really need? A feed, a sleep, a change. It's not rocket science. Any idiot could do it. But nothing I did was to Softie's satisfaction. And at some point you throw up your hands and say: "Alright, you do it." But that wasn't good enough either. Then it was: "So I have to do everything, do I?"

'But, you know, it seemed to me like Softie was the only one who thought I was doing a crap job. Matilda and me, we actually get on great. I mean I'm obviously not seeing her as much as I'd like at the moment, but she loves me. She likes being out with me. She doesn't care about having strawberries all cut the right way, and in the right dish. She likes hanging around and exploring. Whenever we're together, old ladies stop us – they cluck, and say: "Isn't your wife lucky to have you?" And I'm thinking, "That's not the way she sees it, lady, I can tell you that for free." And when we were still together, I'd go home and I'd say to Softie: "People think I'm actually a pretty good dad, being out with the baby, and no mum along." And she'd say: "Oh, that's right. I'm lucky to have a husband that does something. Never mind what I do. That's just expected of me. No special praise for me. But when you go out with Matilda for what, one hour a week, it's like you're a saint."

'And it was the same when I stayed in with Matilda, when Softie went out. She'd come back in, and she'd say: "So, what have you done? Lumped her in front of the TV?" It might have been raining, or it might be that we'd already been out. I'd say: "We went out for an hour. Now we're back. There's a limit to how many times we can go out," and Softie would say: "There's a limit to how much TV a baby should watch. Whenever she's with you, she watches *Sesame Street*. She watches *Playschool*. She watches *Dora*. She's watching videos too, isn't she?"

'I'd say: "She likes videos, Softie," and Softie would say: "Children like lollies and they aren't good for them either." So I'd take Matilda downstairs and put her in the stroller and we'd go down the beach and walk from Elwood to Brighton, or up the other way, to Middle Park. And we'd enjoy that. The two of us, we'd enjoy it. I'd sit with her on a bench somewhere and get some pears into her or whatever, but you can be sure when I got home that I would have done something wrong. Not enough sunscreen, or not the right hat. Or then, one time, when Matilda was just learning to sit herself up on her bottom, I don't know, at six months, I turned my back for half a second, and a dog romped over – this was at Albert Park where dogs can come off the leads – and sort of chewed on her. Didn't break the skin. Just nuzzled her, the way dogs will. Matilda cried. She was still crying a bit when we got home. Softie said, "What did you do to her?" Like, what did *I* do? I explained about the dog. Softie went absolutely nuts. She took Matilda from me, was holding her, stroking her back, checking her over, saying, "Oh, poor little you, poor little girl, Matilda, what happened, did a big dog bite you . . . ?" And of course, Matilda picks up on that. She senses the tension. She gets that she's supposed to be upset. She throws her arms around her mum and cries harder, and of course that's justification, isn't it? Justification to get stuck into me. Softie's all: "What if the dog *had* bitten her? What if she'd gotten rabies?" I was like, "We don't have rabies in Australia." But Softie was all, "I can't trust you to do anything."

'And so when Softie went back to work, much earlier than she first said she would, Matilda had to go into day care. I wasn't allowed to look after her. And she started getting sick. Those places are full of germs. The doctor at the hospital actually told us that. He said, child-care centres, they're like Petri dishes of bacteria. But still Softie wouldn't come at me being home with Matilda. She'd rather have her with strangers, cooped up in a cot all day in some nursery with twenty other babies, getting sick. And I thought that wasn't right. Because I was perfectly capable of looking after her.

'And then, absolutely out of the blue, Softie said, "I think we should have another baby." I mean, put that in context, Dr Bell. We were barely even speaking to each other. We were at each other's throats the whole time, and Softie was saying we should have another baby. I could hardly believe it. I said, "Are you crazy?" And that was clearly the wrong thing to say. So then I said, "Don't take this the wrong way, Softie, but there's no way we can have another baby. It's just too hard." And she said, "How is it hard for you exactly?" And I said, "Come on, Softie. Don't give me this. We're still getting up in the night, still changing nappies. And anyway, I thought you hated being pregnant?"

'Softie said, "I didn't hate it." I said, "Remember how you couldn't sleep? Couldn't even sit down properly at the end. How you were always saying you couldn't get into normal clothes?" And Softie said, "Yes, but it was worth it. Unlike you, Garry, I'm willing to make sacrifices for my children." And I said, "Well, you can sacrifice that idea. Just no way."'

Dr Bell said, 'And how did Softie respond to that, Garry? You saying you didn't want another child?'

'Like she responds to everything. She went off at me. Started shouting and screaming. I said, "Come off it, Softie. We're barely coping with the baby we've got. You're exhausted." She said: "If I'm exhausted it's because I'm trying to be full-time parent and full-time bread winner with no help at all from my husband."

'I tried a different tack. I said, "Look, Softie, we've got a good life. We've got a little girl, and she's perfect. But you're forty now. Why take a risk? I don't want to be picking a child up from primary school when I'm sixty. What are the other kids going to think? That I'm the grandfather?"

'Softie said, "That's right, Garry. It's all about you."

'I said, "I'm not saying that, Softie. I'm saying we've been lucky. We've got one daughter. She's perfect. Why don't we leave it at that?" Softie said, "Because I don't want to leave it at that. I want another child. Not for me. For Matilda."

'I had to laugh at that, Dr Bell. I mean, you've got to laugh. I said, "Let's not pretend this is about Matilda, Softie. This is about you." She said, "It's not about me. I don't want Matilda to grow up an only child. What if something happens to us? She grows up alone."

'I said, "Nothing's going to happen to us." She said, "I don't want her growing up alone. I want her to have a sister. Like you had. Like I had."

'I said, "My sister was dead before I even knew who she was."

'Softie said, "Well, what about Beam?"

'I said, "Beam wasn't exactly a playmate."

'She said, "You're cruel to him." And that really riled me. Because it was just wrong. I was never cruel to Beam. I used to beat up kids in the playground when they picked on Beam. I've been a mate to Beam all his life, for all he can be in return. But Softie said, "You're being selfish."

'And then she took her cigarettes and went onto the terrace. I bet she hasn't told you that she smokes, has she, Dr Bell? Doesn't tell anyone. Keeps it to herself. I wouldn't even have been interested in her, if I'd known she'd been a smoker when we met. Filthy dirty things. But she'd smoked a bit when she was at MLC – all the girls had a go at it, apparently – and after we'd been together for a few weeks she told me she still had one sometimes. But then she couldn't because she was pregnant with Matilda. And then she was breastfeeding. But then after Matilda was off the breast she took the fags up again. Stress, she told me. And she was still fat. She thought it would help her lose weight. And that's another thing I think should be taken into account here, the fact that she smokes. I mean, that's not good for Matilda, is it?'

Dr Bell said, 'Well, I don't know that the court will make much of that. Softie doesn't smoke in front of Matilda, does she?'

Garry said, 'Well, I don't know. How would I know? I don't see them together any more, do I?'

Dr Bell said, 'But when you were still living together?'

'Yeah, well, Softie's sneaky. She'd smoke at night, after Matilda had gone to bed. She'd sit out on the balcony, stressed out of her head, choofing away. And on this night, she took her cigarettes from under the barbecue, where she kept them, and she closed the sliding door behind her and lit up a cigarette. And I opened the sliding door, and I said, "I wish you wouldn't do that." And she said, "I wish you wouldn't do a lot of things." And I said, "It's bad for you." And she kind of mimicked me, saying: "*It's bad for you.*"

'So, you know, I went and poured the rest of my wine in the sink and I said, "You're talking about having another baby and you're smoking durries out on the balcony. I'm going to bed." And she didn't even bother to respond to me. So I went to bed, and then I heard the balcony door open and close again, and the taps running and Softie brushing her teeth and the toilet going, and then nothing. She didn't come to bed. Matilda was in her cot. We were trying to get her to sleep through the night in her own cot. Softie wasn't supposed to be going in there all the time, but that night she slept in there on the floor. And I thought, "Alright, I'm in for the silent treatment."

'But then, the next night, she came in to me. She'd had a few glasses of wine. She'd had a few durries. I could smell it on her. I'd been trying to stay out of her way most of the evening, by playing on the computer. She was in such a foul mood. Or so I thought. But then she came in to me. And I'll be honest, Dr Bell, that was something pretty unusual, Softie making the first move. That wasn't her style at all.

'But this night, she came in wearing a slip. A nice, lacy slip. And I thought, "Whoa. What's going on here?" And she came into bed, and kind of initiated things. And because that never happened, I knew what was behind it. I said, "I don't want to ruin the mood but I don't want another baby, Softie." And she said, "It won't happen. I'm still breastfeeding a bit." Which she actually wasn't. And which I later found out doesn't work anyway.

'I thought: you sneaky cow! But not in a bad way. I mean, I was that horny, I just let myself go. I actually thought, "Okay, if it happens, it's worth it." That's how long it had been. And afterwards, I said to her, "That was good," and she sort of rolled over, and made a kind of joke with me about it, like she'd liked it.'

Dr Bell said, 'And that pattern of Softie initiating sex, did it continue?'

'For two or three days, yes. Because she's a crafty one. She would've timed things right. She would've known she was ovulating or whatever they call it. And she knew I wouldn't say no to sex. What bloke would?'

Dr Bell said, 'You think she was actively trying to get pregnant?'

Garry said, 'Of course she was. And she managed it. But then she lost the baby. And if you ask me, Doc, it's actually Softie losing the baby that's behind all this. I'm not saying Softie wasn't mad before she had that miscarriage, but she got a whole lot more crazy afterwards. That's when she suddenly got it into her head that the whole marriage was over, and I had to be thrown over, and everything had to end.'

Dr Bell said, 'When did Softie leave you, Garry? I mean, how exactly, and when? Was there a fight, or did you both agree that it was over?'

'I didn't agree to anything,' Garry said. 'And I can tell you exactly when it happened. It was the Easter weekend, not that long after she'd had the miscarriage. Four weeks after, maybe. I remember that because I got invited to some drinks with my gym mates. Wives could come along, but Softie never much liked the blokes from my gym. I said, "Why don't you come? It might make you feel better." Softie goes, "No, thank you very much."

'Well, I decided to go anyway. I left the flat around 7 pm.

I drove down to the bar. I wasn't going to get drunk. I had a few, then got back in the car, and drove home, about 11 pm. I came in the front door, and the flat was completely dark. I thought, "Right, Softie must have gone to bed." But then I checked our bedroom and it was empty, so I looked in Matilda's room.

'And Softie was in there. She was cradling Matilda, and Matilda's head was sort of lolling back, and it seemed to me that she was fast asleep. And for a minute there, I was absolutely freaked out. I thought, "What's this?" Because you know, the way they were sitting there in the dark . . . the way Matilda's head was falling back . . . I thought, "Holy shit!" Because Softie had just been so weird since she'd lost the baby. Weird and cold and distant, and I don't know, just freaky.

'I spoke to Softie. I said, "Is everything alright?" Because it seemed odd to me that Softie was in there, sitting in total darkness, cradling Matilda who wasn't crying or fussing, but completely asleep. Softie was always complaining about how tired she was. And she was just out of hospital, having lost the baby. Yet there she was, up and sitting in the dark. So I asked her, "Is everything alright?" And she said, "Yes." But she didn't look at me. I said, "Is Matilda alright?" And she said, "She's fine." She didn't look fine. She really didn't. Neither of them did.

'I said, "Do you want me to take over?" She said, "No." And the way she said it, I thought, "Uh oh, something's wrong." Maybe she's had a hard time getting Matilda to go down and she's angry with me, because I'd gone out and left her to it when she was just out of hospital. But, I mean, she'd told me to go.

'I went into the kitchen and put the kettle on and I waited there for Softie to come out, and when she didn't I put my head around the door of Matilda's room and said, "Can I get you a cuppa?" And at that point, Matilda sort of sighed, and I realised, well, she's fast asleep, so why is Softie sitting there with her, in the dark?

'Anyway, Softie says: "No." So I went back into the kitchen, and I was standing there, thinking, "What the hell?" when Softie came out of Matilda's room and walked right past the kitchen, without speaking.

'I followed her, saying, "Softie? What's wrong? Is Matilda alright?" But she didn't answer. She went into our bedroom and sat down in front of the computer. I said, "What's wrong?" And she said, "If you don't know, Garry, I'm not going to tell you."

'I was that confused, Dr Bell. I mean, I assumed Softie was angry with me because she was tired and hadn't been able to go to bed, but now she wasn't going to bed anyway. I went into the bathroom to brush my teeth and I got changed into boxer shorts. I made to go towards Matilda's room to say goodnight to her, but Softie said, "Don't go in there."

'I said, "Why not?"

'Softie said, "She's sleeping."

'I said, "I'm just going to give her a kiss goodnight."

And Softie said, "She's only just settled. You'll wake her up."

'I said, "Are you mad at me because I went out for drinks tonight? You said it was alright."

'Softie said, "I don't care where you go."

'I said, "What is it then?"

'Softie didn't say another word and I didn't want to start a fight, Dr Bell, so I got into bed. I was aware of Softie tapping on the computer keyboard. I must have drifted off a bit but at some point, I noticed that Softie had turned off the computer and gotten into bed beside me. I waited until she was settled and then I said, "Where's my kiss?" She didn't answer me, so we were both lying there, neither of us sleeping, with this strange, tense atmosphere, and after about forty-five minutes Softie got up and said, "I can't sleep, you're snoring." I said, "I'm not even sleeping." She said, "Well, it's your breathing then, it bothers me." And she went to sleep on the couch.

'When I woke the next morning Softie was already up and dressed and half-out the door. This was Good Friday. I said, "Why didn't you come to bed last night?" But she didn't respond. She had Matilda in her arms, and Matilda was reaching for me, and I wanted to take her from Softie and, I don't know, throw her in the air, get her to giggle and break the ice between Softie and me, but the way Softie was holding her, sort of bringing her back from reaching for me, I knew it was a bad idea.

'Now, two or three months before this, Softie had told

me, "Oh, the Easter weekend, we're taking Matilda to a farm stay. You stay on a farm, and the kids are allowed to collect the eggs or ride horses or whatever." So I'm thinking, "When does Softie start packing for the farm?" Because it's clear to me that we're supposed to be going to the farm, but no packing has been done. So I say, "When do we have to leave for the farm?" And Softie says, "I've cancelled the farm." I said, "Why would you do that? I thought you were looking forward to getting away for a few days?" But again, she didn't answer me. She just said, "I'm taking Matilda out for a while. We'll be back later."

'Matilda knows the word "farm" and when she heard it, she started saying, "Cow!" and "Horsey!" She knew perfectly well what she'd been promised: not a trip out with Mum, but a trip to a farm.

'I said, "Where are you going? Why aren't we going to the farm?" But she didn't even answer me. Matilda was there, on her hip, reaching out to me, saying: "Horsey!" But Softie just walked out. I watched her from the balcony, putting Matilda into the backseat of the car. Matilda was fighting her, and crying. But there was nothing I could do except hang around the flat watching a bit of sport or whatever, and then, around 6 pm, Softie walked in again with Matilda. I said, "Where have you guys been?" But Softie still wasn't talking to me. She was still being really cold. Oddly cold. Like she was distracted. She put Matilda in the bath, and then let her crawl around in her duck towel for a while before putting her to bed, and then she said, "I want an early night myself" and went into the bedroom.

'I didn't follow her in there. I thought, "Whatever's bugging her, it obviously needs to burn itself out." So I stayed up late and sort of fell asleep on the couch. And the next day, Easter Saturday, the same thing happened: the atmosphere around the flat was just weird and I couldn't get any sense out of Softie. I was trying to talk to her, but she was making herself busy, taking Matilda in and out of the flat with no explanation as to where they were going. I was saying, "Please tell me what I've done wrong." But she just wouldn't talk to me.

'Next day, we're talking Easter Sunday now – and the first Easter Matilda was really going to, like, remember, or know about – I found Softie in the kitchen with Matilda in her high chair and Matilda's overnight bag on the floor.

'I go, "Why have you got a big bag there for Matilda?" And Softie says, "I'm not sure." I go, "What do you mean you're not sure? Are you feeling alright?" And Softie takes Matilda out of the high chair and puts her down on the kitchen floor, and starts doing the washing up. Then she says there's going to be an egg hunt in the park, near where we got married, actually, and she's going to that. And I say, "Well, I'm coming." Softie looks a bit confused but then she says, "Okay," and so off we go. And suddenly everything's different again. I notice that Softie is smiling and being kind of nice to me.

'So then the party's over, and we take Matilda up to the

flat. Softie runs the bath. I say, "You have a rest. I can do that." But Softie says, "No." And she pushes me out of the bathroom and closes the door. I wait a bit, and then she comes out with Matilda in her duck towel, the hood over her head, and again, for some reason, I'm not allowed to hold Matilda. I get walked right past.

'So Softie goes into Matilda's room and closes the door. I can hear Matilda kind of, you know, fighting sleep, and then sucking on her bottle, and at some point she must have gone off, the way they do. And then Softie comes out of Matilda's room, and I'm about to walk through the door to kiss her goodnight, when Softie shuts the door behind her. She says, "She's asleep. Let her sleep." And she closed the door and stood in front of it. Again, I'm thinking, "She's behaving so bloody strange." I was completely freaked out, actually, the way her eyes were, with too much white, too distant, too strange, like she wasn't properly there, if you know what I mean.

'And so I'm again really worried about Matilda. I mean, you hear stories about mothers going . . . I don't know, Dr Bell. I just was that worried. So I called out, "Goodnight, Matilda!" And Softie looked extremely angry. She said, "You just want to wake her up."

'I said, "I just want to say *goodnight*."

'She said, "I don't want you waking her up." Then she goes back to Matilda's room and gets down on the floor and pulls one of Matilda's little bunny-rug things over her and says, "I'm going to sleep in here."

'I go, "I don't understand this, Softie. Out in the playground today it was like we were getting back to normal and now you've gone strange again." She didn't open her eyes or anything. She just said, "I wanted Matilda to have a good Easter. She's entitled to one good memory of her family life."

'I didn't understand what she meant by that. Did she mean she was leaving me, or what? So I left the room for a bit. Then I went back in and said, "Could you please tell me what's wrong?" Because I was by this stage completely freaked out by her weird mood and her strange attitude to me. I told Softie, "If you would at least tell me what I've done wrong, I can apologise and we can get back on track." And then, this really shocked me, because Softie cried a lot but she never had much of a temper or anything, she kind of threw the rug off and stormed out of the room, and we had an argument in the lounge room, where I was begging Softie to talk to me, and she kept saying, "There's nothing to talk about, Garry." And then she went back to Matilda's room, and got down on the floor in Matilda's room, near Matilda's cot, and she was saying, "Just go out! Go out and leave us alone!"

'Well, what could I do, Doc? I slept alone in our bedroom, and then in the morning Softie informed me that she was *again* going out and this time she was taking Matilda to her sister Dawn's. I said, "Well, I'll come with you. I wouldn't mind seeing Dave." Dave is Dawn's husband. But Softie said, "No, I want to go alone." And again, I noticed that she had

Matilda's bag near her feet, only this time it was still open, and she was stuffing things into it. She took a whole bag of Huggies. She took a box of wipes. She took sippy cups and toys, and some of Matilda's clothes. I said, "It looks like you're going to be gone a while." But she didn't answer me. So I said, "Why don't I come with you?" And Softie said, "Why would you want to do that? I'm just going to be sitting with Dawn, letting Matilda play with her cousins."

'I said, "But your behaviour. It's very strange. Why are you packing so many of Matilda's things?" But Softie went out of the flat and put Matilda into the car seat, and drove off.

'Now, I'm not stupid, Dr Bell. I know when something's up. And so at seven o'clock or thereabouts, when the phone went, and it was Softie informing me that she was going to be staying at her sister's for a few days, I wasn't exactly shocked. Still, I said, "What for?"

'And she said, "I've got a lot to think about." I said, "What have you got to think about?" She said, "I want some time alone."

'To be honest with you, Dr Bell, I was that stressed out I was tempted to say: "You know what, Softie? You do need some time alone. In a mental hospital." Because she was acting crazy. But what I did instead was get in my car and drive around to Dawn's house to find out what the hell was going on. And then when I got there, there were no lights on and it looked to me like nobody was home. So I went home and started calling Softie's mobile but it was switched off. So then I started calling Dawn's house. I must have called three or four times before somebody picked up, and it was Dave.

'The first thing he said to me was, "She's not here, Garry. I think she's gone to a friend's."

'I said, "How did you know it was me?" And Dave said, "Who else would keep ringing the house at all hours? I saw your car go around the block too." I said, "I don't believe she's not there. What friend would she go to? Put her on."

'Dave said, "She doesn't want to talk to you." I thought, "Well, that's not really anything to do with you." I said, "Put her on, Dave." He said, "I can't make her talk to you, Garry. She says she doesn't want to talk to you." I said, "Well, if you don't put her on, I'll come over and bang on the door and wake up the street until she comes out."

'Dave said, "You can't do that." I said, "The hell I can't. You've got my wife there and she's been behaving very strangely lately and I'm actually worried."

'Dave said, "I've told you, Garry. She doesn't want to talk to you." He said, "I don't want you calling the house over and over again. We've got little kids here too." And then he kind of hung up on me.

'I sat back, stunned. Because that attitude to me was bloody strange too. I'd always got on alright with Dave. I mean, Dawn is as much a basket case as Softie, but Dave had always been alright with me. So I punched the numbers back into the phone, but now it was engaged. I kept trying. I stayed up, drinking wine, which probably wasn't the best idea, and trying to get through, but the phone just stayed engaged. I suppose at some point I must have fallen asleep. I woke up on the couch at, I don't know, 5 am or whatever it was. I picked up the mobile and tried again. They'd put the phone back on the hook, and it was Dave that picked up. It sounded to me like he was pissed off. He just goes: "Look, mate, I've told you, she doesn't want to speak to you and I don't want to have the phone off the hook 24–7. I want you to stop calling here."

'I said to him, "Put yourself in my shoes, Dave. This is your wife who has run off with your kid with no explanation. What would you do?"

'He said, "I'd man up, Garry. I'd man up and not be hassling her every five minutes. I'd be giving her a bit of space to sort herself out. Because what you're doing is harassing her, and how's it working out for you? Because she's crying here."

'Then he said, "Why don't you just let it alone, Garry? Let her calm down and cool off, and see how things look in a couple of days."

'I told him, "Because I'm going out of my mind here. I'm that worried about what she's doing."

'He said, "Mate, I've been married a lot longer than you. You guys are going through a rough patch. I'm telling you, give her time to get her head together." So what could I do, Doc?

'I put the phone down. I went and turned the computer on. I called up the history. I was thinking, "I'm going to find out what this is about. Because it can't be that she wants to have another baby with me one minute and she's out the door the next." And from the history, I could see that I was right: she was planning to leave me. There was pages and pages of stuff designed to help get her out of the marriage: divorce lawyers, the Women's Legal Service. Custody lawyers.

'I thought, "This is bullshit." I started calling her again. Her phone was still off. I started out on Dawn's number again. I'll admit, I was a bit like a madman, just dialling and redialling and then, I don't know, around six o'clock that night, she finally called me. She goes: "It's me." And I go, "What the hell are you playing at? Where are you?" She goes, "I'm with Dawn." And then she goes, "I want to stay here for a while" and, "I'm confused."

'I'm like, "You're confused? I'm sitting here all day not knowing what the hell is going on and *you're* confused? I want you to come home." And she goes, "I don't want to come home, Garry. I've got a lot of things to think about."

'And the thing that was freaking me out, Dr Bell, was that it wasn't like she was upset. She didn't have the same upset voice she'd sometimes had when she was in the flat. She was absolutely dead calm.

'I go, "Don't sit there talking to Dawn and carrying on. Come home and tell me what I've done wrong. Because we're not going to sort it out with you being there and me being here."

'She goes, "I need some time to think."

'I go, "You can do your thinking here."

'She goes, "No, I can't."

'I go, "Well, how long are you going to be away?"

'And of course, that's exactly what she wanted to hear. She wanted me off her case. She didn't want me in her ear. So she kind of perks up. She goes, "Oh, not long. I just want some time." I was, "Yeah, but how much time?" And she was, "Oh, not long."

'Not long. I mean, that was such total bullshit. From the history, on the computer, I knew what she was up to, which was to divorce me, as soon as she could. She'd already decided she wasn't coming back, and so, if she had her way, Matilda wasn't coming back either. And yet for some reason, there I was, like a dickhead, saying, "Alright then, Softie. You take your time. You think things through. We're a family and we're going to work this out."

'So she gets off the phone. A day goes by and then another day. I'm hanging around the flat like a limpet on a log. I'm doing my best not to call but I'm, like, checking my phone messages every five minutes. But Softie doesn't call me. I'm having restless nights. I'm getting through the wine. Then I try calling her. And she picks up, but she's all strange again.

'I'm like, "Are you thinking of coming home?" And she's, "Oh, no, not yet." And I'm like, "Well, how long is this going to go on?" Because it was shitting me, you know, being pulled around like a bloody puppet, not knowing where things were at.

'So I go, "I know you've been looking for a divorce lawyer. I saw it on the computer."

'She goes, "You're snooping on me now?" I'm like, "What am I supposed to do when you won't tell me what's going on?" She goes, "I don't want to talk about this now, Garry. I'm so tired. I'll call you again tomorrow." But she doesn't call. I have to call her, and the mobile's off. I'm thinking, "What's she playing at? Like, is she going to work? And if she is, is Matilda at child care?" Because by this stage I haven't seen Matilda for what, four days? So I start calling Dawn again. And Dave picks up. And I'm getting pretty sick of talking to Dave. I just go, "Put her on." And he goes, "She doesn't want to talk to you." I'm like, "I don't give a shit, Dave. Put her on." And so there's a bit of shuffling on the line and then Softie comes on. And I go, "What are you playing at? You said you were going to call me. I want to know what's going on. And where's Matilda?"

'She goes, "Matilda's sleeping." And I'm like, "Where's she sleeping?" She goes, "In Corey's room." Corey is Dawn's little boy. They've got Corey and Imogen.

'I go, "Since when is she allowed to sleep in some other kid's bed?" Softie's like, "It's only for a couple of days." And then she says, "She's safe here." I'm like, "What's that supposed to mean? Like she's not safe with me?"

'She goes, "Look, she's fine." And I go, "You sounded more normal yesterday, Softie, and now you're all weird again. What happened?" She goes, "What makes you think anything's happened?"

'I go, "Because you're acting all weird again."'

'She goes, "I'm going to hang up now." And she does hang up. So I get in the car and drive around to Dawn's. And Dave sees the car, and Dave comes out. And he just goes to me, "Garry, mate" – again with the *mate* – "you can't do this. You can't just come around here."

'I go to him, "If you've got my daughter in there I've got every right to be here. I want to see her." And Dave's all, "Softie needs some space, mate. Can't you just give her a few weeks to sort herself out? She's been through a rough time."

'And I'm like, "A few *weeks*?" Because up until this point I've been led to believe she wants a few days to think things through. Now it's a few weeks. And why are we even pretending that she has any intention of ever coming back? I mean, am I so stupid I can't see that she's shot through with my daughter, and she's not coming back?

'So I said to Dave, "I don't want to make a scene here but I'm going in that house to see my daughter." And he's all, "No, you're not." I'm like, "You don't want to try to stop me." And Dave is all, "That's my house, Garry, and you're not welcome in it." I'm, "I'm not welcome now? I'm shut out now, am I? That's where we're at now, is it, Dave?"

'He's like, "She needs some space, mate." And, well, I just lost my rag, Doc. I was shouting, "You let me see Matilda!" And a light in the street came on. Like, a house light across the road. And Dave says, "You're waking the neighbourhood. If you don't go, mate, I'm going to have to call the police. I'm not having you come here, making a racket, waking up the neighbours."

'I'm like, "Go on then, you call the cops. Because I'm sure the cops will be very interested to know that my daughter's in there and I'm being banned from seeing her."

'And Dave's going, "Just go home, mate." *Mate.* "Go home, give Softie some space. She's not coming out. You're not going in. Just get back in your car and go home." But I'm thinking, "No, I'm not going home. She's got no right." So do you know what I did? I drove to the cop shop. I go to the cop, "I want to speak to an officer. My wife has taken my daughter out of our flat, and she won't let me see her."

'A second cop comes out. He's sympathetic. He takes me into a private room. He wants to know how long Softie's been gone. I tell him, "Nearly a week." He says, "Well, there's not much we can do. She's not actually breaking any laws." I go, "She's not breaking any laws? She's got my daughter and she won't let me see her. Isn't that kidnapping?"

'The cop says no. He goes, "She's the child's mother, isn't she? So no, it's not kidnapping." I'm like, "But she won't let me see my daughter. How can that be right?" The cop goes, "Have you got a lawyer?" I'm like, "A lawyer? What would I need a lawyer for?" He goes, "Look. Take my advice. Don't go hanging around whatever house she's at. You'll get yourself in trouble. That's stalking. That's harassment. You need to get a lawyer."

'I go, "She's got my daughter in there, and she's not in her right mind and *I* need a lawyer?" The cop goes, "You need somebody who can advise you. I promise you that you don't want to make a scene outside that house."

'And that's when I got the first sign that the system was going to be stacked against me.'

Dr Bell said, 'And did you get a lawyer, Garry?'

'Not straight away. Because the next day, Softie rings and says, "I want us to see a family counsellor. I've made an appointment. It's in a fortnight." I go, "What's a family counsellor? And what do you mean, in a fortnight? What happens in the meantime?" She goes, "It's somebody who can maybe help us. And a fortnight was the best she had. It was the soonest she had."

'I go, "There must be other counsellors." But she says, "No, this lady was recommended to me. She's supposed to be able to help. It's Relationships Australia and they're all backed up." So I said, "That's fine, I've got no problem with that. I'll see her in a fortnight, but I want to see Matilda now." And that's when it dawns on me how tough she's going to be. She says, "I want to see this lady first. It's important to me, Garry. It's how I want to do things." I go, "If you don't let me see Matilda, I'll go to court." Softie says, "You're not going to get a court hearing in under a fortnight. That system's totally clogged up too." I go, "And how do you know that, if you haven't been asking?" To which she has no answer. Then she goes, "I'm to blame for the backlog in the Family Court now?" And then it dawns on me, Doc. Why are we even talking about court? Is that really where we're headed? So I say, "Where's Matilda now?"

'Softie says, "She's having a nap. We've been at the beach with Dawn and Corey." I say, "Oh, that's nice for her! So I can take it that you're off work, are you? I'm not allowed to see Matilda for, like, five minutes, but you can take days off and do whatever you like with her, is that it? What beach did you go to?"

'Softie goes, "I'm just trying to do what's right for Matilda, Garry."

'I go, "Why aren't you at work, Softie? What's going on?"

'Softie says, "I haven't been feeling well." I go, "What's wrong with you?" Softie says, "I'm not sure. Will you come and see the counsellor with me, or not?" And I go, "Well, when can I see Matilda?" Softie says, "She's having a nap. She fell asleep in her towel, straight out of the bath. She had a big day at the beach." I say, "Then call me when she wakes up." And Softie says, "Alright." I say, "Promise?" and she goes, "Promise." I go, "Alright. I'll see the counsellor if you promise to call and put Minty on the phone." But does she? Does she *hell*. I don't hear a word.'

Dr Bell said, 'I take it you were frustrated?'

'Well, what do you bloody well think? Of course I was frustrated. So I called her again. Dave picked up. He said, "Mate, can you just chill? You're getting Softie all worked up. Every time you call she gets all worked up. I'll get her to call you, alright? I'll get her to call you. I'm going to hang up now. I'm going to politely hang up. Good night, Garry. Do not call here again."'

Dr Bell said, 'And did he hang up?'

'He did. So I thought, "Okay, I'll wait a day, and call her again." But when I rang she didn't pick up. So I said into her message machine, "I'm going to the gym now, Softie. I'm going to be one hour. And if you haven't called me by the time I get back, I'm going to take you to court." And she must have been listening to the messages. She must have thought: "Okay, here's my chance." She got into Dave's car, with Dave, and they drove straight over to the flat, assuming I'd be out, and they started clearing the joint out.'

'Did you catch them at it, or find out when you got in from the gym?' Dr Bell asked.

'I caught them at it. I was taking the stairs to keep fit. So I came onto the third floor, where we lived, and there was Softie, standing there in the flat with Dave, obviously stunned to see me. She'd been hoping, I suppose, to get in and out while I was gone. She nearly jumped out of her skin when I came up the stairs with my gym kit on.'

Dr Bell said, 'Did you get the sense that Softie thought you were perhaps waiting to catch her there?'

Garry said, 'I don't know about that. She always thinks the worst. But that wouldn't be right. I wasn't spying, or stalking, or whatever. I go to her, "Well, hello," and it actually felt weird seeing her standing there, when I hadn't seen her for what, two weeks? And she goes, "Uh, hi, Garry. I've just come to get a few things." She was moving pretty quickly, getting things from her drawers and clothes on hangers, and Matilda's toys, stuffing them into bags.

'I go, "Looks like you're planning on being away a while."'

'She goes, "I don't know, Garry. I don't know. I just need time to think."'

'I go, "I thought you said we could talk to a counsellor."'

'She goes, "Look, yes, it's all so confusing. I need to get my head together."'

'I say, "Where's Matilda?"'

'She says, "She's with Dawn."'

'I say, "How is she?"'

'She goes, "She's great, she's great, she's loving being with Imogen and Corey."'

'I go, "You don't think she'd love being with me? You don't think she misses her dad?"'

'She goes, "Look, yes, it's just I've got some things to work through."'

Dr Bell said, 'Garry, was there a part of you that was willing to accept that Softie might have been telling the truth? That she'd been through a relatively rough time, with the loss of her second baby and she might simply have meant what she said, that she needed some time out?'

Garry said, 'Yeah, well, my interest wasn't in that. My interest was in when I was going to see Matilda. So I go, "Yeah, well, whatever problem you've got has nothing to do with when I can see Matilda." She goes, "I know, I know." I go, "So, when can I see her?" And she goes, "I don't know."'

Dr Bell said, 'What was Dave doing during this time, Garry?'

'Oh, Dave, he's going, "Are we good to go?" He just wants to get out of there. And Softie goes, "Yeah. I think so." Then she says, "Oh, the ladybird. She needs her ladybird." Like, Matilda had this little ladybird thing that you can sit in and ride around on. I go: "Well, here's the deal, Softie. If Matilda needs her ladybird, she can come here and use it." She goes, "Oh, Garry. Don't play games. You know how she loves that ladybird." I go, "You're accusing me of playing games?" And then Softie goes, "Okay. Whatever. I've got to go."'

Dr Bell said, 'She was giving you the very strong impression that she just wanted to get out of there?'

Garry said, 'Yes, but like I say, it was like she wasn't thinking straight. I go, "When are you coming back?" She goes, "I don't know, Garry." I go, "Am I supposed to hang around here until you do know? Is that the deal?" She goes, "I don't know, Garry." And so I go, "Well, tell me this, Softie. Do you still love me?" And she just goes, "Oh, Garry." Like, not yes, not no. I go, "Come on, tell me. Do you? Did you ever?" And then Dave steps in. Steps in and says, "Come on, Garry. Don't hassle her." And he starts going down the hall, towards the lifts, carting all her stuff and Matilda's stuff, and Softie just follows him, and they go down in the lift and get into Dave's car.'

Dr Bell said, 'You followed them out?'

Garry said, 'Of course I followed them out. I needed to know what was going on, Doc. Not that it did me any good. Following them out, I mean. Softie had got in the car.

She was in the passenger seat, looking straight ahead, doing everything she could not to look at me. Dave was reversing the car. I was tapping on the glass, saying, "Talk to me," but Softie wouldn't put the window down, and Dave just drove off.'

Dr Bell said, 'And from there? What effort did you make from there to see your daughter?'

'Right, well, this was when it started to get even trickier. I kept calling and asking to see Matilda, and Softie started to go, "Oh, you're harassing me." It was fine for her to turn up at the flat in the middle of the day to clear the place out, but when I tried to talk to her, that was stalking. She'd go, "Garry, I want you to stop this. I've asked you to give me some space," or something like that. I'd go, "I want to know exactly what you're playing at, Softie."

'Softie goes, "I'm trying to do what's right for me, and what's right for Matilda." I go, "What are you on about?" Because that sounds like *bullshit*. Just total bullshit. Softie goes, "Alright, Garry, if you're going to get angry I'm going to hang up." And she'd hang up.'

Dr Bell said, 'I don't suppose you were ready to give up, though?'

Garry said, 'No. I called her at work. And that's when I found out how far out the door I already was. Because she was using her own name again. When she picked up, she goes, "Softie Monaghan." And I said: "So, all that hoo-ha about how we had to get married so we'd all have the same name and now it's all Softie Monaghan again, is it?"

'She goes, "I don't want you calling me at work, Garry."
I go, "Well, you don't answer the mobile. You won't pick
up at Dawn's. I want to see my daughter." But she just says,
"I'm hanging up now."'

Dr Bell said, 'And, Garry, was there a point when Softie
actually said, "Look, Garry, it's over?"'

'Not to me in person she didn't. She didn't have the guts
for that, obviously. No. I got up in the night, like, to go to
the toilet, and as I was passing by the kitchen, I saw this
white square sticking out from under the door. I went over
and picked it up. Softie must have come past in the night to
deliver it. I put my head out the window to see if she was still
around but I couldn't see her. I sat down in the kitchen and I
opened the envelope. And I knew already what it would be.'

Dr Bell said, 'Do you still have that letter, Garry?'

'Of course I do. I've brought it with me. I made you a
copy, actually. Do you want a copy?'

'I don't really need to keep a copy. Why don't you read
it to me, if you feel like that's something you want to do.'

There's a pause on the tape here. You can't pick it up on
the transcript, obviously, but it's there on the tape. My guess
is, Dr Bell is waiting for Garry to find the letter. There's a
sound, like paper being straightened. Then Garry starts to
read.

Dear Garry, he says.
  *I am writing to tell you that our marriage is over. I
will not be coming home, and neither will Matilda.*

I don't want you harassing my family, my friends at work, or me.

I am putting this in writing: I do not wish to see or speak to you, meaning I want no further contact with you, Garry.

When I say none I mean NONE.

Do not call me. Do not text me. Do not email me. Do not try to reach me through my family. Do not call my workplace. Do not call my sister, Dawn.

This letter is also to inform you that I intend to apply for full custody of Matilda. It is best for her to stay with her mother, while she is so young. You have no means of support. You cannot put a roof over her head.

I am willing to negotiate a timetable for access, a few hours a week, until Matilda starts school. More than that will be confusing for Matilda.

Please do not draw this out and waste our money by fighting a battle you cannot win, Garry.

'And then, you know, it's signed: Softie Monaghan.'

There's more silence here, and then a noise like Garry rolling the letter into a ball.

Dr Bell said, 'How did you take it, Garry? What did you do, once you'd read through it?'

'What do you think I did?' said Garry. 'I got a lawyer.'

Dr Bell said, 'And your lawyer is . . . ? Where did you find your lawyer?'

Garry said, 'Through the Men's Rights Action Team.

They're on the internet. They recommended him to me.'

Dr Bell said, 'And what has his advice been, so far?'

Garry said, 'He's been brilliant. I said to him, "My wife's gone off her rocker. She reckons the marriage is over, and she wants full custody of our little girl." And the lawyer goes, "She won't get it." And that was the first time I was told, you know, that Softie didn't have all the power she thought she had. My lawyer goes, "You've got more rights than you think, Garry. And Matilda's got a right to a relationship with you." He asked me, you know, what I did for a living. I said I was setting up a business. He said, "So, you've been home with your little girl since she was born? You haven't worked?" I go, "Yeah." He goes, "Right, well I'm happy to inform you that you're not just entitled to 50–50 custody. You are the primary carer. If your wife is working, and you are not, you, Mr Hartshorn, are the primary care-giver."'

Dr Bell said, 'At which point, they suggested that you go for *sole* custody of Matilda?'

Garry said, 'Right. I told them, "Well, I've been researching a business plan and Minty's been in child care," and they said, "Doesn't matter. Your wife works full-time. You don't. You are the primary carer." And they drew up the application for custody, and we whacked it straight into the Family Court.'

Chapter Fourteen

I'm speaking only for myself here, but to my mind there's a couple of things you never want to see in life, and one of them's an application for somebody to take full custody of your child. I'd never seen such a document myself, until I found Garry's application for custody of Matilda in one of Frank's white files. It's a short document, sharp and to the point, and to my mind it's not pretty reading. In fact when I first saw it, I thought, 'Imagine being Softie getting that. Your whole stomach would go into a knot.' And it obviously gave Softie a fright. She told Dr Bell, 'I couldn't believe Garry would do that. The application was for full custody of Matilda, and it was full of lies. Garry claimed he was Matilda's full-time carer, which was not the case. I was home the first six months, after which she went to crèche. The idea that he'd take her away from me – her mother – to live with him . . . I couldn't believe it.'

Dr Bell said, 'And when you received the application,

I assume by post, how did you respond, Softie? Did you call Garry, ask to meet and talk . . . anything like that?'

Softie said, 'I had no desire to speak to him. I went and found a lawyer of my own, obviously. But my lawyer wasn't encouraging. She told me Family Law *had* changed a lot in recent years. She explained the *Shared Parenting Act* to me. She said that fathers are entitled to equal time with their children after a divorce. I said, "But Matilda's two years old!" And they told me, age doesn't matter. *Breastfeeding babies* are in shared-care arrangements. I said, "That's ridiculous!" And they said, "But that's the law now. The law says that if the mother works and the father doesn't, the father gets half the time, unless, you know, Garry's an axe murderer or something."'

Dr Bell said, 'You know that isn't quite true?'

Softie said, 'I do *now*. But then I was in a panic. I was thinking, "I want to end my marriage, but how can I, if it means I might lose my daughter?" I said to my lawyer, "We have to fight it." She said, "We'll fight it, but believe me, he'll get a decent chunk of time." I said, "What is a decent chunk of time?" My lawyer said, "To make sure she knows both parents, she has to spend time with both parents." I said, "Well, what if I just leave? What if I go to Sydney? I could get a transfer to Sydney." My lawyer said, "You must know you can't move." I said, "*What*? But I'm an adult! Surely I can live wherever I like!" She said, "Well, yes, *you* can move, of course you can, but you can't take Matilda. She'll have to stay near her father." I said, "How close to him do I have to be?" And she said, "Oh, about thirty kilometres. For the next fifteen years."

'I was astounded, Dr Bell. I said, "But how can that possibly be in Matilda's best interests? To be shuttling between houses? Where the parents are trapped and miserable? To never know where she's supposed to be? Is she to have two of everything? Two lunch boxes? Two bags? Two beds?" And my lawyer, she was very sympathetic, but she said, "I'm sorry, but that's the way the law is now, Mrs Monaghan."

Dr Bell said, 'What was her advice to you, Softie?'

'Well, I asked her to do whatever we could, to stop Garry getting sole custody. That was the first thing, explaining that I was actually the primary carer and that Minty has been in crèche. There have been no occasions when Garry has had exclusive responsibility for Matilda. We pointed out that, yes, I had always had to be the sole breadwinner, but Garry had had the opportunity to work and hadn't bothered, and I shouldn't be penalised for that. And we pointed out that Garry had joined these groups on the internet concerned with "men's rights" after divorce, groups where men advocated violence against women, and hatred of women.

'We said Matilda's best interests could be served only by living with me, at least until she was much, much older. And we put forward emails and voicemail messages Garry had sent me during the time we'd been separated, to show how frightening he'd become.'

Dr Bell said, 'Do you have any of these messages with you? Could you read one for me?'

Softie said, 'I do. I've got them here. Shall I read them now? Onto the tape? Okay.'

And then she started to read:

You're a fat cow is what you are, Softie. You're a fat cow with a mental problem. What you're doing is un-freak-ing-believable. I have not done one thing wrong! I do not DESERVE to be treated like this! That is my freaking daughter you have in your possession. I have a RIGHT to see her.

If you want to leave ME there is nothing I can do about that but you cannot cut me out of MY DAUGHTER'S life.

I will fight for my rights, Softie. I will fight for Matilda's right to see me. Like it or not, we are bound by OUR relationship to OUR daughter who is not YOUR property.

Whatever happens to us, WE – not you alone but WE – are in Matilda's life forever TOGETHER. That is MY RIGHT and HERS.

Dr Bell didn't say anything, at least not that I could hear. Softie went on, 'He left another message on Dawn's mobile, which we had transcribed. Shall I read it? Okay:

Whatever happens between Softie and me, Matilda is

MY daughter. I have a right to a relationship with her. You have no right to interfere. YOU HAVE NO RIGHT TO BE LOCKING ME OUT OF A HOUSE WHERE MY DAUGHTER IS. DO NOT MAKE ME TAKE ACTION YOU WILL REGRET!!!

'But it was this last attachment, Dr Bell – this letter that Garry sent me – that was most disturbing, and we thought it might sway the judge:

My darling Softie,

    I'm writing this without the lawyers knowing. I just want to reach you.

    I know I haven't been the best husband. I know I haven't been the best father. But I love you. I love Matilda. I love our family.

    I feel like I was lost before I found you and now I'm lost again. I want to get back what we had. I want us to be a family again.

    Please stop and think about what you are doing.

    You are a smart lady. So you should know that our family is the only thing that matters to me.

    I'm not saying that we should just go back to the way things were. You've explained that you were unhappy and I can see that now. I'll do whatever I have to do to make you happy.

    The truth is, I need you, Softie. I need you, and I need Matilda. Life without my two girls is empty. I sit on the weekends, lonely with nothing to do. I cannot see a reason to keep living without you. It's not the life I want, and I cannot see any future for myself if you don't come back to me.

Chapter Fifteen

It seems to me that pretty much every bloke, if his wife upped and left and took the kids, would have a moment where they thought, what's the point? Why go on?

I realise there's this idea out there that blokes don't give a rats, that they'll just go and find a younger model, and so on, and, maybe because of all the celebrity divorces you read about – Greg Norman having to pay out $100 million, or Paul McCartney, fighting with that one-legged girl over whether he had to pay so she can get her hair done three times a week – people think, oh, it's only ever about the money.

In my experience, when a bloke gets left and the children get taken, it's pretty much never about the money.

Blokes I've seen in that situation, they're shattered, just smashed, when it happens. The drinking that goes on, and the bawling, of grown men who never cry – or aren't supposed to – well, it's clear to me that a wife walking out is like a sledgehammer to a bloke, and you do hear them saying: 'Right, I might as well end it.'

The thing that's harder to spot is when they actually mean it. To my mind, it's when those blokes start saying dark things about the kids – you know the kind of things I mean; you'll have seen those stories on TV – that you've got to start taking the raving seriously, but again, it's much easier to think, oh, it's the drink talking. Or, he's beating himself up about things. Give him time and he'll sort it out.

I want to be clear here and say my Brian, he was crushed when Nerida threw him over for another bloke and there were days when he'd be curled up on the bed, boots and all, punching the pillow, saying, you know, what the F did I do to deserve it? But – and even Nerida would say this – he kept those feelings away from the kids, and when the time came to settle on the house, he gave it to her, lock, stock and barrel, saying, you and the boys are going to need some-where to live.

What that meant was that Brian would have to go home to his own mum, which is hardly ideal when you've been a family man, king of your own castle and so on, but what else was he going to do? Put Nerida and the boys out on the street? That's not the way we raised him. I'm not saying that Pat didn't resent Nerida for ending up in the house, after the hard work Brian had done to get a deposit together, and then working night shifts during the marriage because they pay a bit more, trying to get some sleep in the day and not being able to do it after Jett and Bax arrived, because they wanted to jump all over him.

'Nerida does the dirty, and ends up with a house,' Pat would say. 'Our Brian never does a single wrong thing, and ends up in the poorhouse. You tell me how that's fair, Barry?'

How could I tell her it was fair? It's not fair. But Brian was right: you can't turf a young mum and three boys into the street. And the main thing for Brian was to do the right thing by the boys, and not let them suffer just because he was suffering.

I've said before that it seems to me Dr Bell was trying hard, in all the hours he spent with Garry and Softie, to get them off the path to war.

He had his work cut out for him, especially with Garry. He was in quite a bit of pain, and that's understandable. He'd married the woman he'd got pregnant, and then she'd taken off, and taken his little girl too. My advice to him would have been to do what Brian did: wait it out. See what happens.

But Garry was armed with lawyers from the Men's Rights groups, and they were making no bones about the fact that a custody battle of any kind is a war against the wife. Go for custody, they were saying. You're not working and she is, so you're the primary carer. And if you get custody, you'll get the flat. And she'll have to pay maintenance. That's only fair. Women have been doing it to men for years.

I've got to be honest and say I had a sense of foreboding as I started to hear Garry talking about taking the case to the Family Court, trying to get all those things that his lawyers said he could. But I'm not going to jump ahead. I'm going to take you through it the same way I went through it, one step at a time.

The first hearing Garry had to go through, it was called an 'interim hearing', meaning it wasn't supposed to be the first and last word on the matter. An interim hearing is what the court holds, well ahead of a full hearing. It basically gives the judge – in this case, Frank – a chance to look at both parents and to read through the reports the family counsellor puts together for him. Then he can make a quick decision about whether either of the parents is likely to do something stupid, and if not to set up a roster of where the kids will live and how often they'll go around visiting, while Mum and Dad go to war over the house, the super and the arrangements, long term.

If you're wondering how I know that, having not seen a custody case up close and personal myself, it's because I took the time to educate myself, meaning I got back in touch with Pam Harris and explained to her that I'd reached that point in Frank's files where the case was going to court, and I was a bit worried about whether I was going to be able to follow it all – work out what the different forms and orders meant – so could I come out and maybe borrow some of her expertise?

'You come any time,' Pam said. So I got the train, then the tram, walked up that paved drive with the box plants on either side. Pam answered the door. Ron was home.

'Barry,' he said, shaking my hand. He disappeared after that – out of sight, although I could hear him pottering around – while Pam and I talked. I asked her if Frank was already sick when Garry's case came to his court.

'It started with a cough that he couldn't shake,' Pam said. 'I brought in Benadryl and that didn't help. He went to his own GP to get a script, but that didn't help either. I remember him saying to me, "This is one of those coughs that doesn't want to leave." Then he started saying he had a pain in his back, near his kidney. It was Betty who said he should have an X-ray. And it turned out that his left lung had filled with fluid. They drew a sample of fluid and sent it for tests, and the results came back: lung cancer. It had already spread to the lining of his chest.'

I said, 'It seems bloody unfair, given Frank never smoked.'

Pam smiled and said, 'He told me he might have had one or two with you.'

I said, 'Oh, well, okay. Once we had a packet, between the two of us, in the mid-morning, boiling sunshine, on a hill out behind the school. Neither of us took it up, though. My Pat, she smoked right up until Brian was born, but I never got a taste for it, and neither did Frank.'

Pam said, 'I don't recall Frank being bitter about having lung cancer. There was the shock, obviously, of suddenly being unwell. He had to undergo tests, and quickly: blood tests and so on, and that ate into the time he was able to give the court. He was given the name of an oncologist – I don't know his full name but he called him Dr Paul – and when they met to discuss the results Dr Paul said the cancer had started in his lung and spread to his chest. Frank told me, "Pam, treatment is palliative," meaning there was no way to cure him, only to buy time.'

I said, 'Did they give him any idea how long he had?'

Pam said, 'I don't know if they do that. But yes, he knew, or seemed to know, that it already had quite a hold on him. He told me he'd need six or eight weeks of chemotherapy, at Peter MacCallum, and even that was just to buy some time. Being the kind of man he was, he didn't take much time off. He just took his paperwork from the court into the treatment room with him. There were recliners. He'd sit with six or seven others, with nurses carrying bags of what he called "the poison" to hook up for him. He'd read, or try to read, through whatever documents he had.'

I said, 'I can see him doing that. Never not reading something. He could read getting a dink on the back of my bike.'

Pam said, 'They warned him about the cancer treatment. That he wouldn't necessarily handle it well. He'd lose his hair and his taste buds. There were a few months when he couldn't keep down the morning egg. At one point a rash of small red bumps, like pinpricks, appeared down his shins and across the backs of his hands.'

I said, 'It must have slowed him down?'

Pam shook her head. 'Not exactly. He kept coming into the office. You'll know how passionate Frank was about clearing divorces. "It's bad enough," he used to say, "that people have to end their marriages – the death of all that hope. They shouldn't have to sit around waiting for someone like me to put a stamp on it for them." But there were days when he was tired. I'd find him sitting, focused on nothing, not even the ceiling. There might be a binder of reports in front of him, but it would be untouched. And there was a week when he was absent. He had to have a small operation to drain fluid from his lung. They put him on new drugs that worked a little better. But with the kind of cancer he had, new problems kept popping up. He'd get pain in the bones. And then, just when I was starting to think that things really weren't looking very good at all, Barry, he rebounded. The tumours shrank a little. His blood count improved. One of the nagging infections cleared up. He gained some weight.'

I said, 'He must have been hoping it was a cure.'

'Oh, he knew there was no cure. Everyone was quite clear on that point. But it was lovely to have a rebound. Dr Paul was very pleased with him. I recall Frank saying: "Pam, I'm to get an A as a patient."

'He knew he was on borrowed time, so he was determined to make use of what he had. And he was excited about the changes that were coming in. Shared care for fathers. He was passionate about that.'

I said, 'That law – shared care – had that already come in when Garry went to court?'

Pam said, 'It was in. And Frank had already had a bit to say about it. He was one of those who thought the pendulum *had* swung too far in favour of the mothers. Under the old laws, I mean. Fathers would come to court, and they could hardly believe what had happened to them: "It's like my wife has taken a wrecking ball to me. I was married. Now I'm not. I had kids. We got on great. Now she's saying I can see them every other weekend. How is that fair?" And Frank was sympathetic. Because that's not fair.

'But lawyers would tell their male clients, "Your wife is the primary carer. The children are still young. One weekend a fortnight, and half the school holidays – it's a good deal. Or as good as you'll see." So when Garry's case came up, and the shared care laws were in, and the opportunity was there for Frank to make a statement about the new regime, well, he took it.'

I said, 'I've read the judgement. He really let Softie have it, didn't he?'

Pam looked grim and said, 'Yes, I suppose he did.'

Chapter Sixteen

I'm guessing there are going to be a lot of people out there who have never seen a proper court order, meaning the document handed down by the court, after the judge has had a look at both sides of the argument. I hadn't seen one myself until Pat got hers in the mail. To my mind it's worth having a look at the one Frank handed down at the end of the first hearing with Garry and Softie. If nothing else, it shows you what frame of mind he was in.

Monaghan & Hartshorn [2007] FMCAfam 17689
FAMILY COURT OF AUSTRALIA

Applicant:	MS Softest MONAGHAN
Respondent:	MR Garry G. HARTSHORN
File Number:	MEL768979 of 2007

SUBJECT CHILD: **MATILDA MONAGHAN HARTSHORN**
PRESIDING: JUSTICE FRANCES BELMONT
BROOKS.

I have before me a great number of documents relating to what I shall call the battle for ownership of Matilda Monaghan Hartshorn.

I see that both her parents are here. I'm pleased that they are, because I'd like to take the opportunity, early in what I fear will be a long and bitter battle, to tell them what I think of what they're doing to their child.

I'm not speaking here about their fight for custody of her. I'm speaking here about their decision to get divorced.

Let's not fool ourselves about what divorce is. Divorce is a failure of parenting. It does more damage to children than just about anything else that might happen to them in the years before they become adults. It takes from them the only things they hold dear. It breaks up their home. It destroys their sense of family. It removes them from the comfort of having one bed, in one safe, secure, familiar house, where they go to sleep every night of the week. It fills them with sadness and, probably, guilt. They can't help but think that they must somehow be to blame. It sets them up for a world in which nothing is certain and nobody can really be trusted.

So, why do parents do it?

Sometimes because they have no choice. There is violence in the marriage, or drunkenness, and abuse. The children are at genuine risk of harm if the parents stay together.

But that's not the case here, is it? The problem here is that the parents are merely unhappy. Matilda's mother, in particular, is unhappy.

I've read through the report that my friend Dr Ian Bell has put together after sitting with both parents. And it is very interesting. Dr Bell has obviously gone to a great deal of trouble, talking to Matilda's mother for many hours about her decision to leave the marital home and take her child with her. He speaks of an 'irretrievable breakdown of the relationship' between the parents. He speaks of a 'disconnect' between the couple; that there is 'profound dissatisfaction' with the way things have turned out between them. And that is one way of looking at it.

Another way of looking at it is to say that Matilda's mother has decided to give up. She doesn't like the man she married and promised to love forever. She can't stand to look at he who gave her the gift of a child. Her husband, Garry, doesn't do things the way she'd like them to be done. And so she's decided to quit. Which would be one thing, if there were no children involved.

But there is a child at the centre of this divorce, and her name is Matilda. I have an enormous number of documents before me, and yet I have been unable to form a picture of Matilda. How is she coping since her parents separated? Is she reaching the developmental milestones we'd expect of a child of her age? Is she walking and talking? Does she clap and sing and play? Does Matilda understand what is going on between the adults in her life? Has anyone spoken to her about it? If so, how does she feel?

To my mind, it's worth reminding ourselves that Matilda is a child. She's not a vase, or a Persian carpet, or even a Persian cat. She's a little girl who is two years old.

To my mind, she has the right to stay in the home she's always known, with parents who love her, and who strive, selflessly, to make her childhood a safe and precious one.

But that's not going to happen, because Matilda's mum has taken it upon herself to tear the family unit in half.

That's her choice, of course. Divorce is entirely legal. You don't even have to have a good reason. I'm quite certain that Matilda's mother is telling herself that Matilda will get over it. Kids are so resilient these days, aren't they?

Actually, they're not. What the research about divorce says is that it is devastating for children. But there is one thing that parents can do to ease the path ahead for children of divorce. They can try to get along and co-operate with each other. They can ensure that their children see and know and are able to love both of them, and make the process as pleasant and trouble-free as possible.

And so I turn to Ms Monaghan's application. It's for full custody of Matilda. She's not seeking to share the care of this little girl with her former husband. She's not proposing any kind of compromise that would allow Matilda to frequently see her dad. She's saying, 'Matilda should live with me. And she can see her dad for a few hours, on Saturdays, every other week.'

As a Family Court judge, I have some experience with this kind of arrangement, and let me tell you what would happen, were I to grant that application. Matilda would start

off seeing her dad for a few hours a weekend once a fortnight. That would soon dwindle to once a month. Matilda
will get older and she'll start to tell her mum that she can't
be bothered going to see her dad on the weekend. She'll
want to be with friends. Her mother has already shown, with
this application, that she's not that interested in supporting
a relationship between Matilda and her dad, so she'll say,
that's fine, and she'll call Matilda's father and tell him his
daughter's not coming. He will object and Matilda's mother
will say, 'Well, it's not my fault. I can't force her to want to see
you.' And Matilda will become one of the one-in-five children
who never see their father after divorce, or who see them
once a year, at Christmas, or on their birthday.

Now let me turn to Mr Hartshorn's application. It, too, is
for full custody of Matilda: he's not interested in compromise,
either. To my mind, his position is one demanding of some
sympathy. His wife has already left the home, with the child.
She's made it very clear that she wants nothing to do with
him. He must know what's ahead if he doesn't fight, and fight
hard, for access to his little girl.

So, what can I do? Well, the couple has come here for
orders, so I will give them some orders.

My order is that Matilda will live in a week-about arrangement with both parents, until she reaches the age of
eighteen.

Now, I can see the lawyers getting to their feet. I don't
have the power to do that. This is an interim hearing. And
that's fine – I fully expect my order to be appealed. Everything

I've read and everything I've seen in my decades in this court tells me that this couple is in this for the long haul. Marriage, they couldn't hack. Divorce, they can go at for years. They'll take my orders today and find ways to get around them. They'll keep coming back here until each of them is broke and everyone around them is exhausted.

And why? They'll tell you it's because of Matilda. They want what's best for Matilda. How curious, then, that what's best for Matilda is missing from almost every document I have in front of me.

Now, I'm the kind of bloke who respects authority and I hope it goes without saying that I've never been inside a court house in my life. That being the case, had I ever been faced with a judgement like the one Frank handed down to Softie, I'd have been mortified. I'd have been ashamed of myself. I'd have wanted to pull my socks up, improve my behaviour. See whether there wasn't a way to work things out with Garry, so at least the divorce would have been smooth, if the marriage couldn't be.

But that's not how Softie reacted. Softie was straight onto her lawyers, telling them to 'do something', meaning appeal Frank's decision to give Garry shared care. And she wanted Frank dismissed from the case altogether, on the grounds that his judgement proved what everybody said, that he was biased against mothers, and against her in particular. Lawyers being lawyers, they were happy to give getting rid of Frank a go – more money for them – but in their defence, they did tell Softie there wasn't much they could do about the orders themselves. Garry *was* going to be allowed to see Matilda, whether Softie liked it or not. And I'm not sure anyone can fault Frank for that. There was no reason – or none that I could see – to think that Matilda wouldn't be safe with Garry. No evidence that he'd ever done anything really wrong.

Which is why, after reading through the judgement, and putting the next tape of Dr Bell's into my little tape deck – well, what I heard, it shook me in my shoes. Not because I didn't know it was coming. Pat had warned me, after her Googling of it. No, it was more . . . The strangeness of it, coming after Frank had given Softie such a dressing-down. The timing . . . But I won't jump ahead. I'll just say the next tape in the collection, recorded about a month after Frank handed down his first orders, was Softie. And the first thing that struck me was that it didn't sound like her. Softie's voice had gone all high, and strange.

'I picked Matilda up from Garry's last Friday and it was clear to me, from the moment I put her into the car, that something was wrong,' she said. 'She was wriggling, squirming, fighting me, and I thought, "Okay, she's wrung out, she's not slept properly." Because she never sleeps properly at Garry's. He doesn't understand about bedtimes. He revs her up, when he should be calming her down. And besides that, Dr Bell, you know probably even better than me, children need routines. They can't cope with unpredictability. One day here, one day there, Mum there, and then

Mum not there. But this upset was something different, more than normal – it was like something had happened. Matilda was thrashing at me, like I was the enemy.

'At first I thought, okay, what awful things has Garry said about me? Because I'd picked Matilda up from McDonald's and Garry was there, leering at me, so smug, still so thrilled with having had his win in court, and he tried to harangue me in the McDonald's playground, saying, "Look, she's fine, she's fine, she's had a great time with me." And like a fool, I'd engaged with him, saying, "If she's fine, it won't be because of your influence, it will be because of your mum and Rick, Garry." Because I knew, as well as anyone, that Garry wasn't looking after Matilda on his own. He was collecting her from me and taking her to his mother's house – to Joan and Rick's – and he was getting Joan to help him, on those weeks when he had Matilda. There's just no way he could have done it by himself. And I was grateful for that, because his mum, at least, understands what Matilda needs, in terms of proper meals, and that kind of thing. I mean, Joan raised two boys and Rick has always been fantastic with Matilda, giving her horsey rides and that kind of thing.

'I could see Garry wanted to get stuck into me about that, but I made it plain that I wanted no conversations about the court in front of our little girl.'

Dr Bell said, 'Did Garry respect that?'

Softie said, 'Oh look, Dr Bell, Garry's mood since Justice Brooks handed down his judgement . . . let's just say, he's enjoying having the upper hand. Let's put it that way.'

Dr Bell said, 'And what was it about Matilda that made you think that something had happened?'

Softie said, 'Right, well, as I said, the way she reacted when I put her in the car was strange. And then, when I got her home I took Matilda out of the car, and she was still fighting me, scratching at me.

'I got her inside the house – I'm still at Dawn's – and I put down her little suitcase – she has her own little Dora suitcase, with a pull-along handle. I bought it to try to make the handovers fun, and I've been showing her how to pack and unpack it, trying to bring some routine into the mess. And I put it down and that calmed her a little, because she likes to unzip the case when we get home and take things out of it. So I let her unzip it, and the first thing I see is a feather boa. A feather boa, Dr Bell.'

Dr Bell said, 'I take it that was something you didn't pack?'

Softie said, 'That was certainly something I didn't pack. A feather boa? For a two-year-old? With feathers coming off it, getting breathed into her throat? It's exactly the kind of thing I would never give Matilda. What if she wore it to bed? And rolled around and choked herself? It's totally inappropriate. So I made a note to put that into my diary.'

Dr Bell said, 'Diary? Is that for the court?'

Softie said, 'Yes, for the court. My lawyer told me to keep a diary. To keep a close eye on Matilda, noting any changes to her behaviour . . . But anyway, Matilda kept going through the case. She was on her knees, taking out this, taking out that, and then she gripped herself – her private parts, Dr Bell – and said, "Wee wee." And that has never happened before. Matilda's still in nappies. I'm not potty training her. I've decided, with everything that's going on, that it's too much for her. Another change, when she's got enough to deal with.

'Then Matilda said, "Potty." And I thought, well, okay.

'Now, some of her little friends have a potty. There's a potty at crèche. Her cousins had a potty. But I was still fairly surprised to hear Matilda say potty, Dr Bell, because we don't have a potty in the house.

'In any case, I told her, "I'm going to run the bath, Matilda. You can do a wee-wee in the bath." She was quite hysterical. She was saying, "No, no, no, no," and she was stripping herself out of her clothes, and ripping at the sides of her nappy, and no matter how I tried to hold her, calm her down, get her to stop, she kept saying, "Wee-wee, wee-wee," like weeing in her nappy was something she could no longer do. I couldn't imagine what the matter was, so I took off her nappy and there she was, standing naked from the waist down, holding her private parts, saying "wee-wee, wee-wee." It looked to me like she was in considerable discomfort, like she was really holding on, and I thought, what should I do? Hold her over the toilet, so she could go? So I did that. I took her by the underarms and held her over the toilet, and she went in it.

'It occurred to me obviously that Garry must have been trying to toilet train her, which was very wrong of him to do without consulting me. In my view, Matilda's not ready. And that's the problem with this whole ridiculous shared-care situation – you have two parents doing different things without communicating. So I made a note to tell Garry to stop whatever potty training he was doing, and then I ran the bath and tried to put Matilda into it, but she was screaming and crying, which she'd never normally do – she loves her bath! – and she was clinging to me. And as soon as I attempted to lower her into the water she was screaming, "No, Mummy, no, no, it hurts my wee-wee."

'I could not work out what was going on, Dr Bell, so I kept Matilda on my hip, and emptied the bath and took her out to the lounge room and popped her down on the floor. And she immediately returned to the little suitcase, and picked up the feather boa, and she draped it around herself. And the way she was standing there, Dr Bell, I felt sick. I felt physically nauseous . . .'

Softie paused. Presumably, she was trying to compose herself. When she continued, her voice was pretty much strangled.

'There was something about the way she was standing, Dr Bell. She had her hip cocked. Cocked to one side. She was naked, and she'd got one little hand . . . it was . . . she'd got . . . she was holding herself, Dr Bell . . . She was standing there with a feather boa around her neck, hip cocked, holding herself . . . holding her private parts and looking at

295

me like . . . like . . . like . . . with this *expression* . . . such a grown-up expression . . . And I knew. I just *knew*.'

Dr Bell spoke very quietly. He said, 'What was it you knew, Softie?'

Softie said, 'Something had happened to her, Dr Bell. Garry had . . .'

Dr Bell said, 'Had what?'

Softie said, 'Isn't it *obvious*? Do I really have to say? He'd *interfered* with her. He must have done.'

Again, very quietly, Dr Bell said, 'That's quite a leap, Softie. What makes you think that?'

Softie said, 'What else could it be? Where else would she learn that? To stand like that? To leer like that? With the feather boa! And the pose! It was like something from pornography! Where does a little girl see that kind of thing? Little girls, they're always *copying*. They don't just come up with that kind of thing. And so the first thing the next morning I went to our GP. I was waiting there when her rooms opened. I said, *please*, it's an emergency. I asked for a lady doctor. I told her what I'd seen. Straight away she agreed to do an examination. I could hardly stand it. I was sobbing and sobbing. I was trying to help, trying to take off Matilda's clothes, and Matilda was saying "*No, no, no,*" and fighting hard, and it actually took both of us to get Matilda out of her clothes, she was fighting so hard, like she knew what was going to happen.'

Dr Bell said, 'Was the doctor able to conduct an examination, Softie? What was her conclusion?'

Softie was crying hard. 'But that's the most frustrating thing!' she said. 'She said she couldn't be one hundred per cent sure that anything had happened! She said there was nothing . . . nothing *broken* or red, or *obvious*. But that doesn't mean anything, Dr Bell! That could just mean he is being very careful not to get caught! You can abuse a child without leaving any signs of it! Everybody knows that. But there were signs of it – to me, anyway! Only she – the doctor – couldn't see them!'

Dr Bell said, 'And what did the GP advise, Softie?'

Softie said, 'Oh, well, she said, "It's an inconclusive thing! But you have to have further examinations. You have to have this looked into." And I said, "But the court says I'm to hand Matilda over to Garry every other week! How can I do that?" And the GP was absolutely on my side. She said, "No, no, you don't have to do that. You need to tell the court that you have new concerns. You need to get an order, suspending his rights. You mustn't leave her in harm's way!"'

Chapter Seventeen

I've said before that I don't keep secrets from Pat, and I'd told her often enough that if anything of interest came up she'd be the first to know. And so pretty much the moment I'd composed myself, after listening to Softie getting so upset, I went inside, carrying the little tape deck, and I said, 'Pat, I want you to listen to this.'

I had a feeling Pat would make a fuss, saying, 'I've told you before, that case doesn't interest me. It's not for us to involve ourselves in that kind of thing. And don't you think I've got enough on my plate with Brian?'

So before she had time to argue I took her gently by the elbow and said, 'Pat, please.' I sat her down in the sunroom, put the headphones on her, and pressed play on the tape. You'll know by now that Pat's not the type to give in easily. She was saying, 'What's all this about? The headphones don't fit! I can't hear it properly. Who's it supposed to be?'

I said, 'It's the mother of that little girl Matilda Hart-shorn. Listen, Pat, just listen.'

The room fell silent.

I watched Pat's face as Softie's voice came filtering through. She looked a bit confused at first, and then she relaxed into the sound of Softie's voice, but then, when it became clear what Softie was going to talk about, her expression, it looked almost frightened . . . all the same reactions I'd had when I'd first heard what Softie had to say.

I tried to interrupt a bit. I kept saying, 'Where are you up to?' That kind of thing. But Pat had her brow furrowed, and she waved me away. I was anxious so I went into the kitchen and faffed about, before coming back out.

Pat was still listening intently. 'Where are you at?' I whispered, but again, she waved her hand, shushing me. That particular tape is about twenty minutes long and I was that fidgety towards the end I couldn't stop moving from one foot to the other. When it was over, Pat put her thumb down on the stop button without saying a word.

'Do you think she's telling the truth?' I said.

'Of course she is,' said Pat.

I said, 'You don't think she's making it up?'.

Pat said, 'Why would she make it up? Who is saying she made it up?'

'I don't know, Pat,' I said. 'I've got to tell you, it feels odd to me, hearing that. Frank has only just told her – Softie, I mean – that she's got to share custody of Matilda. I know she sounds convincing. But isn't it a bit convenient?'

Pat said, 'Well, what did Frank say?'

The truth is, at that point, I didn't know. But the files made it clear. He'd put a stop to shared care, so Garry could be investigated. And what had Garry said? I didn't know, so I went to the next tape in Dr Bell's collection, and there was Garry going berserk about the things Softie had said.

'This is absolutely not right!' he said. 'This is totally wrong! Softie has gone into court, and she's made the most disgusting allegations. She's told lies and more lies.'

Dr Bell said, 'I can see how angry you are, Garry. Tell me your immediate reaction to hearing the allegations against you. What did you say?'

Garry said, 'My immediate reaction? What do you think? I was like, "You must be joking." I said to my lawyer, "This is just *bullshit*. Why would I abuse my own child?" Has Softie ever said to you, Dr Bell, that she thought I might be a ped? Has anyone ever said that I might abuse Matilda? Before I got 50–50 custody? No she hasn't! Because it's complete crap. It's made up to bolster her case! It's a scam.'

Dr Bell said, 'What was your lawyer's advice, Garry?'

Garry said, 'My lawyer! He's bloody hopeless. You know what Softie's done, don't you? She's gone back to the court. She's made a formal allegation against me to the police. And now the court is telling me I can't have shared care of Matilda any more, because they need to do an investigation! And while that bullshit investigation is being done, I can only see Matilda for two hours a fortnight! *Two hours a fortnight!* With a supervisor! And not even in my own home! In what they call a contact centre! And this guy – the judge, Justice Brooks – is supposed to be on the side of dads! I'd hate to see a judge that was on the side of mums! Maybe they'd just stick me in jail with no trial! They've taken Matilda away from me. And this isn't right, Doc. I'm being judged before a trial! I'm guilty before being innocent. My lawyer's said I have to go along with it; I've got no choice. An allegation's been made. They have to investigate. And the judge, he's all: "This is regrettable. This is unfortunate. But we must investigate."

'I'm like, "I've got to prove myself innocent? In what court of law? That can't be legal. I've done nothing wrong." He goes, "That's the way it is. They've got to investigate. They're not going to let you have Matilda unsupervised, not when an allegation of sexual abuse has been made. Imagine the outcry! It's too risky. From their point of view – we know this is bullshit – but from their point of view, what if Softie's telling the truth?" I said, "So, it's my word against hers? And until then, she wins? And I don't get to see Matilda, now, for how long?"'

Dr Bell said, 'Well, you can see Matilda, can't you, Garry? In the contact centre?'

Garry said, 'In a contact centre! Which is torture. Have you ever *seen* one of those places, Doc? There's bars on the windows! There's a security guard on the door. You've got to go through your pockets when you get there. They want to see ID. No ID, no getting through the door. Then you sit and you wait until they give you permission to see your own kid! It's so wrong!

'I've got to go through all this *crap* – this absolute crap – to see my own child! And that's before we even get to what Softie's now putting Matilda through.'

Dr Bell said, 'Matilda's seeing a child psychologist?'

Garry said, 'Yes! With dolls! They told me she was going to have to go to some special kid doctor who would give her dolls. Have you heard about the dolls, Doc? Anatomical dolls. Dolls with big willies. They're giving her dolls with giant willies – I've looked them up on the internet – and they're saying to her: ever seen one of these before? A doll with a big dick, with wool around it. Like that's not going to, you know, have an effect on Matilda, seeing that? I said to my lawyer, "How can that be the right thing, giving a girl a doll with a big willy sticking up?"'

Dr Bell said, 'Did your lawyer explain how the dolls work?'

Garry said, 'I don't give a shit how they work! Sure. They told me. Somebody says to Minty, "Did you see something like that before? When did you see that? Was it hanging down? Was it sticking up? Does your daddy have a thing like that sticking up?" What must that be doing to her? I can't believe they would put a child through that. That *Softie* would!'

Dr Bell said, 'I take it you've been sent for an evaluation, too, Garry?'

Garry said, 'Oh, too right! You bet I have! It's not enough to put Minty through it. Oh no, it's part of the game, isn't it, to punish me as well. It's out-bloody-rageous!'

Dr Bell said, 'Where did they send you, Garry?'

Garry said, 'To one of those experts that specialise in kiddy-fiddlers of course! To some clinic at the Rialto in the city, where you have to go and everybody knows why you're there! And I couldn't find the place. I kept getting lost. I went into the hotel in the end. I put my head down on the reception desk. I was that close to bawling my eyes out. I go to the girl on reception, "I just want to see my little girl." And she was some poor innocent concierge. But she turned out to be nice about it. She goes, "Where are you supposed to be?" I told her, and she walked me to the sliding door. She points me in the right direction. She goes: "You walk 500 metres. You'll see the lifts." It was really nice of her. All these weeks, feeling like a . . . I don't know, like the lowest form of life, and she was being kind to me. So anyway, I finally got in there. I was a bit late. It wasn't like here, Doc. There was a woman at reception. She was talking on the phone, not even looking at me. I could tell she thought I was a ped. Because I was late, I said, "I'm Garry Hartshorn. I have an appointment at 11 am." She didn't say a word to me. Not one word. She stuck her finger up in the air, like I was to be silent. She kept talking on the phone and only when she was well and truly done did she go, "Your name again?" Like she wouldn't have known who I was. She gives me a piece of paper, clipped to the clipboard. She says, "You've got to fill that out." I think, "Great, so now there's a record of me visiting the kiddy-fiddler specialist!" But I fill it out. I'm just about done when the door opens, and this bloke comes out.'

Dr Bell said, 'Was it Ross Street?'

Garry said, 'That's him. It was Ross Street. Ross the ped specialist! I follow him in. All the time, I'm thinking, "Who's been in here before me? What weirdos, what freaks?" I sit down and he says, "You're Garry Hartshorn?"

'I go, "That's right."

'He goes, "I'm Ross."

'I go, "Right, Ross."

'He goes, "Tell me why you're here, Garry."

'I go, "I've been told to come."

'He goes, "By the court?"

'I go, "That's right."

'And he goes, "And there's an issue here . . . why don't you tell me what the issue is?"

'I mean, Dr Bell, like he didn't bloody know! I go: "The issue is, my wife won't allow my daughter to see me."

'He goes, "Yes. Anything else?"

'I go, "You know as well as I do! My ex-wife claims I'm a kiddy-fiddler. Just saying the word makes me sick."

'Dr Street said, "I understand you deny the allegations against you, Garry?"

'I said, "Of course I bloody do." And I told him, "They're complete bullshit."

'He goes to me, "Well, then, why do you think Softie has raised them?"

'I go, "Power! Control! To get rid of me! I don't know. How would I know? You're the psychologist." Not that what I said mattered. I was pretty sure this bloke was on Softie's side.'

Dr Bell said, 'What makes you say that?'

Garry said, 'The things he said. The way he put them. He said, "Are you working, Garry?" Like he wouldn't know that I'm not working.

'I go, "Not at the moment, no. I've been a bit stressed out."

'He goes, "Are you on any medication, Garry?" Again, like he wouldn't know.

'I go, "Sleeping pills."

'He goes, "How long have you been taking sleeping tablets?"

'I go, "Since this thing started."

'And then he goes, "And what about before this started? Any anxiety?" Like he was setting me up. I go, "I've got no anxiety! I've got rage at being called a ped!" Then he goes, "Your wife says you had little interest in caring for Matilda before the two of you separated, but now you've decided to potty train Matilda."

'I go, "So what?"

'He goes, "Have you told your wife about the potty training?"

'I go, "Of course not. I'm only to do what she says, don't you know? Softie freaks out about anything I do. We kept it to ourselves. I told Matilda it was like a game, and when she remembered to go, we'd celebrate ourselves."

'He goes, "Celebrate how?"

'I go, "Oh, you know, Matilda used the potty! Good girl, Matilda! Let's wash out the potty! Let's put it in the toilet."'

'"And don't tell Mummy?"'

'"And don't tell Mummy . . ." And then it dawned on me. Then I could see what he was getting at! You can see what he's getting at, can't you, Dr Bell? He was heading down the path of, well, what other secrets do you have? And I'm, like, you've got to be joking! What is this? A set-up?'

Dr Bell said, 'It sounds like you couldn't wait to get out of there.'

Garry said, 'Too right I couldn't. But then this bloke, he goes, "When was the last time you saw Matilda?" And I go, "It's going on six weeks."'

'And then he goes, "Would you like to see her now?"'

'I go, "Of course I would." Because I don't quite get what he's saying, which is, "Would you like to see her now, as in *now*."'

Dr Bell said, 'Matilda was *there*?'

Garry said, 'That's what I said! "Matilda's here?"'

'And he goes, "She's here."'

'I go, "What's she doing here?"'

'He goes, "I'm to observe the two of you, Garry. Didn't anyone tell you that?"'

'I'm, like, "Nobody told me anything!" I'm going, "Where is she? When can I see her?"'

'And he goes, "Well, why not now?" And he picks up the phone, and presses a button and goes, "It's Ross. Yep. Okay. Could you bring Matilda in? Thank you."'

'And then, you know, the door opens, and all I can hear is "DADDY!" And there's Matilda, and she's across the room, and I'm thinking, "You're so big! When did you get so big! Look at you! Your hair's so long!" Because, you know, even when it's only been six weeks, they grow so much! And this bloke, Ross Street, he's going, "Alright, Garry, alright, you two. I've got some reading to do. Why don't you two sit and play while I do my reading?" I'm, like, sit and play? With him sitting there? But, whatever!

'So, you know, we sat and played, and Matilda was laughing and happy and going "Daddy, Daddy, Daddy!" and sort of bouncing up and down. And I was going, "I've missed you, Matilda!" And we were both, *"I love you."* *"I love you too."*

'We got down on the floor. There was this basket of toys. We got stuck into that. Ross Street never left the room. He was making like he was working, but I could tell, Dr Bell, he was actually keeping an eye on us. I put him out of my mind. I thought, "Just get into this, and enjoy this. Just be normal, show him you're normal." There were blocks, so we built stuff. There were teacups, so we had a tea party. And then Ross Street sort of came over and said, "Okay, Matilda, time to go." And Matilda didn't want to go! She was perfectly happy to sit and play with me! And she started crying her heart out when he said she had to go!'

There is a pause on the tape here. Then Dr Bell says, 'Have you seen Ross Street's report, Garry?'

Garry says, 'No.'

Dr Bell says, 'Would you like me to read parts of it to you? The parts I think you'd be most interested in?' Garry pauses for a minute. Then, when his voice comes back on, it's much quieter.

'Okay,' he says. 'What does it say?'

Dr Bell clears his throat: '"Matilda showed unambiguous excitement at the prospect of seeing her father and when the two were brought together for observation, her response was one of joy. There is genuine attachment between the two and it is difficult for me to conclude that Garry Gary Hartshorn poses any threat to his daughter, Matilda. On the contrary, it seems to me that Matilda is missing him."'

Chapter Eighteen

I probably don't need to tell you that there was only one more tape in the collection after that. One more tape, filled mostly with Softie, speaking like she was being strangled.

'I'm not going to hand Matilda over to an abuser,' she said. 'I'm sorry, Dr Bell, but I will not do it.'

'She sounds desperate,' I told Pat. She had finally agreed to help me listen to these last tapes and was sitting beside me.

Dr Bell said, 'Softie –'

Softie interrupted him. 'No, Dr Bell. I will not do it. I *cannot* do it. There's not a court in the land that can make me do it.'

Dr Bell said, 'It's important to remember that the court has no evidence that what you're saying about Garry is true . . .'

Softie, at this point, is pretty much shrieking. 'The court is taking the word of a man who has spent half an hour with Garry over the word of *me*, Matilda's mother. Who is this Ross Street, anyway? How can we trust him? What does he really know?'

Dr Bell said, 'He's a psychologist, Softie. He's dealt with a lot of men who have a history of child abuse. He's extremely experienced. He's said quite clearly that you have no reason to be worried. Matilda is in no danger from Garry. There's no evidence at all.'

Softie said, 'I don't care about his experience. And there is evidence! I'm gathering more evidence every day. This morning I took Minty out of her nappy on the change table, and her hands went straight down! Straight down, Dr Bell! Like she knew to cover up! And she won't sleep alone any more. I'll try to leave her alone in her room, and she'll be screaming: *"MUMMY! DON'T GO, MUMMY!"'*

Dr Bell said, 'Your lawyer's explained to you that none of this constitutes evidence for use in court?'

Softie said, 'She has! But that's just ridiculous! It's like, never mind what I think! I'm only her mother! What does that count for these days? In that court? Nothing.'

Dr Bell said, 'It's not just that Ross Street didn't find any actual evidence of abuse.'

Softie said, 'You don't understand. Matilda's not going to blurt everything out to a stranger! That session . . . the one with the dolls, I had to tell Matilda, "We're going to meet a nice lady!" But Matilda's a very bright little girl. She can tell when something's up. We walked in and the lady said, "Hello, Matilda. I'm Dr Lisa." I said, "Say hello to Dr Lisa, Matilda." But Matilda was too busy hiding behind my legs. She knew something was up. There were toys in the room. The psychologist said, "Would you like to play with some toys, Matilda?" Then she says to me: "Oh, you'll have to leave the room!" I was very anxious about that, Dr Bell. How could I trust the process if I wasn't allowed to sit in? I was very worried that she wouldn't pick up on little clues, things only a mother would notice. But I didn't have a choice, did I? I had to leave the room. Had to leave Matilda in there, with all those strange dolls and a lady she'd never met before in her life. And afterwards, the lady says Matilda made "no disclosures". She said, "We showed her the toys. Matilda didn't seem interested in the doll." I couldn't believe it, Dr Bell. I'm being told: "She made no disclosures!" She's been with a stranger for less than an hour! She's two years old – what do they expect?'

Dr Bell said, 'Has the court instructed you to see a psychologist, one that specialises in these kinds of cases, Softie?'

Softie said, 'Yes, it has! And my lawyer said I had to go! So now I'm being sent for a strange appointment with a woman who seemed to think that the sexual abuse of children is quite normal! She said to me, "At this stage we have no evidence that Garry has done anything to Matilda. But let's say he did. How would you feel about that?" I could hardly believe it. I said, "How would I feel about it? I'd murder him. It's revolting." She said, "I want you to try to separate those feelings – your disgust about sexual abuse – and ask yourself this: do you believe that Matilda would be harmed by being touched in an inappropriate way by her father?"

'I said, "Of course she would be harmed!" And she said, "I know this is difficult. I want to see if you can see it from the perpetrator's point of view. Let's assume Garry has touched Matilda in an inappropriate way. Now let's assume he doesn't know what he's done is wrong."

'I said, "What are you talking about? Everyone knows it's wrong!"

'This lady says: "Not everyone thinks that way, Softie. But let's assume Garry does know it's wrong, and he'll never do it again. That he admits it, and gets treatment. Would you deny him a role in Matilda's life forever?"

'I said, "Yes! Absolutely, yes!"

'She said, "But what about Matilda's need to know her father?"

'I said, "Well, he wouldn't be her father any more! He'd be a monster!"

'She said, "But can you see that whatever he's done, she might need him in her life?" And I had to say, "No, I cannot. I absolutely cannot!" I got quite upset, Dr Bell. I was saying: "If he's abused her, he's lost his right to be her father!" And then, of course, there's the fact that I know he abused her. Meaning I've got no doubts. I'm in no doubt at all. I know what's gone on. And I cannot believe that the Family Court is now going to try to force me to hand my little girl over to a man that I know – I just *know* – is going to hurt her. Ask any mother, Dr Bell, what would you do? Ask any mother. They'd say the same as I'm saying: "I'd rather die than do it."'

Dr Bell said, 'Softie, I'm sure your lawyer has explained this to you. If the court orders that shared care resumes, and you refuse to allow Matilda to see her father . . . if you obstruct the court . . . I don't need to tell you, Softie, you're going to need to prepare yourself for the possibility that the judge is going to remove Matilda from your custody, and give her to Garry, who *will* let her see *you*.'

Softie said, '*I cannot, I cannot, I will not, I cannot . . .*'

Dr Bell said, 'Because the one thing a court wants to see, in a custody case, is parents that are co-operating with each other. They want to see that you're helping Matilda get along with Garry. Helping her keep in touch with him. Letting her know that you approve . . .'

Softie said, 'I do not approve!'

Dr Bell said, 'And that's going to be a problem for you. Because if you go into court, and you say: no, no, I don't want Matilda to have any kind of relationship with Garry, the court's going to say you're "unfriendly". That's a legal term, Softie. The court is going to say Garry wants Matilda to have a relationship with her mother. But her mother is opposed to a relationship between Matilda and her father. So the only way Matilda can have a relationship with both parents is if Matilda lives with her father.'

Softie by this point was barely even mumbling. 'No, no,

no, I cannot, cannot . . .' She said it over and over again, 'I cannot, I cannot,' and, 'Please, you can't make me do it,' and, 'I just can't, Dr Bell' and 'For God's sake, this is child abuse. It's cruel. It's torture. It's vicious and malicious and I just *can't* . . .' until Pat and I couldn't bear it any more and switched off the tape.

'How awful!' Pat said. 'But surely Frank didn't make her do it? Surely he didn't take that man's side?'

I grimaced. 'I think he was going to try,' I said. I handed her the last of Frank's documents, a transcript of a court hearing.

'Are the parties here?' asked Frank, according to the transcript.

Counsel for Garry, Michael Sanderson, said, 'If it pleases the court, your Honour, my client, Garry Hartshorn, the child's father, is here.'

Frank said, 'Alright. And Ms Monaghan?'

Counsel for Softie, Nadia Filiminov, said, 'If I may, your Honour, we're having some difficulty locating our client.'

Frank said, 'She knew to be here at 10 am?'

Ms Filiminov responded, 'We did give her those instructions, yes.'

Frank said, 'Has she been called?'

Ms Filiminov said, 'She has.'

'On the speaker system?'

'Yes, your Honour.'

'Have you spoken to her this morning?'

'Not this morning. No.'

'You're sure she's not in the waiting area?'

'We don't believe so.'

'We'll take a brief adjournment,' Frank said. 'Call the mother's home, her work, her mobile. You've got ten minutes.'

Ten minutes passed.

Frank said, 'Well? No appearance?'

Nadia Filiminov said, 'Not that I can see.'

Frank said, 'I suppose I don't need to be told that the child isn't here either?'

Nadia Filiminov replied, 'That's right, your Honour. The child doesn't appear to be here either.'

Frank said, 'And I take it you've tried all the numbers? Is she at her place of work?'

Ms Filiminov said, 'We have not been able to locate her at all, your Honour, nor anybody that knows her where-abouts at this time.'

Frank said, 'So, she is missing?'

Ms Filiminov said, 'It seems that way, yes.'

Frank said, 'I don't need to tell you that she's therefore in contempt of this court, I suppose?'

Nadia Filiminov said, 'No, your Honour.'

Frank said, 'Very good. So long as you understand that. So long as you understand how hard I come down on those who treat my court with contempt. I hereby issue a recovery order. I want the child, Matilda Monaghan Hartshorn, found and placed in the temporary custody of Victorian Human Services. And I want the mother brought to me.'

Chapter Nineteen

Back when Pat and I were first married, there was a word for women who upped and left a marriage without so much as a note on the kitchen table. They were called bolters. 'She's done the bolt,' that's what people said. Done the bolt, or done a runner, or shot through, and it was like everyone accepted it.

Women in those days didn't necessarily work, and they might not have any money, so if they upped and bolted and took the kids, everyone assumed it must be for a good reason because it wasn't easy to do. It took some guts. And that was Pat's reaction, when she heard what Softie had done with Matilda.

'She did a runner,' she said. 'And I can't blame her. You can see the path the court is on. They're going to make her hand over the girl. And no mother would do that.'

I couldn't disagree with her. No mother would hand over their child to a man they believed to be a monster.

But . . . what if it wasn't true? That was the bit that got me, and it was obviously the bit that got Frank.

I don't say Matilda was making it up. She was two years old. She'd have no idea about those kinds of things, or she shouldn't, anyway. But the timing of it . . . I couldn't get past that. How could anyone be sure that Softie was telling the truth?

Was that what Frank meant, when he said he'd mucked things up? But that didn't make sense. It seemed to me that he was going to dismiss the allegations. He was going to give Matilda back to Garry.

I was so confused about the whole thing, I did something I wouldn't in ordinary circumstances do. I went looking for Dr Bell on the internet. It seemed to me he was the person most likely to have an informed opinion on whether Softie was telling the truth. So I wanted to know, what did he think? Was Softie right to take off? And what had become of her?

I located Dr Bell's office and I called him up, and I can't tell you how stunned I was to find that he had been waiting to hear from me. 'You're the chap that's been handed the Hartshorn matter,' he said, when I introduced myself. 'Pam Harris told me you might call. Have you been through everything?'

'I have!' I said, maybe too eagerly because I was completely taken by surprise. 'It's ended pretty abruptly. Softie hasn't turned up for court. I don't know what I'm supposed to do next.'

'Why don't you come in, Barry, and I'll see if there's anything I can add,' he said.

Dr Bell's office wasn't as upmarket as I'd imagined. There was no secretary or anything like that. There was a water dispenser and some plastic cups and copies of *New Idea* on the coffee table. There was a buzzer on the wall you could press, to get Dr Bell's attention. I pressed it, and then I sat and waited until he came out.

You know how it is when you've been listening to somebody's voice, and you've got an idea as to how they might look, and sometimes you get it completely wrong? Well, as with Pam, Dr Bell looked exactly as I'd imagined. He had a white beard, white moustache, and a full head of white hair, like Colonel Sanders of Kentucky Fried.

He took me into his office. There were a couple of hairy facemasks from Papua New Guinea on the walls, and on the desk a coconut that had been carved to look like a monkey wearing a pair of wire glasses.

I sat down in the guest chair and then realised it was probably the one that Softie and Garry must have sat on. That unsettled me a bit. There was a bit of small talk between Dr Bell and me: did he know Frank personally (yes) and how long had I known him, and so on.

'It's quite a job he's given you,' Dr Bell said, 'going through an entire case, not even being paid.'

'Do you object to me having your tapes?' I said.

'That depends,' Dr Bell replied. 'Are you going to put them to good use?'

I said, 'I don't know what that means exactly. I feel I've not got the full story. I know Softie hasn't turned up for court. Pat – that's my wife – she tells me she's never been found. She's seen stories on the internet.'

Dr Bell said, 'That's right. The police traced her movements after that hearing, although not for two weeks. It seems like she left the country two days before she was even due in court.'

'Why did they take so long?'

'It's not difficult to leave the country unnoticed.'

'Not with a child? In a custody dispute?'

'Not at all. If you're a parent who's worried about that kind of thing – that your partner may take off – you can ask the court to put the child's name on the airport watch list, and that's going to set off an alarm, but Softie's name was never on it. Why would it have been?'

'I just assumed parents couldn't leave the country with their kids.'

'They can't, legally. Illegally, they do it all the time.'

I said, 'Do they know where she went?'

'Bangkok. Then London. She got off in London. And hasn't been seen since.'

'The police can't find her?'

'What police? We don't have SWAT teams of police to send over to London, combing the ground looking for parents who have done a bolt.'

'The London police don't help?'

Dr Bell scratched his beard on the side of his face, like a man will do when he's really got no idea how to proceed.

'Scotland Yard, they've got a bit on. And, of course, Softie may not be in London any more. The borders in Europe, they're all down. Softie and Matilda, they can pass through to Paris. To Frankfurt. To the Netherlands. Who knows where they are. Which is why Garry had no choice, really, other than to go the nuclear route.'

'The nuclear route?'

'Media coverage. He went looking for media coverage. And he got lucky, if you can call it that. In most of these cases, where the mum has done a runner, you're hard pressed to get journalists interested. Half the readers are going to say, well, she probably had a reason to go. Or, that doesn't sound like anyone's business but their own.

'But Garry did hold one card. Matilda wasn't just any missing child. She was Rick Hartshorn's granddaughter. And Rick was a bit of a celebrity. So that's how Garry managed to get publicity. If you've looked on the internet, you've probably seen it. For a while there, he was speaking to anyone who would listen. And now, of course, he wants to go that route again.'

I said, 'How so?'

'With you.'

'With *me*?'

Dr Bell said, 'Well, that's the point of this, isn't it? To help Garry find Matilda?'

I stood up. I said, 'Whoa there, Dr Bell. I'm not sure that's my business. I have no way of knowing . . . I mean, how can you be so sure? Maybe Softie's telling the truth. Why am I going to get myself involved in this? I couldn't live with myself, if I delivered up a child into the arms of a kiddy-fiddler.'

Dr Bell looked surprised. 'Barry,' he said. 'Have you talked to Garry Hartshorn? Have you talked to Pam about what happened?'

'I don't think I know what you mean,' I said. '*What* happened?'

Dr Bell said, 'Rick Hartshorn died . . .'

'I know that.'

'And . . . Look, Barry, you should talk to Garry. You should call him. He's waiting for you to call.'

'What do you mean, he's waiting for me?'

'Well, that's the point of all this. You're supposed to contact him.'

And so, I called him. And it was just as Dr Bell had said, he wasn't at all surprised to hear from me.

'You've read about my case?' he said. 'Are you coming over?' He told me where he lived, and it was Edgewater Towers. That surprised me. He was in Softie's flat. But then, why wouldn't he be? It was his home when they were married and Softie never turfed him out.

I drove there. It felt strange parking in the big car park out the back. I kept thinking about Garry taking Matilda out of the car that first time, when they got back from the hospital when Matilda was still in the capsule, and Softie was already so upset about whether things were going to be alright.

I pressed the button – 3A – and there was Garry's voice again. Not friendly. Not unfriendly. Just: 'So you're here.' Then there was a buzzing noise.

The building has got one of those doors that buzzes, and you push it open, but you've got to push while it's buzzing. It's not as smooth an operation as it should be, and it took a couple of goes to get me inside.

I started to wonder what on earth I was doing there, meddling in other people's business. Actually, I was pretty close, when I stepped out of the lift, on that third floor, to turning around, getting back in, and going back to my own life.

But Garry had already opened the door to his flat.

He was standing at the end of the corridor with his jeans on, a boot in the door, holding it open, looking down the hall for me, and so there was no turning back. What kind of man sees the person he's looking for and hightails it?

I said, 'Garry Hartshorn?'

He said, 'That's me.'

I strode towards him, stuck my hand out. He took it, and I saw parts of a tattoo, sticking out from under his shirt sleeves. He looked like he hadn't shaved, and his attitude – well, it was defensive. Like he recognised that he was about to go through another round of having to defend himself, when he was sick of having to defend himself.

I followed him back into the flat. It was painted like a woman might paint it – peach colours, with photographs of Matilda all around, but it was also pretty obvious that a man lived there, alone. There was a Vic Bitter carton standing near the bin, in the kitchen, piled high with empties. There was a smell like fried eggs, or beans, or maybe beans on toast. There wasn't a piece of fruit or a vase of flowers. There were sliding doors – those Stegbar ones – going out onto the balcony. There would have been a good view but the glass was dirty and anyway the sea outside was grey. On the balcony I saw two sets of hand weights, like that was where Garry did his lifting.

It's obviously a bit awkward, when you meet a fellow and you've just spent weeks listening to him on tape. Not that Garry minded. He seemed to know full well that I'd been doing that. And it seemed that he'd been waiting a while for my visit. He was prepared.

Laid out on the coffee table in front of him were letters he'd written to his local member, and to the local papers, to the cops, and Family Court judges, and reporters, and even to the PM, desperately trying to find somebody who would believe him, when he said he hadn't molested his daughter.

'Thinking back now, when Softie whacked those papers into the court, saying that I'd abused my own daughter, my life was basically over,' he said.

We were sitting in the little space that gets called the lounge room in those two-bedroom flats. There was a poster of dolphins on the wall in an aluminium frame. I remember thinking it was exactly the kind of thing that Nerida would love. The carpet was a bit stained, but the flat was basically pretty clean. There was one of those fake brass hat stands, with a motorcycle jacket hanging off it. The jacket was dirty, and the stand had gone a bit green, maybe from seaspray.

'There was never going to be any evidence that I'd done anything wrong, because I would never do anything like that,' Garry said. 'And Softie must have known that. However much she hated me, she must have known that. And she must have known that your mate, the judge, Frank, was going to rule in my favour. And that's why she took off before anyone had a chance to stop her. You expect the cops to help you. You think: this is basically an abduction. She's taken my kid. It's against court orders, but the cops just go: oh, we don't have a lot of manpower. They won't go to Softie's old workplace and ask any questions. They won't, like, go through her email, or sit Dawn down and make her say what she knows.

'When it comes down to it, basically what they said was: you're going to have to find her yourself.

'I go, "How am I supposed to do that? Bug Dawn's phone? Break into her email?" Because to my mind, if anyone knew anything, it was Dawn. That was where Softie had been living. That's where she took off from. But according to Dawn, Softie didn't tell her where she'd gone for Dawn's own protection – so Dawn wouldn't have to lie in court if she was asked. So what else could I do, Barry?

'I got a publication order. You know what that is, I

suppose? It means you can talk about the case. Normally, you can't talk about a case in the Family Court. People are entitled to their privacy. It's your business what's going on in your life. But when somebody's run off with your kid, you can get a publication order. You can talk to the media. And that was my biggest mistake.'

I've got to say, I agreed with Garry about that. Months before I even went to see him, my Pat had let me know that everyone on the internet said Garry's wife had taken off because he was a paedophile. And he kind of triggered that storm, by taking the case to the media. I watched while he dug out the first story that was published. It was in the *Herald Sun*, under the headline: *Hunt for Car King Grandchild*. There was a picture of Matilda – she had dark blonde curls, with a chewed, plastic sippy cup in the corner of her mouth – and there was a picture of Garry, with his biceps and his tatts, saying, 'We were involved in a custody dispute and, like so many women these days, my wife decided that our daughter didn't need her father. But times have changed. The law now recognises fathers' rights.'

The caption under the photograph, said, 'Hands-on Dad: Garry Hartshorn is missing his daughter, Matilda, granddaughter of Car King Rick Hartshorn.'

Looking at it, I couldn't help thinking Garry didn't do himself too many favours posing with the short-sleeved shirt and his biceps bulging. Like I say, I'm not a journo, but I did wonder if the bloke who wrote the caption – 'Hands-on Dad' – wasn't having a sly go at Garry.

'The story got picked up by the talkback radio stations,' Garry said. 'But half the people who called in were saying, well, why did she run off? She must have had a reason.' Then I got a call to go on a morning talk show on TV. It was that *Mornings with Yvonne* show, with the host, Yvonne whatever-her-name-is-now. And two seconds before the camera started rolling, she warned me, "I'm going to ask you the hard questions."'

Garry was on his knees at this point, messing about with a DVD collection, trying to find the one he wanted, putting it in the machine, holding the remote control, finding the bit he wanted, talking non-stop.

'I thought, "What's she on about?" There was no time to find out, though. She was talking to the camera, saying: "Up later in the show, we'll have the first of all the celebrity chefs . . . blah de blah . . ." and then – here, you watch.'

I watched. Yvonne's been on that morning show for, what, fifteen years? And I don't mind her. She's pretty good at what she does. She looked into the camera and said, 'But first, the news story we've all seen: this girl, Matilda Hartshorn, who is the only granddaughter of the car giant, Rick Hartshorn, is missing. Taken out of the country by her mother, in a custody dispute. We've got the little girl's father, Garry Hartshorn, here with us today. Hello, Garry.'

Garry said, 'Hello.'

Yvonne said, 'So, tell us, Garry, how are you related to Rick Hartshorn?' And Garry said, 'He's married to my mother. So, technically, I suppose, he's Matilda's grandpa.'

Yvonne said, 'And how is it that you are able to talk about your story? Because it's the case, isn't it, that Family Court matters, they're normally held in secret, aren't they?'

Garry said, 'Well, that's right, but Softie – that's my wife – didn't have the right to take my daughter out of the country, and the Family Court has given me permission to try to find where she's gone.'

Yvonne said, 'And your wife – Softie – do you know why she took Matilda out of the country?'

Garry reached forward with the remote, paused the video.

'See, Barry, watch here. Watch. Because this is where I realised I was being ambushed! Here's where she produces this email, which is supposed to be from Softie, saying: "I had to leave. I had no choice. I believe my husband is a sexual predator, and the court was going to make my little girl live with him." You watch. It's a complete ambush.'

He pressed play. Yvonne produced the email and did, indeed, read out, on live television, that Garry was suspected of molesting Matilda. Garry paused the video again, freezing it on his own, shocked face.

'So, look at me, Barry. I'm sat there, like a rabbit in the headlights, thinking, "Now everybody's going to say: oh, right, she took off because he's a ped!" So I go, "That's just not right. That's not right."'

He played the tape. To Yvonne, he was saying, 'That's one hundred per cent wrong. I have never done anything to hurt Matilda, and I never would do anything to hurt Matilda.'

Yvonne was saying, 'But, Garry, Garry, no, listen a minute, Garry, your wife, your wife, is saying . . .' Garry kept interrupting her. 'That's not right, that's not right, you have no right to say that on TV.'

Yvonne said, 'But you're the one who called the media, Garry . . .'

Garry said, 'I called in the media because I've got to find Matilda.'

Yvonne said, 'Well, you've made the decision to go public, and we're not in the business of telling only one side of the story.'

Garry said, 'You've got no right to raise allegations that are complete lies! I'm not the criminal here. Softie is the one who has run off.'

Yvonne said, 'But you're the one making a public spectacle out of it, aren't you, Garry? And not telling the whole story, it seems. Because these emails we received from your wife, after you went on radio, tell a different story. And they say that your wife has the support – the financial support – of your stepfather.'

'Rick Hartshorn is not my stepfather.'

'He's married to your mother! Didn't you just say that?'

'He is.'

'But now you're saying he's not your stepfather.'

'I'm adopted. And Rick Hartshorn has got his point of view. But the allegations against me are bullshit.'

They bleeped out 'bullshit', but you could see Garry's mouth forming the word. What they didn't bleep out was Garry's expression. It didn't look good for him at all.

'And now watch what she does!' Garry said, wielding the remote. 'She kind of wraps things up: "Alright, that's Garry Hartshorn – son, *adopted stepson*, I should say – of the car king Rick Hartshorn, talking about the hunt for his daughter, who is missing and whose wife, ex-wife, says she had no choice other than to flee." I mean, how do you think I felt about that, Barry? I'd gone in there, in good faith, and they'd basically reported whatever Softie said about me, which in my view ought to be against the law. So I came off the set, basically feeling like my head was going to explode. I was thinking, "What else can anyone do to me, now?" And then the *Herald Sun* reporters went along to interview Rick Hartshorn, and completely destroyed me.'

He was back in his media file, digging out the story the *Herald Sun* published, after the *Yvonne* interview.

'Here, you read it,' he said.

I read it. The story ran under the headline: 'Car King Backs Mum of Missing Child'. It seems like the reporter had heard Yvonne saying, 'Your wife has got the support – the financial support – of Rick Hartshorn' and had gone out there, to find out why Rick was supporting her and not trying to get Matilda back. Hartshorn was quoted as saying:

Softie's done what she's done. I don't pretend to know the ins and outs of it. But I do know that children belong with their mother, especially little girls.

I can't approve of what Garry's doing, trying to hunt

them down. To my mind, a mother's got a duty to speak up if she thinks her child isn't safe.

I've known my daughter-in-law for a while, and it seems to me that whatever she's done, she's done it for a reason, and that reason might be flawed, that's not for me to say, but hunting her down when she's sheltering with a child, doesn't seem to me to be the way to handle it.

And as for Garry, well, as most people know he's adopted. We don't know his family, his genes, so it's hard to judge, isn't it? They say the apple doesn't fall far from the tree.

When the journalist asked him if he knew where his grandchild might be, Hartshorn said:

All I know is, she's got enough money to stay away as long as she thinks she should.

Asked if that meant that he had funded her flight from Australia, he said:

I think I've said enough. I'm sure your readers can figure it out.

I said to Garry, 'How did you take it?'
Garry said, 'I picked up the phone, and got Mum. I said, "Put Rick on." She tried to head off the confronta-

tion. She said, "Oh, Garry. This isn't good. I don't want all this trouble. Rick isn't well. He's been so tired. He probably had no idea what he was saying."

'Rick had cancer by this stage, you see. But, I mean, that didn't stop him from being a prick. I said, "Put him on." And, for once in my life, I let Rick have it. If anything good has come from this, it's that I finally let Rick have it. I said, "What are you playing at, Rick?" Rick said something like, "I don't like your tone, Garry." And I said, "I don't really give a shit, Rick. What's all this I read in the paper, you taking Softie's side?" Rick said he wasn't taking sides but he wouldn't have Softie "hunted down like a dog".

'So I go to him, "If there's a dog in this, Hartshorn, it's you." And it felt good to say that.

'But, you know, it did me no good. I was still branded a ped on national TV, and now in the paper. And straight away, people's reactions to me changed. Ask anyone. I mean, I still had a few mates. It was all they could do to go out with me in public. One afternoon I got home to find some dickhead had put a hose pipe through my letterbox and put the water on. The residents here weren't that happy. They wanted me out. But the building is strata. They can't force me out. I just try to keep to myself.

'Having that label put on me, it's obviously become more difficult to get anyone interested in helping me find Matilda. Who's going to want to do that? At the anniversary of when she disappeared, I rang every reporter I'd ever met and said, oh, it's been a year. And some of them did a story saying, "It's been a year." But you can't do that every anniversary.

'So what did I have left? I've got the website, and maybe when it's Missing Children's Week, or some reporter some-where wants to do a story on the failure of the Family Court, they'd call me and say: okay, Garry, show time. So, I was actually at the point of thinking, you know, this is running out of steam. I'm running out of ways to bring attention to this, and I was starting to think, I'm never going to find my girl. But then I got the camera, and, you know, it kicked things off again, and now I'm starting to think, well, not only will people maybe *want* to help me now, they really need to help me, because there's a lot at stake.'

Does any of that make any sense to you? Because, I've got to tell you, I sat there, not understanding, not for one minute, what the hell Garry was going on about. Camera? What camera?

I cleared my throat. I leaned forward a bit on the couch. I said, 'Excuse me here, Garry, but you've lost me.'

Garry said again in a matter-of-fact tone of voice, 'Yeah, well, it is hard to get your head around.'

I said, 'I'm sorry, Garry . . . what is?'

And that's when it dawned on him that I had no idea what he was on about. 'Shit!' he said. 'Shit, Barry. No, no, no. Christ. Shit. Are you telling me you don't know . . . ?'

I said, 'Know what?'

Garry said, 'Don't you know about this already? You're telling me you've come here and you don't know about this? You're still thinking Softie might be telling the truth about me and Matilda. Shit, Barry!'

I said, 'I've got no idea what you're talking about, Garry.'

'Well, why are you actually here?' he said. 'I got the impression from what you said on the phone that you were up with all this?'

Again I had to say: 'Up on *what*?'

'Jesus Christ,' said Garry.

He reached into one of his boxes and picked up a digital camera. 'You're going to tell me you don't know about this?' he said, shoving it towards me.

I admitted I had no idea.

'This camera is Rick Hartshorn's. I told your mate, the judge, what was on it. I told the lady too.'

'Pam?'

'The judge's secretary.'

'That's Pam.'

Garry said, 'So I've told everyone, and you come here saying you don't know. I don't get that. I thought that was why you were here. To help me.'

I said, 'Right, well . . .'

'You know about me being adopted, right?'

I said, 'I do.'

Garry said, 'You know my old man, John Cooper, he died?'

'I do.'

'You know Mum got married again? To Rick Hartshorn? You know all that?'

I nodded.

Garry said, 'Right. Well, then, you know what kind of bastard Hartshorn was.'

I said, 'For giving Softie the money to run away, you mean?'

Garry said, 'Not for that! For Christ's sake, I can't believe this. Don't tell me I'm going to have to go through this shit again? Nobody has told you what happened? Alright, I'll tell you. I was a kid. John Cooper had died and I wasn't entirely sure about the new bloke who was living in our house. I started wagging school. There was a creek near our house, under the railway bridge. There were no fish in it but rabbits were in plague. There was a chemical that farmers used to kill them.'

I said, 'Ten Sixty?'

Garry said, 'Right. Rabbits dropping dead everywhere from the Ten Sixty. And one particularly big rabbit had got caught in some branches, overhanging the creek. I'd seen it a couple of times, and tried to reach it with a stick. So I was doing all that – wagging school, poking this rabbit with a stick – when I saw something out of the corner of my eye. And it was my new step-dad, Rick Hartshorn.'

I said, 'Down by the creek?'

Garry said, 'Right. And I remember thinking, "Shit, I'm in trouble here. I'm meant to be at school. And now Rick's turned up, probably looking for me, probably now going to strap me." But Hartshorn goes, "That's a good size rabbit. Here, let me help." And he takes the stick and starts poking at the rabbit. And he's got longer arms. He gets the rabbit out easily enough, and he's wiping the slime off it, and saying, "Look at the size of the bastard. What do you reckon we should do with it?" And I'm thinking, "Okay, I'm not in trouble." Because Hartshorn was saying, "Maybe we can knock the head off and keep it, like a trophy."

'I go to him, "Mum won't let me keep it. She'll make me throw it out." But it was like he wasn't listening. He goes, "Have a close look." And then he goes, "You know what would be good? If you dried the skull out, you could use it as a bookend. You got any books back at home? Picture books?"

'I go "No," and he goes, "You got no books? Or no picture books?" I go, "I don't read much." And he goes, "If you haven't got books, what are you reading? Magazines?" I said, "I don't have magazines. I have comics." And he goes, "Magazines are better." Then he goes, "What about your dad, though? He must have had magazines? Magazines with girls in them?"

'Now remember, I'm not much more than twelve years old. I had no idea what he was on about, Barry. I was basically still a kid. Then Rick goes across the creek, striding, one stepping stone to the next. He says, "Want to see a secret place of mine?" I say, "What kind of secret place?" And he says, "Oh, a place where I keep my bullet shells." And, like an idiot, I follow him. We get to this, like, cave, where the ground has been swept. There's burnt wood in a pile, like there's been a fire. Rick goes: "This is my secret place." I don't like it at all, being in there. I go: "I better get back." And he goes: "But wait and see what I've got, first." He heads towards the back of the cave and pulls out a garbage bag, and he says, "You never saw any of your dad's magazines?" And I'm so lame, Barry, I still had no idea what he was on about. He takes a pile of girly mags out of the garbage bag. Old *Playboy* and *Penthouse* – old now, I mean, not old then. This is a long time before the internet. So it's the first time in my life I've seen nudie pics. Rick's opening the magazines and showing me the pictures, saying, "Here, help yourself." And my mind was like a blizzard, Barry. I said, "I better get home." And Rick goes, "Sit down and have a look through. It's good stuff." He was turning the pages. I still remember one of the women: she was on a lilo, like a clear, plastic lilo, in a pool, with her heels on. That's all: heels. I remember thinking, "She's going to pop that lilo, in those heels."

'Rick took a cigarette from his top pocket. He goes to me, "You ever smoked?" I go, "No." Then he goes, "There's some niggers in here. Niggers and chinks. But the chinks have got no tits. You like tits, right? Like, get a load of the tits on that." And he pushes more of the magazines at me.'

Garry paused. I didn't know what to say to him, so I waited until he went on.

'Suddenly, Hartshorn's got his member out, and he's looking at me, and he's saying: "Here's what you've got to do. You've got to give this a good tug. You ever had a stiffy? Get your old fella out. Give it a good pull. Try it." And so I bolted, Barry. I took off down the track we'd come down and I could hear Rick crying after me, "Where you going? You're going to miss the best bit!"'

I said, 'Where did you go?'

Garry said, 'I went home. I found my pushie. I was out of the saddle, just flying home. I was thinking, "I've got to find Mum. I've got to tell Mum." And I ran straight into the house, and Mum was there, and she looks at me, with my hair all on end, and she says, "What's wrong, Garry?"

'I look at her, Barry, and I can't speak. I can't get a word out. I'm thinking, "Shit." Because she's standing at the oven, and she's got her apron on, and she's cooking up a meal, and she's got Beam in the lounge room, watching TV, and she looks that bloody relaxed. That bloody relaxed and happy. I mean, we've been poor. Now things are getting better. Mum's got the Ga-Mini. Beam's being looked after. So I go into my room. Mum comes and knocks and I say, "Go away." Then, I don't know how long afterwards, she calls me for tea. I come out of my room. And there's Rick Hartshorn at the table, with his chops and his peas. Always served first, he was. And he doesn't look up at me. He's making like he's busy with his tea.

'Mum says, "Well, Garry, nice to see you. What was all that about? Flying into your room like you've been shot out of a cannon?"

'And do you know what I do, Barry? Nothing. I do

nothing. I don't look up from my place mat. I don't look at Rick Hartshorn. I never told anyone what happened.'

I leaned back in the chair. 'Until now,' I said.

Garry said, 'Until now. Because who was going to believe me? No one. But then, when he died, I got the camera, and things changed. I had to speak out. And that was why I got in touch with your old mate, the judge, Frank. Only to find out he was dying too. I couldn't let that stop me, though. I had to get a hearing.'

I said, 'What camera?'

Garry said, 'Rick's camera. To be more accurate, Beam got Rick's camera. You know Beam, right? You know he always had a camera? Well, when Rick died, first thing Beam did was take Rick's camera. You've got to understand, Barry, he doesn't do things the same as the rest of us. Doesn't get that he's supposed to be polite about things. He takes the thing out of Rick's walk-in wardrobe, where Rick always kept it, and he says to Mum, "*Mine.*"

'And Mum was like, "Alright, Beam, you've had an eye on it forever. You might as well take it." But the battery's flat and Beam doesn't know how to charge it. So he gives it to me and I charge it up for him, and out of curiosity I flick back through the memory card, and there's a file: M. And what I found in there . . .'

Tears started to flow down his face.

I said, 'Jesus.'

Garry got up from the couch, said, 'Excuse me' and went and stood on the balcony. Then he came back in and said, 'I feel that bloody guilty about this. Because you know, when Softie was going on about it, I was just certain she was trying to have a go at me. I never bloody thought, "Hartshorn's a paedophile." I was thinking, "Hartshorn's a *poofter*." It's not the same thing. I know that. I get that. But for some reason it never occurred to me the old perv would go for Matilda, because she's a girl.'

I repeated, 'Because she's a girl.'

Garry said, 'But then, once I had the camera with the evidence on it, I had to track down the judge to show it to him. Not just to say, look, I was innocent all along. Because what I'd said about Softie was also wrong. She wasn't deranged. She wasn't making anything up. She was wrong about *me* – but she was right about Matilda. So I called Melbourne City Chambers, asking to speak to Justice Brooks. And it was his assistant that picked up and she told me: "You'll have to make an application, Garry. You can't just storm in here saying you've got new information." I could tell she didn't think I would have anything of interest. So I said, "Mrs Harris, I really need to speak to the judge. I'm desperate." And she was firm with me, saying, "You have our sympathy, Garry, but absolutely not."

'So I got back in touch with Dr Bell, saying, please, somebody has to hear me out. He set up the meeting and I handed your judge mate the camera, and said, "I just want you to take it. I want you to do something." I remember how he looked. He was that thin and frail. He had a cane. And he was looking at the pictures of Matilda, and I could see he was going to topple over. He said, "What are you telling me?" And I said, "That's Rick Hartshorn's camera." He said, "I want you to swear to it." And he meant, like, literally. Pam got the Bible and I swore to it. I explained how I came to see the photographs. How the worst part of it wasn't just seeing her like she was – with the boa, and exposing herself – it was the expression on her face, Barry. Little kids, they know when they're doing something wrong, don't they? And you could see how scared she was. Like she was trying to smile. Trying not to get into trouble. Trying to do what she was being told. And be a good girl. But the look she had, it was, where's Mum? Where's Dad?

'So I told your judge friend all that, and he was in shock, I could see that. Like, he'd been thinking that Softie was lying, but now he could see she was telling the truth. Just not about me.

'He asked me one more question: "Is there any chance that these photographs could have been taken by Beam?" And I said, there's no way those are Beam's photographs.

'Frank said, "Because?"

'And I told him, "Beam can't take a photograph like that. A staged photograph. Beam can take a photograph of the carpet. That's all Beam can do. And there's something else Beam can't do. He can't hurt a child. He just can't. It would be like him stepping on a bug. It's something he can't do."

'The look on your mate's face, the judge's face – I can't describe it. It was like: what are we going to do? We've got this little girl here, and she's been . . . she's been abused, and everyone suspects the dad, and it's not the dad. And the little girl needs to know that. And the mum needs to know that. But how do we tell her? Because nobody knows where she is. What she calls herself. Where she's gone. And Rick's dead. So he's not ever going to court. There's going to be no trial that she can hear about.

'So I'm sitting there, labelled a ped, with all the evidence that I'm not one in front of your mate the judge, and all he could say was, "I'm sorry this has happened, Garry."

'I was saying, "You're sorry? *I'm* sorry. I'm sorry my daughter is growing up somewhere with her dad not around, and if she knows she's even got a dad, she thinks he's a monster. And I'm sorry the whole country believed that too."

'Then the judge was saying, "No, you're right. We've got to put it right." But what could the poor bloke do? He was absolutely on his last legs. And all he was saying was, "I'll think of something."

'And then, after his funeral, Pam called and said, oh, he's handing the files to somebody he trusts. A newspaper man. And, I mean, isn't that you? Is that not why you're here, to put things right? To get this story out? To put it all down, so if Matilda does ever come looking, she'll be able to find me? And she'll know not to be frightened. Because I never would have done her any harm.'

Epilogue

Nobody knows for certain what happened to Softie, when she fled Australia.

Nobody knows what she's told Matilda, about her dad.

Does she say, 'I don't know for sure who he is, little one'?

Or does she say, 'I'm sorry, Matilda, but your daddy passed away. He died'?

One thing's for certain: Matilda probably doesn't remember Garry.

She was two when she last saw him and she'd be, what, four now?

Four.

Amazing when you think about it, isn't it?

How fast the time goes.

As a father of four and now a grandfather of twelve (thirteen, if you count Ethan, and I certainly do), I can tell you that happens with all kids: they're grown up before you know it. Nobody who has little ones still in nappies, or who is still getting up ten times a night, is going to believe this, but you turn around one day and, snap, they've gone.

They're heading off to school, with massive shoes and sun hats, and school bags they can hardly carry. They're riding bikes around the neighbourhood, and then they're learning to catch the bus, and before long they can drive.

You come home one day, and they're talking about moving out, or getting married, and then they're having kids of their own. And when they do, by God, you can't believe your luck!

Grandkids!

Because it's true what I said earlier: having grandkids is so much easier than having your own. You don't have to walk the halls, trying to get them off to sleep. You don't have to sit up till all hours, wondering where the hell they've got to, and thinking when that door opens: 'I'm taking the wooden spoon to their backside.'

That's not your job. Your job is to slip them lollies.

Mum can say, don't climb all over Grandpa. He needs his rest. You can say, come sit on my lap. Tell me about school today. And when you get sick of sticky fingers in your ears, you can send them home.

Unless you're not seeing them, of course.

Like we weren't seeing Jett, Baxter or Ethan. By the time I'd finished writing out all of Matilda's story – setting the record straight for her, and for her dad, it was pretty much Christmas. I'd just finished posting the last of this manuscript to Pam, so she could proofread it, and I'd come home to find Pat sitting on the lounge-room floor, surrounded by toys and Christmas paper. Pat doesn't often cry – she's stubborn like that – but she was crying.

I went straight to her and said, 'What's gone on, love?'

Pat said, 'I went shopping for Jett, Baxter and Ethan today. And the girl in the toy shop, she said, "How can I help you?" I said, "I'm not really sure. I'm shopping for my grandsons." And she said, "Well, what kind of things do they like?" And do you know what I had to say, Barry? I had to say: "To be honest with you, I have no idea." I have no idea. It's been so long now since I've seen them, I'm not sure I'd even know them if I saw them in the street.'

I said, 'Oh Pat. Don't say that. You'd know them, Pat. They'd know you too.'

Pat said, 'No, Barry, they wouldn't know me! And if they did recognise me, it would probably make them *run* because who knows what Nerida has been saying about what I'm like. Not that I love them and miss them, that's for sure!'

I didn't know what to say to that. I mean, there was my Pat, unwrapped toys at her feet, wiping the back of her hand under her nose, her heart just completely broken, and no real prospect of knowing any peace, in what should have been the best days of her life.

I said, 'Pat . . .'

'No, Barry,' she said, putting up her hand like a traffic cop. 'Don't tell me not to make any more fuss! I'm going to make *more* fuss. When the courts open next year, I'm going to go. I'm going to fight for those children. It's like they said on *A Current Affair*. We need more granny power. And as for these gifts' – she signalled towards the toy shop bags – 'well, I've decided *not* to wrap them. Brian wants me to wrap them. "Wrap them up, Mum, and I'll make sure the boys get them," he said. Well, *no*. What I'm going to do is wrap up an *empty* box and put it on the doorstep with a note inside saying: "We'd like to give you a present, but we have no idea what you want for Christmas because your mother won't let us see you!" *That's* what I'm going to do.'

I don't know what came over me, but I said, 'No.'

It was like Pat didn't hear me. She said, 'It's the only choice I've got, Barry.'

I said, 'We're not going to do that, Pat.'

'Well, what am I supposed to do?' she said. 'Brian's all, "Oh, why can't you two just make peace?" Like I'm the one who should make the first move? Why should I make the first move?'

I said to Pat, '*Somebody's* got to show some common sense.'

'Well,' she said. 'It's not going to be *me*.'

She couldn't hear herself. Like so many people caught in these kinds of disputes – 'I'm not talking to so and so, because she did this or that' – she couldn't even hear the absurdity of her own argument any more. So I said, 'Okay then, Pat, if it can't be *you*, then I suppose it will have to be *me*.'

And with that, I picked up the toys, still in their bags, and I walked out to the car. Pat was following along behind, saying: 'What exactly do you think you are doing, Barry?'

I didn't answer, except to say: 'If you want to come, Pat, you come.' And, to her credit, she did. She got into the passenger seat. Her face was white with worry. Of course she knew where I was going, and what I was doing, which was taking matters into my own hands for once, for everyone's sake.

I didn't say a word to Pat in the car. I simply drove directly to Nerida's house. And when I got there, I drove right into the driveway, parking up behind Nerida's car. You'll know the kind of house Nerida's got: triple-fronted, they call it, with three sets of windows along the side. Somebody comes up the drive, you know they're there. They just can't miss you.

I stopped the car. I got out, opened the rear door, and took out the boys' toys. I marched up to Nerida's front door, with Pat by the arm. And I knocked.

I knocked, and at first nothing happened. I knew I was taking a risk. What if Nerida shouted out, 'Get off my property!' But I was acting on a hunch. Even if she didn't miss us, she'd have to know that the boys did. And it's a wicked sort of person who won't let their kids see their grandparents when they're right outside.

So I knocked again – and this time, the door opened a crack. I thought, don't tell me she's got the bolt on? Don't tell me I'm going to see Nerida's face peering through the gap, saying, 'If you don't leave now, I'm calling the cops.'

But it wasn't Nerida. It was little Jett, with his jet-black hair and cheeky-monkey face, and he was grinning at me.

Behind him, I could see Baxter, and behind Baxter, running down the hall, I could see Ethan. And all of them were just grinning their heads off, and rushing to get the locks on the door undone, and Jett, he was shouting, like with real joy, 'Nan! Pop! Mum says you can come in!'

Reading Group Questions

1. *Matilda is Missing* is a story about a bitter divorce. Divorce itself has become more common in Australia in the past forty years, in particular since 'no-fault' divorce came in. Do you support 'no-fault' divorce? Do you believe that divorce has become too easy?

2. *Matilda is Missing* is also about a custody dispute in the age of shared care. What is your opinion on shared care? Does a child have a right to know both their parents after divorce? To what lengths should the Family Court go in order to ensure that children see both parents after divorce?

3. Who should decide whether shared care is appropriate in any given circumstance? Should the court decide? Should there be exceptions to the rule?

4. The first character introduced in the book – Barry Harrison – has no real connection to Matilda, besides being the one chosen to tell her story. Why do you think the author decided to tell the story from the point of view of a third person, and not from the point of view of one of the parents?

5. Barry and his wife, Pat, are grandparents who are being denied access to their own grandchildren, because of divorce. How widespread is this problem? Should grandparents have more rights in the Family Court? Should grandparents be allowed to ask for custody arrangements that would give them the legal right to see their grandchildren on a regular basis?

6. What do you think of the lengths Pat goes to in order to try to force herself back into the lives of her grandchildren?

7. What impression did Softie make on you? Why do you think she married Garry?

8. What did you make of Garry? Has he been damaged by his past? Why did he marry Softie?

9. Do you think couples that want to get married should be made to undergo some kind of counselling, either by the church or by trained professionals? Do you think couples should have counselling before having children?

10. Had you been the judge in the case, what decision would you have handed down at the first interim hearing? And how would that have changed, as Matilda got older?

11. Had you been either the judge or the Family Court psychologist, would you have believed Softie when she brought up her fears about Matilda being molested?

12. What is your view of the decision Softie took to take matters into her own hands?

GHOST CHILD

In 1982 Victorian police were called to a home on a housing estate an hour west of Melbourne. There, they found a five-year-old boy lying still and silent on the carpet. There were no obvious signs of trauma, but the child, Jacob, died the next day. The story made the headlines and hundreds attended the funeral. Few people were surprised when the boy's mother and her boyfriend went to prison for the crime. Police declared themselves satisfied with the result, saying there was no doubt that justice had been done. And yet, for years rumours swept the estate, clinging like cobwebs to the long-vacant house: there had been a cover-up. The real perpetrator, at least according to local gossip, was the boy's six-year-old sister, Lauren . . .

Twenty years on, Lauren has created a new life for herself, but details of Jacob's death begin to resurface and the story again makes the newspapers. As Lauren struggles with the ghosts of her childhood, it seems only a matter of time before the past catches up with her.

I CAME TO SAY GOODBYE

It was four o'clock in the morning. A young woman pushed through the front doors. Staff would later say they thought the woman was a new mother, returning to her child – and in a way, she was. She walked into the nursery, where a baby girl lay sleeping. The infant didn't wake when the woman placed her gently in the shopping bag she had brought with her. There is CCTV footage of what happened next, and most Australians would have seen it, either on the internet or the news. The woman walked out to the car park, towards an old Corolla. For a moment, she held the child gently against her breast and, with her eyes closed, she smelled her. She then clipped the infant into the car, got in and drove off. That is where the footage ends. It isn't where the story ends, however. It's not even where the story starts.